"I've got ninet
married to me
that period."

"But I thought..."

He could only guess what she probably thought. He'd told her yesterday that it was a ninety-day marriage and he meant it. That didn't mean he wasn't planning on giving his all for the show.

Paul leaned closer to her, so close he could smell the sweet caramel scent of coffee on her lips. She instantly stilled as her eyes lifted to his, a question there. He didn't know why he'd gotten into her personal space, only that he couldn't step away now that he was there.

Against his better judgement, he reached out and twirled a strand of her blond hair around his finger, feeling the silky texture of it, before he tucked it behind her ear. Her hair was just as soft as he remembered.

Kyleigh looked at him, as if unsure. "Why'd you do that?"

He lifted a shoulder. "Because I wanted to."

Somewhere in the background, Paul heard Gregori moving, getting a better shot of them. It was background noise that wouldn't distract him as he enjoyed the nearness of his wife.

His wife.

His mouth ticked upward. "Whether you like it or not, Mrs. Rodriguez, for the next ninety days, you're mine."

Dear Reader,

Every boy band has a "bad boy," and Paul Rodriguez has proudly accepted that label over the years. When his reputation jeopardizes his position as host of *First Comes Marriage*, a reality TV show that marries strangers, he knows he'll do anything to save his job. The show's director decides to film their next season in Holiday Bay, the town where his career started. Paul is shocked to discover that one of the contestants is none other than Kyleigh Sinclair, his former high school girlfriend. He decides to marry her himself, knowing that the predicted record ratings will secure his role. But as the two spend time together, Paul realizes that he's ready to retire his bad-boy ways so he can win back the woman he never forgot. Now he has ninety days to convince Kyleigh that, this time, he's not going to let her go.

Paul is one of my favorite characters. On the surface, he seems like a one-dimensional figure who only cares about fame and everything that comes with it. But once you realize what truly drives him, I think that most people can relate to him in some way. His story is about survival—that no matter what life throws at you, you find a way to keep going and push through.

I hope you love Paul and Kyleigh as much as I do. For more about my books, you can visit my website, kellistorm.com, where you can also subscribe to my newsletter.

Kelli

FIRST COMES
MARRIAGE

KELLI STORM

SPECIAL EDITION

MIX
Paper | Supporting responsible forestry
FSC® C021394
www.fsc.org

Harlequin®
SPECIAL
EDITION™

PLEASE RECYCLE THIS PRODUCT IS RECYCLABLE

Recycling programs for this product may not exist in your area.

ISBN-13: 978-1-335-18023-0

First Comes Marriage

Copyright © 2025 by Kelli Du Lude

Harlequin Enterprises ULC
22 Adelaide St. West, 41st Floor
Toronto, Ontario M5H 4E3, Canada
www.Harlequin.com

HarperCollins Publishers
Macken House, 39/40 Mayor Street Upper,
Dublin 1, D01 C9W8, Ireland
www.HarperCollins.com

Printed in Lithuania

Kelli Storm graduated with a BA in public relations from Grand Valley State University. Harlequin published three of her books in 2025! Her debut young adult fantasy also came out in October 2025. Kelli resides in the Great Lake State with her three rescue dogs and a fifteen-year-old fish named Henry O'Malley.

Books by Kelli Storm

Harlequin Special Edition

Challenge Accepted

His Small-Town Challenge
The Fake Dating Dare
First Comes Marriage

Visit the Author Profile page at Harlequin.com.

For my brother, who got sucked into becoming
a reality TV fan by accident.

Chapter One

Kyleigh Sinclair tried to comprehend the words scrawled across her ancient laptop screen.

We appreciate your submission to be a contestant on the hit show, *First Comes Marriage*. Congratulations! Your application has made it to our final round of consideration, and we'll be in touch shortly with our decision.

Kyleigh blinked hard as she stared at the email. This had to be a mistake. She would never submit her name to some stupid reality show that married complete strangers. Even if she was interested—which she wasn't—there was no way she'd submit her name to a show hosted by her ex-boyfriend from high school.

Once upon a time, she'd thought he was the love of her life, and she'd been silly enough to think he felt the same way. But as soon as Paulo Rodriguez signed his contract to join Holiday Boys—the biggest boy band of all time—he changed his name to Paul and dumped Kyleigh. On prom night, no less. He sent her a text telling her they were over, while she'd been sitting at home, waiting for him in her prom dress.

She had zero desire to be anywhere near him again, let

alone marry some stranger in front of him. It'd be too humiliating.

The bell above her shop rang, giving Kyleigh a welcome distraction. She relaxed slightly at the sight of one of her closest friends, Julie Reynolds. The redhead owned the shop across the street from Kyleigh. She was also married to Jake Reynolds—local hometown hero and Paul's fellow Holiday Boy. Julie glowed these days, content in a marriage that made most people sigh with envy.

She swayed up to the store's butcher-block counter and placed a bag on top.

"I was craving a pasty, so I picked up one for you while I was at it," Julie explained.

"Aren't you always craving pasties these days?" Kyleigh teased.

Julie was heavily pregnant, expecting her first child with her husband. While she was very open about her asexuality, she and Jake made their marriage work. To avoid any possible media leaks, considering Jake was still an incredibly popular singer, they'd conceived their child the old-fashioned way. Kyleigh had secretly worried how that might change the dynamic of her friend's marriage, given that sex wasn't normally a part of their relationship, but the couple seemed closer than ever.

Kyleigh's stomach growled as the scent of Franki's Pasties reached her nose. "You're my savior," she said as she reached inside the bag and pulled out the takeaway container.

"You doing okay?" Julie asked as she rubbed her belly. "You were looking a little stressed when I walked in. Business still going okay?"

"Yes, that's not the problem," Kyleigh said. She removed

the container lid. Her mouth watered at the sight of the crusty pasty smothered in vegetable gravy. "Business is better than ever actually. It helps that Jake is always seen going into your store." She smiled at her friend. "Whenever it's rumored he's in town, I typically get a large influx of customers who hover in my store keeping an eye out for your husband. They usually end up buying something while they're here."

Julie started to grin, but her face changed into a wince, and she rubbed her stomach again.

Kyleigh's motherly antenna shot up. "You okay?"

"Yeah, the baby's just kicking more than usual. She's ready to come out, I think," Julie joked.

Kyleigh grabbed the compostable plastic knife and fork that came with the food. "She? Did you finally decide to find out the baby's sex?"

"No, we're still waiting on that," Julie said. "But I feel like we're having a girl. Jake insists that the baby is a boy though, so we'll see who's right."

"What does Dylan think the baby is?" Kyleigh asked, mentioning Julie's stepson.

"I think he's secretly hoping for a boy since his mom gave him a sister already, but he said he'll be happy either way." Julie tilted her head, her high ponytail slipping to the side. "But don't change the subject. What was making you look so stressed when I walked in?"

"It's nothing," Kyleigh assured her, deciding the whole email was a silly joke that should have ended up in her spam folder instead of her inbox. "I received a weird email, that's all."

"About what?" Julie asked curiously.

Kyleigh shook her head. "It said I was being considered for that ridiculous show, *First Comes Marriage*."

Julie's eyebrows darted up. "Paul's show. Did you enter it?"

Kyleigh's lips twisted downward. "Of course not. First off, I have no interest in appearing on reality TV. Second, I would never appear on something hosted by Paul Rodriguez, of all people. And third, even if I was desperate enough to marry a complete stranger, I certainly wouldn't enter a show that's filmed out in California. I can't leave my store that long."

The concern on Julie's face morphed into unease, and Kyleigh's internal alarm started to sound. Very few people knew that Kyleigh and Paul had ever dated. Due to her father's disapproval of Paul, they'd kept their relationship a secret and avoided being seen together. Since Kyleigh was a couple years older than Julie, her friend hadn't known Kyleigh and Paul were once a thing until Kyleigh told her a few years ago.

"What?" Kyleigh asked as Julie tried to regain her composure. "What's that look for?"

"Um…well—" she started to say.

"What?" Kyleigh asked again, her tone a little sharper as a sense of impending doom washed over her.

"It's just that… Paul told Jake they're planning on filming the next season of *First Comes Marriage* in Holiday Bay. Apparently, the network executives saw the town when the Holiday Boys did that charity concert here, and they think it's the perfect setting. Finding love in a small town and all that jazz."

Kyleigh's stomach lurched. "You can't be serious."

Julie nodded. "Paul said the network wanted to try something new. From what he told us, they're supposed to start filming here within the next few weeks."

Kyleigh swallowed hard. "And is Paul still the host?"

Her friend looked at Kyleigh in sympathy. "There's no reason why he wouldn't be. He's been the host for years. I think he would have told Jake if he'd been fired, but he hasn't mentioned anything."

Kyleigh peered back at her laptop screen, which was now black. The blankness couldn't erase the memory of that email announcing she was a possible contestant. On Paul Rodriguez's show.

She tried not to panic. "They can't just randomly enter people, right? There's no way that can be legal."

"I would assume they pick people for the show who actually *want* to be there." Julie tried to sound encouraging, but Kyleigh could see the doubt in her eyes. "Listen, I'll ask Jake about it after work tonight. Honestly, this whole situation is probably nothing to worry about. I'd bet you anything that the email was sent by mistake."

Kyleigh gave her a weak smile. "Thanks, Julie. I appreciate you looking into it. Let me know what Jake says."

"I will," Julie assured her, then glanced down at her smartwatch. "I should get back to my shop so Greta can have her lunch break. I'll call you later, okay?"

"Sounds good," Kyleigh replied.

After her friend left, Kyleigh did her best to put the whole thing from her mind. She didn't want to think about the bombshell Julie just dropped on her. Or the fact that there was a strong chance she'd see Paul Rodriguez again in the very near future. Holiday Bay was a small town. It was hard to avoid people even if you wanted to.

Kyleigh was hosting a crochet class later that night, and she forced herself to focus on that instead of the guy she dated two decades ago. She owned an arts and crafts store, Kyleigh's Knits. Between her own perseverance and a small loan from her parents, she'd started the shop a little over fifteen years ago. It took a couple of years to get the small business rolling, but now her store was one of the most popular spots in the community, thanks to the variety of classes she offered.

Entering the store's craft room to start getting things set up, she went over to her cabinet where she stored the yarn and needles for her workshops.

The bell above the shop rang again, but before she could walk back to the front, she heard her daughter call out, "Mom, where are you?"

"In the back, setting up for the class tonight."

"Can I use your laptop? I'm having trouble with mine, and I need to finish my homework."

Kyleigh let out a soft sigh. "That's fine."

Holly was in eighth grade now. Her life had seemed to change overnight after she officially became a teenager. Gone were the days of playing with dolls until bedtime. Now, she spent most of her time on her computer, which was even older and more outdated than Kyleigh's. While they weren't struggling by any means, their money was tight enough that Kyleigh couldn't afford to spend any extra income on things they didn't need. She lived by the philosophy *don't replace it unless it's broken*. Unfortunately, Holly's computer had lived long past what it should have, and Kyleigh was going to need to replace it soon, especially with high school right around the corner.

"Yes!" she heard Holly shout a few moments later.

It was rare to hear her daughter get excited about anything these days. Aside from puberty making her hormones rage, she'd been having issues with some of the other girls at school.

During Valentine's Day the previous year, Holly's school

raised money for new football uniforms by selling candy grams. The football players had gone around delivering grams to students throughout the day, announcing to everyone who the recipients and senders were. Holly's bullies had sent one to a boy she had a crush on, stating it was from her with love, broadcasting her feelings to the whole school. She had been mortified, coming home in hysterics.

The bullying had gotten crueler since. Kyleigh had brought it up to the school numerous times, and they'd finally made some half-hearted attempt to solve the issue by having the kids watch a video on bullying. Their solution hadn't solved anything. It didn't help that the mother of Holly's main bully was president of the PTA. Kyleigh was at her wit's end about the whole situation and had begun to look at alternative solutions for Holly's education.

Kyleigh headed to the front of the store to see what had caused Holly's happy reaction. She found her daughter staring at the computer screen. She's pulled her blond hair—so much like her mother's—into a high ponytail. Her blue eyes sparkled, and she wore a bright smile on her face.

"What's up?" Kyleigh asked.

"This!" Holly shrieked. She turned the computer so that Kyleigh could see that her email was still open, the announcement from *First Comes Marriage* glaring back at her.

Kyleigh shook her head. "Oh, ignore that. It was sent to me by mistake."

"It wasn't, though," she responded.

The proud expression on her face had Kyleigh's eyes narrowing. "Do you know something about this?"

Her daughter's elation made her look younger, like the sweet kid who used to follow her around the store, instead of the sullen teen that spent most of her days in her room.

Holly squinted at the screen. "I entered your name, but I didn't think you'd actually have a chance."

Upon that announcement, Kyleigh marched over to the counter and snapped the laptop shut to get her daughter's full attention. "What do you mean, you entered my name?"

Holly rolled her eyes like it was obvious. "I saw on social media that they were looking for contestants between the ages of twenty and forty who lived in the area. All I had to do was enter your name, age, upload your picture and click an agreement that the show could film you."

"Wha—why on earth would you do that?" Kyleigh asked.

Holly quirked her head, causing her long blond pony-tail to tumble down her left shoulder. "Don't you think it's time you got married again?"

Her jaw dropped. "What? Why on earth do you think I need or want that?"

She was perfectly fine with her status as a divorcée, thank you very much.

Holly waved her hand around the store. "No offense, Mom, but all you do is work and take care of me. You don't have much of a life."

She tried not to get too hurt over that. "I have a life."

"Having wine nights with Meg and Julie on occasion doesn't count. What about a relationship with a man? When was the last time you hooked up with someone?"

Kyleigh tried not to blush. "What in the world? I'm not discussing my sex life with you."

"I'm just saying, it's time for you to get back into the dating pool. You haven't dated anyone since you and Dad broke up."

It was true that Kyleigh hadn't been involved with any-one since Dan left her to move to the Upper Peninsula. He'd met some woman named Ginger shortly after the divorce, remarried and had three kids with her. Considering he'd always told Kyleigh that he never wanted kids, and he rarely saw Holly, it stung her more than she wanted to admit.

"Okay, even if I wanted to date someone," Kyleigh finally said, "why do you think I'd ever want to be on a reality TV show?"

"It's such a funny show. The dates are ridiculous, and the host is super-hot. You'll have so much fun, and even if the marriage doesn't work out, at least you'll get to spend some time with Paul Rodriguez. He's really cute. Did you know he's dating Monica Valdez? Do you think he can get me her autograph?"

Kyleigh tried to ignore the way that news made something unpleasant crawl inside her. Paul's sexual escapades over the years had become legendary. Who cared if he was dating some tacky reality star who only made it big thanks to her leaked sex video?

"Well, I'm not doing it regardless," Kyleigh told her daughter firmly.

"What?" Holly had the audacity to look shocked. "You have to!"

"I absolutely do not, and if this is how you're going to spend your time on the computer, maybe you don't need one anymore."

Holly gave Kyleigh a familiar look that said her daughter clearly thought she was being unreasonable. She had that expression practically patented.

"Okay, I shouldn't have entered your name," Holly admitted. Kyleigh folded her arms over her chest. Her daughter wasn't one to give in so easily. "But what about me?"

Kyleigh's fingers tapped against her crossed arm. "What about you?"

"You're always telling me that the store is my legacy, right?" When Kyleigh merely lifted an eyebrow in response, Holly said, "Think of the publicity being on the show could give the shop. This could set us up for years to come. Decades even."

A master manipulator, that was what her daughter was. But…this *would* put the store on the map in a way it never had before. It'd be nice to buy things they could really use. A new car. New technology for both her and Holly.

No! The whole notion was absurd.

And yet…

"What do you say?" Holly asked, her eyes pleading.

Kyleigh had no interest in going anywhere near Paul Rodriguez. She'd only seen him a couple of times in the past twenty years—at Julie's wedding and the pre-wedding party—and that had been enough.

Still, what Holly said did make the idea somewhat tempting. The extra publicity couldn't hurt the store, and if Kyleigh ended up selected as a contestant, the whole experience would only be temporary.

With her mouth forming a thin line, Kyleigh said, "I'll think about it."

Chapter Two

Paul Rodriguez sat in his office chair, an unhappy expression marring his face. He watched his show's director pace back and forth in front of his black granite desk.

"Shawnee, would you please stop moving, you're giving me motion sickness," Paul finally snapped as he reached for his mug of coffee. He wished it was something stronger, but he didn't drink. Or he should say, he *rarely* drank. After a drunk driver killed his parents when he was younger, he rarely resorted to alcohol for anything. The last time he'd had something was at Jake's bachelor party, and that was only because—

Shawnee gave him a dirty look. "Had a rough night, did you?"

Rough didn't begin to cover it.

Paul had had enough of his girlfriend, Monica Valdez, using him as a prop for her reality show, *Just Monica*. When they first started sleeping together, he'd been flattered by her attention, of her wanting to showcase him on her show. But it quickly lost its appeal when her team's camera crew started following them everywhere, and he realized she didn't really want him. She wanted the fame attached to his name.

So he dumped her. Which led to her screaming at him

for a full hour until he walked out of her apartment. He'd celebrated the failure of yet another one of his relationships by coming home and revising his twelve-step plan to launch his own production company for the hundredth time. He'd been up way too late the previous night, and now he felt queasy from the lack of sleep. And he really didn't appreciate his director demanding to see him at seven-freaking-o'clock in the morning.

"I take it you haven't been on your social media this morning?" Shawnee asked him.

Shawnee was around his age, a complete ballbuster, and one of his closest friends. For that reason, he didn't snap at her like he wanted to. She'd probably whack him upside the head if he did.

Paul rubbed at his dark brown eyes tiredly. "Until ten minutes ago, I was sleeping soundly in my bed, so no, I haven't checked my socials."

"Then let me enlighten you," Shawnee replied. She pulled out her phone and turned it on before slapping it in front of him.

It took Paul a minute to get his vision to focus. When it did, his eyebrows shot up. "This is what you woke me up about? Monica throwing a tantrum on Insta?"

From what he could gather, Monica was telling everyone that *she* dumped him. It amused him, but he didn't really care what narrative she wanted to tell the world, as long as he never had to see her again.

"This is serious, Paul," Shawnee said, snatching her phone. "She's telling everyone you're a commitment-phobe."

Paul looked at his now empty coffee mug with longing. "She's not wrong. Also, I'd like to point out that she and I dated for three months, tops, and she's now telling everyone that *she* broke up with me. How does that make me the problem here? It's not like we were engaged or anything."

There'd only ever been one woman he'd loved enough to consider marrying, but her father had quickly convinced him that he was a nobody from the wrong side of the tracks—not good enough for his little angel. But Paul didn't want to take that particular trip down memory lane this early in the morning.

"Monica isn't just someone you can brush aside," Shawnee warned, resuming her pacing. "She has a large social media following, and people are listening to her. Including network executives."

Paul's brain had started drifting to what he was going to ask his chef to cook for breakfast, but the mention of the network brought his attention back. He gave Shawnee a cool look. "Can you get to the dammed point?"

She glared at him. "Fine. Paul, you're a forty-year-old man acting like a playboy. You've told more than one reporter that you'd sooner set yourself on fire than ever get married—"

"Oh, please, I haven't said that to anyone since I was in my twenties—"

Shawnee waved him off impatiently. "I'm going to level with you. It isn't a good look to have someone who's clearly anti-marriage hosting a show that's sole purpose is to sell people on the idea of marriage. And from the conversation I had with the network, they're thinking maybe it's time to make a change."

Paul stiffened. "What kind of change?"

Shawnee looked reluctant. "I've heard some rumors that they're thinking about going with someone younger. Someone who's already married."

Paul raked his fingers through his wavy, dark brown

hair. "Those sons of— This is my show, dammit. I literally own the rights to it—"

"You own forty-nine percent of the rights. The network owns the other fifty-one percent, and if you remember, they also added an escape clause in your contract that if they wanted to change hosts, they could."

Paul barely remembered the details of his contract. He'd been too elated that the show would open doors to the entertainment industry in a way being a Holiday Boy hadn't. Because of that, he hadn't paid much attention to the fine print.

Paul's heart sank. He couldn't lose *First Comes Marriage*. It was his flagship show. In fact, over the past couple of years, he'd been working hard on starting his own production company. His dream was to film the best of reality TV before branching out into other parts of the industry. TV shows. Film.

For him to do that, he needed the networks to believe in him. Reputation was everything in this town. He thought he had enough power and respect from being the long-standing host of *First Comes Marriage*. But his credibility had taken a hit when a show he'd successfully pitched ended up canceled before it started. He'd planned a show around his fellow Holiday Boy, James, who restored old homes in Detroit. When James discovered his husband was having an affair with the director, he understandably bailed. Without James, the show folded.

Paul didn't hold anything against his friend. James handled the situation much better than he would have. If it had been him, he would've done something to end up in prison, like his brother.

Unfortunately, when it came to his professional career, the fiasco had tarnished Paul and his ability to deliver a high-quality show. He shouldn't be surprised that the network was trying to replace him. They probably thought he was washed up. A has-been.

A failure.

Just like Kyleigh's father always predicted he'd be.

Paul rubbed a hand over the bristles on his face. He looked at Shawnee with exhausted eyes, feeling every bit his age. "What do I need to do?"

"We need to make this season the biggest one we've ever had." She walked over to the chair on the opposite side of him and reached into the gray laptop bag she'd left there earlier. She pulled out her tablet and powered it on before handing it to him. "Here's a list of the contestants we've chosen for the final round of applicants. We need someone that screams Midwest values. Someone different than anyone else we've had on the show." She gave him a stern look. "And it'd be great if we could find someone who's actually interested in the groom they're marrying, instead of making googly eyes at you."

"Good luck with that," he said with feigned arrogance. It was true that more than one bride applied to the show in hopes of landing Paul himself, instead of a groom. Sometimes he consoled their eventual failed marriages by giving them one night of pleasure. At least, he used to. He'd been getting more wary about it over recent years.

He flipped to the first application before letting out a snort. "Abigail Leonard. Aged twenty. Daughter of Alise and Stu Leon—oh hell no. First off, we're not considering having someone on the show that's not even old enough to drink—"

"Please, when has that ever stopped us from—"

"Not to mention, I got to third base with her mother behind the high school stadium after my football team kicked her boyfriend's team's ass in ninth grade. Forget it. That'd be super awkward. Especially if she made googly eyes at me, as you put it."

Shawnee gave him a disgruntled look. "What are the chances there will be someone in this selection that you haven't had some form of sex with?"

Paul gave her a rakish grin, but it instantly dropped when he looked at the next contestant. "I haven't slept with this one, thank god. Opal Beaumont. Daughter of Clarice and Mayor Beaumont."

Shawnee peered at the screen upside down. "What's wrong with her? She's cute, has that Midwest look about her. Has connections to the town that viewers will love to see."

"She's also a pretentious snob." Paul had heard enough horror stories from his bandmate, Tyler, about the Beaumonts. Tyler's wife, Meg, was once engaged to Opal's brother, Lucas. The Beaumonts had gone out of their way to treat Meg like absolute garbage. He'd rather quit the show than have that woman anywhere near his set. "She's an absolute no."

Shawnee threw up her hands. "Fine. What about the next one? You can't object to her. She's as Midwestern as they come. Single mom, owns a small business in town and just happens to be a blond goddess."

Paul flicked to the next application and instantly froze. He couldn't believe what he was seeing. He'd never forget that face for as long as he lived. He'd certainly dreamed about it enough over the years.

"What?" Shawnee said impatiently. "You can't seriously object to her."

Paul didn't hear her. He was too busy staring at the picture of Kyleigh. The last time he saw her was at Jake and Julie Reynold's wedding. She'd gone out of her way to pretend he didn't exist that night. He couldn't blame her. He hadn't ended their relationship in the best way.

Paul had been so stupid back then. He and his friends had just signed a contract with Phil "Big Poppa" Cummings, officially becoming the Holiday Boys. Big Poppa had promised he was going to make them superstars, richer than they could ever imagine.

Paul had been ecstatic and eagerly drove to Kyleigh's house in Holiday Bay to tell her the news. He'd wanted to take her with him, his mother's engagement ring in his pocket. But Kyleigh hadn't answered the door when he knocked. She'd apparently been at the salon getting her hair done for prom, which was later that night.

Instead, her father, Brock Sinclair, answered. Brock had been the town's sheriff at the time, and he'd never approved of Paul dating his daughter.

After Paul's parents died, he and his older brother, Dominic, lived with their aunt. Aunt Esperanza had barely managed, needing to work three jobs to support them. Between the loss of their parents, and their only remaining family gone at all hours, Dom spiraled. While Paul lost himself in performing, letting his music distract him from his grief, Dom had no outlet and instead became angry. He fell into the wrong crowd, earning himself a horrible reputation. His relationship with his brother strained to the breaking point. Before they knew it, Dom burglarized a store in Holiday Bay—caught by none other than Brock Sinclair.

As far as Sheriff Sinclair was concerned, Paul wasn't any good for his daughter. When Paul foolishly blurted out his plan to marry Kyleigh, the sheriff pointed out that he had nothing to offer her. That all he could offer was poverty. Paul tried to explain that he'd just signed with a manager, and he was on the verge of becoming rich and famous.

Brock laughed in his face, telling him to get serious. What were the chances of him actually making it big? He told Paul that if he truly loved Kyleigh as he claimed, he'd let her go.

And when that still hadn't motivated Paul to give her up, the sheriff went after Paul's greatest weakness. He threatened Dom. Brock told Paul that if he didn't end things with Kyleigh, the sheriff would do everything in his power to make sure his brother never got out of prison.

With that threat lingering in the air, he shut the door in Paul's face, leaving him stunned, his hateful words carved into Paul's brain.

No matter how furious Paul was with his brother, he knew that Brock could and would use his influence to prolong Dom's sentence. Paul couldn't be responsible for that.

And he couldn't ignore what else the sheriff said.

Paul was nothing and had nothing to offer Kyleigh. His parents never had much money. It strained their marriage before they died. He'd witnessed firsthand how working multiple jobs had exhausted his aunt. His grades had never been much, and he never planned on going to college. What could he offer Kyleigh if Holiday Boys failed?

A whole lot of nothing. As much as it killed him, Paul knew he had to let her go.

But as he walked away from her house, he promised himself he *would* make it big. He'd become the biggest success the world had ever seen. He'd become wealthy. Popular. And then he'd come back for Kyleigh while shoving his success in Brock Sinclair's face.

He started receiving phone calls and texts from Kyleigh later that day. He ignored them all until he finally responded, I'm leaving town tonight. I'm sorry I can't be with you right now.

Her texts stopped after that. His phone went silent. He didn't hear from her again. He went on to do exactly what he promised himself. Holiday Boys blew up. He invested his money well and became wealthier than he ever could have dreamed. He fell in love with the entertainment industry, and the camera loved him back. He became a star.

Then he went back for Kyleigh.

But it had been too late by then. She had met some guy in college and was engaged by the time Paul returned. He found out later that she'd had a kid shortly after getting married. As much as it killed him, Paul had no choice but to finally, truly, let her go.

In an effort to forget her, he fully embraced his bachelor status, sleeping with anyone from groupies to contestants on his show. No matter how many women he slept with, though, he couldn't forget Kyleigh. She haunted him like a specter.

"Hello, earth to Paul," Shawnee said, waving her hand in front of his face, breaking his fixation on the tablet. "What is it?"

"I can't..." His voice choked, and he cleared it forcibly. "I can't have Kyleigh on this show."

Shawnee let out a tired sigh. "Let me guess. You fooled around with her, too."

"I didn't fool around with her," Paul rasped. "I loved her."

Her eyebrows shot up. "Come again? I didn't think you were capable of the emotion."

Paul gave her a hostile look. "Funny."

"What happened then? I've never seen you respond to any woman like this, let alone a picture of one."

He glanced back down at Kyleigh's face. She was forty

like him, but she had aged beautifully with her gorgeous blond hair and blue eyes, her face maturing to perfection.

Paul shook his head to clear it. "What did I know? We were kids. Just teenagers."

"I see," Shawnee said slowly.

"Look, these contestants aren't going to work." Paul shoved the tablet across the desk before jumping to his feet. "Send me another list. I'm going to take a shower."

"Sure," she said.

After Paul left, Shawnee grabbed her phone to call her cameraman. "Gregori, it's Shawnee. I need you to gather the crew and fly out to Holiday Bay. I want to start rolling on our female contestant's first interview. Can you meet me there on Tuesday?"

"Sure, boss," Gregori responded. "Where are we meeting you?"

Shawnee looked down at her tablet.

"Kyleigh's Knits."

Chapter Three

The store was busier than normal due to buzz going around town that a camera crew had been spotted checking into the local hotel. Speculation had been rampant all morning that the crew was a part of *First Comes Marriage*. Kyleigh's stomach had been in knots ever since a customer told her.

Was Paul with them?

Not that she cared.

Thanks to Hollywood being at their backdoor, people started gathering on Main Street, hoping to get a glimpse of whatever was about to descend on their quiet community.

"I put my name in for the show," Charlotte Hoeks told her. The leggy twenty-two-year-old purchased a book on *Origami for Beginners*. "I would just *die* if I got selected."

Kyleigh kept her face as neutral as possible. When Holiday Boys were at their peak, a magazine had listed a hobby each boy loved. Paul mentioned origami. He'd been really good at it, too. Back when they were dating, he'd given her a whole collection of different birds and animals he'd made from paper. She'd kept them in a keepsake box under her bed, but after he dumped her, she'd thrown it away.

Sometimes Kyleigh regretted that. She probably could have sold them on some auction site and made a small fortune for herself.

"I wish you luck," she told the younger woman after handing her the receipt.

Charlotte left, and Kyleigh's shoulders drooped. She could feel a headache coming on. Sighing tiredly, she pulled out her tablet and started walking around the store to do inventory.

The bell above the shop rang, and Holly entered. "Hey, Mom."

"Hi, sweets," Kyleigh replied. She paused when she looked at her daughter's puffy eyes. "What happened?"

Holly didn't meet her eyes. "Nothing."

Kyleigh walked over to her and grabbed her daughter's chin, gently lifting it so she could see Holly's face a little better. She sucked in a breath when she saw Holly had a fat lip.

"What on earth?" Kyleigh muttered. "Who did that to you?"

Holly pulled her head away and turned her face. "No one. I tripped and hit my mouth when I leaned down to get a drink from the water fountain at school. It's not a big deal."

Kyleigh's head ached a little bit harder. "Honey, I can't help you if you don't tell me what's going on."

"Nothing! Can I just go do my homework or something?"

Kyleigh's lips firmed before she let out a little breath. "I put those cheese snacks you like in the fridge in my office."

"Thanks." Holly didn't say another word as she headed to the back room.

The bell rang again, and Kyleigh pushed away her worry and put on another forced smile. "Hello, is there anything I can help you f—"

Her greeting died as four people entered the store carrying various cameras and lighting equipment.

A man in his early sixties with gray hair and a deep tan pointed to a younger man. "Set that one up over there, Leroy."

"You got it," Leroy said, walking over to one of the aisles and setting a tripod down.

Kyleigh hurried around the counter. "Excuse me, what are you doing?"

"Setting up," the older man told her, like it should be obvious.

"Yes, but why?"

The doorbell rang again, and a tall woman with short red hair walked in. She wore a dark gray business jacket with a matching pencil skirt and had a no-nonsense look to her. "Are you Kyleigh Sinclair?" she asked.

Kyleigh glanced at the cameras getting arranged before turning back to the woman, a sickening dread making the acid in her stomach erupt like a volcano. She swallowed hard so she wouldn't throw up. "Yes?" she said after a pause.

The woman's stern face lit into a bright smile. "I'm Shawnee Roberts. Congratulations. You've been selected as our female contestant for the hit show, *First Comes Marriage.*"

"What? No, I—"

A screech resounded from the back of the building before Holly came flying toward her. She ran into Kyleigh so hard she caused her to stagger on her feet. Her daughter wrapped her in a hard hug.

"I knew it!" Holly shouted. "I knew you'd get selected."

"Who's this?" Shawnee asked, holding her hand out to Holly.

"I'm Holly Meadows, I'm her daughter," she said as she shook the older woman's hand.

"Nice to meet you, Holly," Shawnee replied before turning her attention back to Kyleigh. "You're actually our first contestant to have a child. It'll be a fresh twist. In fact, I think this is going to be our best season yet."

"Holly," Kyleigh said firmly. "Go back to your homework."

"But, Mom—"

"Go!" Kyleigh's voice left no room for argument.

Her daughter let out an angry humph before stomping back to the store's office.

Kyleigh waited until she disappeared before asking, "Holly's not going to be on the show, will she?"

Shawnee frowned in confusion. "Well, yes. You did read over the agreement, didn't you? It gives us consent to film *all* aspects of your life. I have the full contract with me that I'll need you to sign before we wrap today. But let's get you in front of the camera and make sure this is a good fit before we finalize everything."

"Well, you see…" Kyleigh didn't know how to begin explaining the situation she found herself in. "About that. I didn't actually—"

She intended to explain that she hadn't signed the agreement. That after further consideration, she was going to pull her name out of the show. The store was doing well enough. She didn't need their help with publicity. Could things be better? Sure. But she didn't need to sell her soul to the devil to accomplish her sales goals. And yes, being a contestant would've made her daughter ecstatic, and that was important after everything Holly had been going through lately, but Kyleigh couldn't do it. The idea of marrying some stranger while Paul watched like she never mattered to him made Kyleigh physically ill.

That was what she planned to say anyway.

And then, the man himself walked into her shop, looking angrier than she'd ever seen him.

To say Paul was furious was an understatement. When Gregori called him to confirm where Shawnee had instructed the crew to start filming, Paul booked the first plane ticket he could get to Michigan. Even though his seat was in coach next to the bathrooms, and he'd dealt with a seventy-year-old woman hitting on him the entire flight. He fully intended to chew Shawnee out, but he came to an abrupt halt when he saw Kyleigh standing in front of him looking like a deer in the headlights.

Her hair was tied in a knot at the top of her head. She wore a navy blue sleeveless knit sweater with leggings that hugged her in all the right places. Even though she'd always been the most beautiful woman he'd ever seen, she was pale and had a pinched look on her face. That expression put a pause on his pulsing outrage. He opened his mouth to ask her if she was okay, but Gregori chose right then to interrupt them.

"We're all set, boss," the cameraman told Shawnee. "We got some nice shots around town earlier and already took pictures of the exterior of the shop."

"When did you—" Kyleigh started to say, but Shawnee talked over her.

"Perfect. Kyleigh, my wife will get you into makeup. Babe, are you ready?" she called out, adoration on her face.

Her wife, Heather, walked over to them from where she'd been standing with some of the other crew. "Yep, ready." She grabbed Kyleigh's arm and dragged her to the back of the store before Kyleigh could get a word of protest out.

That was how this crew worked. No time for chitchat

when money was on the line. Concerns could be brought up later.

Shawnee turned to Paul with the expression of an angel on her face.

Paul gave her a deadly look. "Are you being serious with this?" he snapped. "I told you Kyleigh was a no."

"I know you did."

Paul threw his hands in the air. "Then what the hell are we doing here?"

"You and I both know that she's the perfect choice. She's exactly what this show needs. We have to shake things up and not have the same twentysomethings that we always have." Shawnee held her hand up for dramatic effect and wiped it slowly across the air in front of her as she said, "Picture it. A single mom, who owns a small business in Holiday Bay, is ready to find a second chance at happiness."

Paul's eye twitched. "Okay, then let's find someone else."

Shawnee crossed her arms over her chest, giving him that stubborn look he hated. No matter how many times they butted heads over the years, no matter how much he loved his friend, he knew that expression well. It meant he wasn't going to win this battle.

"I've already spoken to the network, and they agree. Kyleigh's in."

"Dammit." Paul ran his hand through his hair. He started to pace. "You know there's a history here."

"Wasn't that years ago when you were kids?" Shawnee looked at him, matter-of-fact. "You've both moved on."

Had he, though? Had he ever gotten over Kyleigh Sinclair? He'd certainly tried, but had he actually ever succeeded?

Kyleigh reappeared with Heather. A layer of makeup now covered the dark circles he'd noticed earlier under her eyes, and Heather had added blush to give her cheeks some much needed color. She looked stunning, despite the pallor to her skin that even makeup couldn't hide.

"Kyleigh, we're going to do your interview over there," Shawnee announced, pointing with her hand to a wall of fabrics.

Kyleigh looked around the store as if she didn't recognize it.

"First day nerves, huh?" Heather said to her. She grabbed Kyleigh's arm again and guided her toward one of the chairs the team had set up.

Paul gritted his teeth, not taking his eyes off Kyleigh as he muttered, "Who's the male contestant you've chosen?"

"We're still deciding. We've narrowed it down to two."

"I want full approval on that," Paul said, furious all over again. He had no reason to be so mad. This was his job. He'd been marrying strangers to each other for years. This was just business, and Kyleigh's marriage to another man was merely a transaction. The urge to punch something was absolutely ridiculous.

"If you're going to be stubborn about our final choice, then we'll have to—"

"I'm serious, Shawnee," Paul said. "Either I get the final say on who Kyleigh marries, or you find yourself a new host."

Shawnee's jaw dropped at that. She knew how much this show meant to him.

But to hell with Kyleigh marrying some random guy who wasn't good enough for her. There was no way he was about to let that happen.

"Fine," Shawnee finally said.

"Fine," Paul repeated. "Now, if you'll excuse, I'm going to do Kyleigh's first interview."

"What?" Shawnee didn't try to hide her surprise. Usually, she always did the first interview. Paul didn't even see the contestants until later on in the filming.

Ignoring her, he walked toward Kyleigh, determination setting in his shoulders. The last time he had seen her she'd ignored him.

Well, she may have been able to mostly avoid him at Jake and Julie's wedding, but there was no way she could ignore him now.

Chapter Four

Kyleigh sat down in the black banquet chair the crew had collected from her craft room. There was movement all around her as various people continued to get things ready for filming.

Her eyes wandered around the clean white walls of her store, where black iron baskets were filled with different yarns. On the long, open racks behind her were rows of fabrics of all different types. One aisle over were items for drawing and artwork. The store was set up to embrace any hobby that a crafter did. Kyleigh was normally deeply proud of her shop.

Her mind didn't register any of it.

How had this happened?

She wasn't supposed to get selected. She figured she could run with the idea for a bit longer for Holly's sake— her daughter was so enthralled with the whole thing—but she never thought they'd actually choose her. They usually picked girls who were fresh out of college.

No. This was a huge mistake. Kyleigh needed to stop this train before it left the station. She opened her mouth to say just that when movement caught her eye.

Through the brightness of the lights they'd set up, she could see Holly peeking around the corner of one of the shelves. She hopped from one foot to the other, barely able to contain her excitement. The words of refusal stuck on Kyleigh's tongue as her gaze narrowed on her daughter's poor, fat lip. She couldn't remember the last time she'd seen Holly so happy.

Paul walked over to the chair opposite her and sat down with a confidence that would have impressed her if she wasn't so horrified.

The last time she'd seen him at Julie's wedding, she'd done her best to ignore him, but Paul Rodriguez wasn't a man someone could ignore. He had a magnetism that always drew the eye. And she hadn't been the only woman drawn to him that night. More than one lady walked by him, vying for his attention. His reputation with women was legendary for a reason.

The daze in her head cleared at that reminder. She lifted her chin as she looked at Paul.

He leaned back in his chair, eyeing her with a cool casualness she wished she could return.

"What are you doing?" Kyleigh whispered.

"Interviewing you," Paul responded as he straightened the collar of the tight black polo shirt he wore.

"You don't do first interviews," she replied, and then wanted to smack herself when a sly, smug expression popped onto his face.

"Watch the show often, do you?"

Kyleigh gave him a cold look. "My daughter is a fan." She nodded toward Holly.

Paul's head whipped around, noticing the young girl for the first time. Holly went as still as a statue as Paul examined her briefly before sending her a bright, professional smile. Holly let out a squeak and disappeared from view.

Paul turned back to Kyleigh. "She's a miniature version of you."

"So I've been told."

An expression flashed across his face so fast, she couldn't decipher it before it disappeared.

"If you've watched the show before, you know how this works," Paul said. A man who'd introduced himself as Gregori held a light meter in front of her face. Paul continued as if he wasn't there. "I'm going to ask you a series of questions to get a feel for what your ideal man is." He paused, his lips pursing like someone had shoved a lemon down his mouth. He finally ground out, "Any questions?"

"No," she replied.

Gregori gave them a nod before moving behind a camera. "Camera two ready?" he called out, and Leroy gave a thumbs-up.

"Audio?" he asked.

A woman wearing headphones, holding a boom mic over their heads, nodded.

Gregori said, "Everyone quiet, please. Annnnd…rolling."

Paul sent the camera another one of his faux megawatt smiles before saying, "Ladies and gentleman, welcome to another season of *First Comes Marriage*. This season we're taking you, the viewers, out of California and returning to my roots in Holiday Bay, Michigan. As fans of Holiday Boys know, this is where my friends and I met and started the band. And in front of me is our very own Holiday Bay native, Kyleigh Sinclair. Or is it something else since you've been married?"

Kyleigh stiffened at the passive aggressiveness she could hear in the question. "No, it's Sinclair. I never changed it after my marriage."

"Right." His voice was as dry as sandpaper. "Tell us, Kyleigh. What do you hope for in your future husband?"

"I, um…" Kyleigh didn't know what to say. She felt queasy. Everyone around them stared at her expectantly. She never planned on getting married again, so she'd never put much thought into the idea. She certainly didn't feel like talking about her future husband's characteristics with her ex-boyfriend.

"Yes?" Paul said, his features turning smug again. The bastard was enjoying this.

Her chin rose defiantly. "I want someone who understands the meaning of commitment. A man who doesn't run away. A husband who will put us first before his career."

Paul's eyes turned icy as her words hit their target. "What about financial security? From what I remember, that was the most important thing to your family. Do you expect your husband to be in a certain income bracket?"

Anger warmed Kyleigh's cheeks. "Are you insinuating—"

"Let's get back to your former marriage," Paul interrupted. "Why didn't you want to take your husband's name? Should your future husband expect the same thing? Or did your father bully you into keeping it? Many people don't know that your dad used to be sheriff of Holiday Bay. He always was a controlling jerk—"

"What the hell is your—"

"Oookay," Shawnee said, stepping in between them. "Paul, I know you two used to know each other, but I'm going to need you to keep this professional, or you'll have to leave, and I'll take over the interview."

A belligerent smile popped on his face. "I don't see anything wrong with my questions. I think they're perfectly legitimate. People are going to want to know every detail about Kyleigh's life." His eyes locked on hers. "You get that, right? Nothing about you is going to be sacred. People are going to want to know everything about you, from the reason you divorced your ex to your family history. Even if you don't share anything, people have a way of finding out. Are you sure this is what you want?"

Kyleigh swallowed. It wasn't what she wanted at all, and she was tempted to tell them that she never applied in the first place. But something stopped her. Maybe it was Paul himself. It was obvious from the attitude he was giving that he didn't want her as a contestant. She was feeling stubborn enough to do the show just to spite him.

"Why don't we take a ten-minute reset and compose ourselves?" Shawnee suggested.

"Fine with me," Kyleigh responded. She jumped up on legs that shook. Without looking at anyone, she marched across the store's brown vinyl floor toward the back where the bathroom was. Closing the door behind her, she walked over to the sink and gripped the edge of the counter until her fingers turned white.

How dare he?

Who the hell did Paul Rodriguez think he was? She'd watched the show enough times to know they never dived into personal questions to start. It was usually silly innocent things like asking her about her ideal date and finding out what her astrological sign was. They never dissected their contestants' lives like that.

How dare Paul act like that! He was acting as though she had wronged him somehow. Had he forgotten that *he* dumped her? Once upon a time, she'd loved Paul with every fiber in her soul. And he left her with nothing but some half-ass text breaking up with her. Now he acted upset because she'd moved on with her life? To hell with that *and* him.

Any thoughts about abandoning the show disappeared.

She was going to go through with it. She was going to marry a complete stranger. She couldn't wait to see Paul's face when she said *I do* to someone else. If she was lucky, maybe her future husband might actually be the guy for her.

Determination settling in her, she walked over to the door and shoved it open. It hit someone who let out an *oof.* Paul rubbed his shoulder.

"What?" she snapped.

"Look, I came to apologize to you. I shouldn't have started the interview like that."

"Fine." She went to brush by him, but he grabbed her arm.

"Can you stop?" he said, his face lined with irritation.

"What?" She glared at him.

"Stop walking away from me."

"Me?" This man's freaking audacity. "I'm not the one who walks away from people."

"I…" Paul looked at her in frustration before gently dragging her back into the bathroom. The door closed behind them with a snap. He let her go to run a hand through his dark hair. "You can't be serious about this, Ky."

Kyleigh's heart flipped at the nickname. Despite the easy shortening of her name, she'd always gone by Kyleigh. Paul was the only one who ever called her Ky. "What aren't I serious about?" she said, her voice tight.

He walked toward her, and she took several steps back until her hips hit the sink. Paul placed his hands on either side of the counter, caging her in.

"You can't be serious about this show. You don't want to marry a stranger."

"Don't I?" she responded.

"That's not who you are. You've always overanalyzed

everything, from your test scores to which song to do for karaoke."

Kyleigh thought back to that summer they first met at performing arts camp. At the time, Kyleigh had thought about becoming an artist. Paul always knew he was going to be a singer. They both arrived at the camp in very different circumstances. Her parents had paid for her, always making sure she lacked for nothing growing up. Paul had received a scholarship for singing and acting. But despite their different walks of life, they'd connected on their first day when Paul offered to help carry her bag to her lodging.

On their last night that summer, the camp held a karaoke showcase, and Paul and Kyleigh sang together, receiving a standing ovation. Later, they'd sneaked off and made love for the first time.

Her face heated at the memory. Her hands touched his chest. She meant to push him away, but she couldn't get her arms to cooperate. She said shakily, "You don't know me anymore."

"Don't I?" Paul responded lowly. He moved toward her until they were bare inches apart. She could smell the fresh mint of his breath, the rich woodsy scent of his cologne. Goose bumps broke out on her arms at his nearness, and he stared at her skin in fascination.

"I forgot how reactive you are," he murmured almost to himself as he ran a finger lightly over the raised bumps. She shivered, and his lips curled into a smile that wasn't fake like his earlier ones. This one was sensuous, filled with promise.

He closed the distance between them, the heat of his chest rubbing against her breasts until she could feel her nipples harden in response.

His lips brushed against her ear, and she arched against him in phantom response.

"You can still back out, you know," he whispered. "You don't need to marry a stranger. I know you don't really want to do this."

The spell he'd captured her in instantly broke. She pushed him away, and he took a few careful steps back.

"Who says I don't?" she asked to be contrary.

Her skin burned with embarrassment. While she felt the need for a cool shower, he appeared completely casual, as though she had no effect on him whatsoever. What little pride she had when it came to him shattered around her feet.

Until he snapped, "You think I'm really going to step aside and let you get married on my show?" He didn't try to hide the anger boiling under the surface of his composure.

It unleashed her own anger. The pent-up hurt that she'd buried years ago, and the fury she felt now over his reaction to her being on his show. Kyleigh wasn't blind to what Paul had been up to since he left her. He very much lived the lifestyle of a playboy and had slept his way through countless women. Yet, if Kyleigh wanted a shot at love, he freaked out?

Screw that!

Stiffening her spine, she maneuvered past him to the door. "If you'll excuse me, I have a contract to go sign."

She walked out of the bathroom and didn't look back to see if Paul followed her.

Paul fumed as he watched the camera crew pack the show's equipment into their rental van. After his first attempt to interview Kyleigh, Shawnee had lived up to her word and kicked Paul off the set. She told him to go wait somewhere else; that she was taking over.

He'd paced outside the building like an angry tiger and watched through the window as Shawnee completed Kyleigh's interview. It was clear that Kyleigh was at ease now that Paul was no longer in the store, her face relaxed, her smile unguarded.

If he closed his eyes for a moment, Paul could still feel the imprint of her against him when they were in the bathroom together, the sweet smell of the cherry blossom perfume she still wore infiltrating his senses. He knew the scent well. It had haunted his dreams for years.

It had taken every bit of his self-control to not react like he'd wanted, which was to feel her lips against his, to explore her mouth with his tongue to see if she still tasted as good as he remembered.

He watched her now as she tucked a strand of loose hair behind her ear. Out of all the women he'd known, no matter how many relationships he'd attempted, no one ever measured up to Kyleigh. It was because of her he had the financial success that he did. He'd been so determined to prove to her and her father that he was worthy of her.

And now he was supposed to step aside and let her marry someone else. *Again.*

Forget that.

Shawnee and Gregori shook Kyleigh's hand and left the shop. Kyleigh headed toward the counter where her daughter sat playing on a laptop. Holly said something to her, and Kyleigh went around the counter to point at something on the screen. He was in awe of how much her daughter looked like her. Even their expressions were identical as they stared intently at the screen.

Had he returned sooner, or if Kyleigh had waited a little bit longer for him, that might have been his daughter—his family—in there. Not that he knew anything about being a family man. His family life had imploded when he was still an impressionable teenager.

"Despite how the interview started," Shawnee said, walking over to him, "I think I managed to salvage the situation."

"Great," Paul muttered as he turned away from the scene inside.

"Is this how it's going to be all season?" his director asked, following him.

"What do you mean?" He headed for his rental car.

"You acting like a jealous lover every time Kyleigh speaks about finding someone else."

"I'm not acting like a jealous anything. You're imagining it."

"Well, that's a relief to hear." Shawnee reached for her phone and pressed a button.

Paul's phone beeped a few seconds later, letting him know that he'd received a text. His foul mood turned completely black as he stared at the pictures of two men about his age.

"What the hell is this?" he growled.

"It's the final list of men we want to consider for Kyleigh's husband."

Paul stared blankly at the picture of some blond guy with dimples. He hated everything about him. There was no way this douche was going to get anywhere near Kyleigh.

"No," he replied simply but firmly.

"What do you mean no?" Shawnee asked, clearly exasperated. "We agreed that you could pick out her spouse, but you have to, you know, *actually* pick out her spouse."

"I said no," Paul replied, deleting the text. "She's not going to marry any of those guys. Because I'm going to marry Kyleigh myself."

Chapter Five

Shawnee stared at him like he'd grown two heads, but after he said it, a huge burden lifted from his shoulders. Giving her a nod, he pulled the keys to his rental out of his pocket and unlocked the door of the red Aston Martin they'd given him.

"You need a ride back to the hotel?" he asked before hopping in. "Or are you driving back with Heather?"

She stumbled after him, falling into the passenger seat. "Heather can get a ride with Gregori. What the hell are you talking about, you're going to marry her yourself?"

"Think about it. If I marry Kyleigh, it'll kill two birds with one stone. It'll not only prove to the world that I can commit despite what Monica said, but my marriage will guarantee record-breaking ratings, securing my role as host for years to come."

And if he got to spend more time with Kyleigh, proving to her—and her father—that he was no longer the same pathetic kid from Clarington, then so be it.

Shawnee was quiet for a moment as he started the car and pulled onto the street. She opened and closed her mouth several times before saying, "Okay, you make a great point. But why now? Why this contestant? Surely you still aren't hung up on her?"

"Come on. We dated years ago," Paul replied evasively. "What do you want to hear? That she's the one that got away?"

"Is she?" Shawnee asked, her tone unusually gentle. Shawnee was typically very blunt in her responses. The fact that she was handling him with kid gloves should have given him a clue that he wasn't hiding his emotions as carefully as he thought he was.

He ignored her question as he took a detour. He pulled into a parking lot and nodded toward the bay in front of him. "See that beach? That's where we'll have the ceremony. I saw someone get married there years ago, and I always thought it was a great spot."

He'd taken Kyleigh to a date at the park shortly after they'd returned home from camp. He'd borrowed his aunt's beat-up car and picked Kyleigh up, ignoring her father's disapproving expression. They'd gone to McDonald's and then to the beach. It hadn't been much, but back then, it was all he could afford. Despite feeling slightly embarrassed that he couldn't offer to take her somewhere more worthy of her, he realized that she hadn't seemed to mind. They'd eaten their meal together and watched the couple marry in the distance. He could still see the awe on Kyleigh's face, could hear the delight in her voice as she talked about how romantic it was as the bride and groom kissed, confirming their marriage vows.

"Logistically, we should have a backup in case it rains," Shawnee said, her mind already going into work mode. "It'll be a pain in the ass to get permits and security. Maybe we should get a list of alternatives toge—"

"No," Paul said firmly. "It's got to be there."

He pulled out of the parking lot and headed to their hotel, ignoring Shawnee's protests about how he was being impractical. From the moment he saw Kyleigh's entranced expression all those years ago as she watched that couple get married, he knew they'd have their own wedding on that very spot one day. Not even an act of God would stop Paul from marrying Kyleigh on that beach.

After saying goodnight to Shawnee, he headed to his room. Paul took a long, hot shower to wash off his day of traveling. It was hard to believe that just that morning, he'd been lying in his California mansion, asleep on the custom-made king-size bed that cost him thousands of dollars. Settling on the motel's lumpy full-size mattress, he grabbed his phone from the bedside table where he'd placed it earlier and called his best friend, Zan.

While all the Holiday Boys were close, he'd always been closest to Zan. It was probably because they were the two outsiders. Jake, Tyler and James grew up together in Holiday Bay. Zan and Paul had grown up in Clarington and attended school together. They'd known each other since they were kids and bonded over their love of music, though Zan had been from one of the few upper middle class families in Clarington, and Paul had lived in one of the poorest.

Paul, unable to get comfortable on his mattress, got up and paced around the room as he waited for his friend to answer.

"Hey," Zan said after a few rings. "Long time, no talk."

"I texted you this morning."

"Yeah, but when was the last time we *talk* talked?" Zan said.

Paul laughed. "Aww, you miss me, buddy?"

"Every single day. I cry myself to sleep at night, hoping and wishing my best friend would pick up the phone and call—"

"Yeah, yeah," Paul said with a snort.

"Who's that?" a young voice said.

Paul's heart melted a little at the sound of his goddaughter, Alice. He didn't have much patience for kids. Well, that wasn't fair. He'd simply never been around them much. The ones he had been around were screaming tweens and teenagers who'd had his face plastered across their walls.

"Hi, Uncle Paul." Alice's little voice came on the line. "Are you coming for my birthday in a few months?"

"I wouldn't miss it. What are you going to be, twenty-nine?"

Her infectious laughter filled his ear. "I'm gonna be eight, Uncle Paul."

"Eight years old already. You're getting too big, bunny."

"All right," Paul could hear Zan say, his voice muffled in the background. "Give me back my phone, you little thief. Go check if your mom needs anything."

"Bye, Uncle Paul," Alice said.

"Bye, bunny," Paul replied.

"Sorry about that," Zan said a moment later.

"You know I'll never turn down the chance to speak with your kids. They're the only children I like."

"Wait until you have your own, you'll think different," Zan remarked, but he always said that.

"Speaking of that, I have some news," Paul said.

"You get Monica pregnant?" Zan asked.

Paul grimaced at the thought. "I'd rather cut off my dick than procreate with her. I always made sure we were extra careful there."

"Sorry, bro, but accidents do happen…"

"Can you stop wishing that on me?" Paul pleaded, squeezing the back of his neck with his hand.

"Sorry," Zan said, amusement in his voice. "So what's your news?"

"I'm getting married."

The sound of the phone hitting the floor jarred Paul's eardrum. He pulled the device away with a wince.

"Dammit," Zan swore from a distance before he came back on, his voice clearer. "I'm sorry, can you repeat that? I think I'm having a connection issue here. I thought you said you were getting married."

"I am."

"Wha…why…who?"

"I'm marrying a contestant from the show. In fact, we're going to be *the* couple of the new season. But don't tell anyone. This is completely confidential information until the promos can go out."

Zan was so quiet that Paul had to check the phone to see if they still had a connection.

"Let me see if I'm getting this straight," his friend finally said. "You're marrying someone on the show. *You.* I… Who is she?"

"Kyleigh Sinclair."

"Kyleigh. As in your ex-girlfriend, Kyleigh?"

"Yep, she entered her name in the show, and despite me telling Shawnee not to select her, she chose her anyway. With all the bad press I'm getting thanks to Monica, it makes sense. Shawnee said the network has been talking about replacing me. This will solve all my issues. They won't be able to fire me if I deliver them their best season yet. People will see that Monica is also full of garbage, and I'm not anti-marriage."

"But it's Kyleigh," Zan said. "Are you sure about this, Paul? I was there, remember? I saw how messed up you were after you two broke up."

Paul's jaw locked. It was true that after they signed their contract and he left town, he went on a downward spiral.

Paul spent too much time acting out and sleeping around. He gained a horrible reputation and officially became the "bad boy" of the Holiday Boys.

At one point, their manager, Big Poppa, had threatened to fire Paul if he didn't pull himself together. The threat of Paul losing his chance at success worked, and he stopped going out so much. He didn't become a saint overnight, but fans greatly overexaggerated his rebellious ways.

"I know what I'm doing," Paul told his friend firmly.

Zan went silent again before he finally said, "I guess I'll offer my congratulations then."

"Thanks," Paul replied, his tone stilted before he cleared his throat. "Listen, that's not the only reason I'm calling. I want you to be here as my best man."

"I'd love to…" Zan said, but there was hesitancy in his voice.

"But?" Paul tried not to feel hurt. He knew deep down Zan would always support him no matter how dumb his choices were. Even if Paul was going into the marriage to save his career, he couldn't imagine his best friend not being there.

Zan let out a sigh that seemed to come from the depths of his soul. "It's Mary."

Paul's disappointment immediately dissipated. "I'm a crap friend. How's she doing?"

Zan's wife, Mary, had been diagnosed with leukemia a few years ago. It seemed as though every medication the doctors tried did little to improve her condition. A bunch of friends and relatives from Zan and Mary's inner circle, Paul included, offered to be stem cell donors, but unfortunately, none of them were a match.

"She's not doing too good," Zan admitted. "The doctors are struggling to get her white blood cell count into a normal range. She's tired all the time. When she doesn't think anyone can hear her, she goes into our room and cries from the pain. I hate it. I hate seeing her like this and feeling so helpless."

"She's a fighter," Paul tried to encourage. "You know she is."

"Yeah." But Zan didn't sound optimistic.

"Listen, forget about the wedding, I'll ask someone else. You take care of you and your family. They're the most important."

"I am sorry, Paul. I wish I could be there."

"I know you do."

"Just…be careful, okay? Kyleigh's a good person. Make sure you don't hurt her."

"There aren't any emotions involved here. I'm not one hundred percent sure what her motivation is for getting married, but the Kyleigh I know wouldn't get married on a whim. I'll have ninety days to figure out what's driving her to do this while giving myself record ratings. Once I figure it out, I'll make sure we both benefit. It'll be perfect."

"Sure, Paul. Whatever you say."

Chapter Six

Kyleigh did her best to ignore the cameras that hadn't left her side since they first appeared in her store two weeks ago. She stepped out of her house, and they were there. She walked around town, and they were there. She did the mundane tasks of restocking her shelves or doing her laundry, and they were freaking there.

Gregori, the lead cameraman, explained that a lot of what they needed was B-roll footage. They'd use different shots of her for promos leading up to the actual season airing. She wanted to tell the crew to leave her alone, to stop following her so she could have a moment to breathe, but she never did. One, the crew was incredibly nice, given they were invading every aspect of her life. And two… there was the Paul factor.

Everything seemed to lead back to Paul these days. Whenever she was tempted to pick up the phone and tell Shawnee she didn't want to do the show, she thought of Paul and his absolute disdain at the idea of her being a contestant. She tried her best to not think about that moment in the bathroom, where he'd stood so close to her she could smell the rich scent of his cologne, something expensive, no doubt. He certainly wouldn't still wear the cheap stuff she'd bought him years ago as a Christmas present. She'd worked at the ice cream parlor at the time, and it had been all she could afford. But the cologne he wore the other day had a lush scent that lingered on her clothes for hours after.

Thankfully, she hadn't seen Paul since that explosive moment between them. She thought he'd be around, given he was the host, but apparently he was busy organizing some things for her future groom.

Her mouth turned down as she finished restocking yarn on her store's shelves. She never thought he'd be so dedicated to finding her a husband.

That's because he doesn't care about you anymore.

Kyleigh brushed that thought aside. She wondered if they'd decided on the groom yet. She knew only a handful of single men her age in Holiday Bay, and none of them would be someone she'd consider marrying. There was Kyle Bishop-Blackenstock, but he was a serial cheater according to his six ex-wives. There was Tom Schneider, who'd gained a reputation around town for belittling women. Maybe it'd be Kevan Walden. He seemed decent enough but was strangely obsessed with his mother.

Kyleigh rubbed her forehead as she headed toward the front of the store. They probably had to go outside of Holiday Bay to find a groom, perhaps to Traverse City or Charlevoix. That wouldn't be so bad. Though she had no intention of staying married to whomever they paired her with, she really hoped they found someone outside of Holiday Bay. Once those ninety days were up, and she got an annulment, she'd have to still live in this town. She could only hope they didn't pair her with someone who was already a part of the community.

Shawnee walked into the store just as Kyleigh reached the counter.

"Good morning, Kyleigh! Gregori." The director beamed.

Kyleigh didn't know the woman well, but she gave off the vibes of someone who took her responsibilities to the show seriously. However, the few times Kyleigh had seen her in the past two weeks, she'd practically been dancing on her feet. Whenever she asked Shawnee about her good mood, the director would only respond that she had a strong feeling that this season would be their best one yet.

"Good morning," Kyleigh returned. She went behind the store's counter and turned on her laptop. "So what's on the agenda today?"

"Dress shopping," Shawnee stated.

"Okay," Kyleigh murmured distractedly as she pulled up a program to track inventory. "What for? Is this like *The Bachelorette* where contestants have to be dressed in formal wear every episode or something?"

"No." Shawnee sounded amused. "But we don't want you wearing jeans and a tank top for your wedding day."

Kyleigh's stomach twisted at that. "Oh…right."

Shawnee looked at her smartwatch. "We should probably head over there. We have an appointment at ten."

"I can't leave the store unattended."

The bell above the door rang, and Wendy, Kyleigh's part-time employee, walked in. Despite Kyleigh's apprehension at Shawnee's announcement, she tried not to smirk at how Wendy was dressed. Unlike Kyleigh, who wore her T-shirt with the store logo on it with a comfortable pair of yoga pants, Wendy *did* look like a contestant from *The Bachelorette*. She'd twisted her mahogany hair into a sophisticated bun on top of her head. She wore more makeup than Kyleigh owned and had on a dress that was better suited for Carnegie Hall than the shop.

"Am I on time?" Wendy asked, flashing a smile at the camera.

"That you are," Shawnee replied with another glance at her watch.

"Oh, Wendy, thank you for coming in today." Kyleigh's cheeks started to burn. "It's just that… I don't have the budget to pay you for extra hours right now."

Shawnee waved her concern away. "The show will cover the cost. We'll need Wendy to cover for you while we're filming over the next few months. You and your husband will have a week off right after the wedding so you can get to know each other."

"I'm happy to do it," Wendy told them before giving the camera another glance.

Shawnee thrust an expectant look in Kyleigh's direction. "Now that we have that all settled, ready to go?"

Swallowing down her reluctance, Kyleigh nodded.

As they headed toward Holiday Bay's only wedding dress shop a short distance away, Kyleigh said, "I'm surprised Paul is letting us put Bridal Barn on the show. I thought you'd fly in some designer from Milan or Paris."

"He's controlling enough of this season," Shawnee grumbled, and Gregori let out a quiet laugh as he trailed after them with his camera. Shawnee plastered on a smile. "From my understanding, Jake Reynolds's wife married him in a dress picked at the Bridal Barn. It ended up in *People* magazine."

"I know," Kyleigh said. As one of Julie's bridesmaids, she had also been featured in the magazine, along with the rest of the bridal party. She thought it would be her only fifteen minutes of fame in her life. She never expected that a camera crew would be following her around Holiday Bay a few years later.

"If it's good enough for Julie Reynolds," Shawnee said,

stopping in front of the shop's entrance, "then Bridal Barn is perfectly acceptable for our show. And speaking of…"

As they entered the store, Kyleigh's two closest friends, Julie and Meg, came up to her. Julie looked beautiful and stylish as always in a blue maternity dress that emphasized her delicate features and perfectly styled red hair. Meg was several inches shorter than her best friend, but she looked equally gorgeous in khaki capris and a green top with a logo for Archer Campground on it. Meg's family had owned the campground for generations. She'd taken over the Holiday Bay location a couple years ago and turned it into a premier stop in Northern Michigan.

"What are you two doing here?" Kyleigh asked, though she was relieved to see her friends.

"We're here for moral support," Meg said, tightening the ponytail of her shoulder length, honey-brown hair.

Jessica, the shop's owner, came out from the back room, her gray hair coiffed in its normal twist. "Ah, here's the lucky bride."

"Hey, Jessica," Kyleigh greeted, giving the older woman a hug. They'd known each other for years, having both served on the board in the past for Holiday Bay's Small Business Association.

Jessica took a step back. She glanced at the camera crew before snapping into a more professional demeanor. "So from what I understand, we're under a pretty tight deadline. We'll need to find you something today."

"Oh…" Kyleigh shifted anxiously on her feet. "We're not in that big of a rush."

"Two weeks," Shawnee said.

Kyleigh whirled to look at her. "What?"

"The wedding is in two weeks," Shawnee replied.

"But...don't you have to pick out a groom first?" Kyleigh tried to reason.

At this, Shawnee's face did a funny little tweak, part amusement, part exasperation. "Oh, don't worry about that."

"Are you serious?" Kyleigh was about to marry the man. A stranger. How could she do anything but worry?

"We found you a groom," Shawnee told her, matter-of-fact.

"Really." Kyleigh felt queasy. "Who—"

"You know I can't tell you anything," Shawnee said. "But I think you'll be pretty happy with the choice. He's a good guy, not to mention handsome and successful. I have a feeling you two will have amazing chemistry. And like I told you before, I know this season will be a smash hit."

Like that mattered. Kyleigh wished again that she'd backed out. This was absolutely insane. In two weeks, she'd be married to a complete stranger.

Paul's stubborn face entered her mind, and she lifted her chin resolutely before turning to Jessica. "I guess we should try on some wedding gowns then."

"Excuse me," Meg said, rushing out of the room with her hand over her mouth.

"Is she okay?" Kyleigh asked Julie.

Julie looked after Meg in concern. "She told me last night she thinks she might have eaten something bad the other day."

"We can postpone this," Kyleigh said, feeling only slightly guilty over using her friend's illness to get out of this situation.

"No!" Shawnee and Jessica said in unison.

Jessica composed herself. "We only have a short window to get this done."

"Exactly," Shawnee agreed.

"Do you know what kind of dress you'd prefer?" Jessica asked.

When Kyleigh stared at her blankly—because honestly, she'd prefer to get married in her yoga pants—Shawnee interceded.

"It needs to be something suitable for the beach."

Kyleigh's attention flew toward the director. "The beach?"

Forbidden memories burst inside her head. Of a date she and Paul had years ago, watching a couple get married on Holiday Bay's beach. It had been the first time Paul ever told her he loved her.

Kyleigh straightened her spine as she shucked away the memory. It was a long time ago. She'd let Paul go after he dumped her, had married another man and had a child with him, for God's sake. Seeing Paul a couple of weeks ago had ruffled something inside her that she had thought was long gone. She didn't need to think about how she'd once believed he was the one. She was about to marry someone else. Kyleigh needed to leave Paul in the past where he belonged.

Following Jessica, Kyleigh entered the changing room, Gregori and his trusty camera close behind.

Jessica pulled the thick curtain closed, blocking their view from the general area. "Now, what do you have in mind?"

"I honestly have no idea," Kyleigh said. "I guess something that's appropriate for someone my age. I don't want my body being shown off to the world."

Not that her figure was awful, and there certainly wasn't anything wrong with other women her age wearing whatever they felt sexy and comfortable in. But she didn't want to be on display with her impressionable thirteen-year-old daughter nearby. Shawnee had told her she could have one bridesmaid, and Holly was going to be hers. She would have loved to have had Meg and Julie in the wedding as well, but apparently she didn't make the rules for her own big day.

"I'll be right back," Jessica said. "You can change out of your clothes and put on the robe over there." She nodded toward a purple silk robe hanging on a hook.

"I'll give you a minute," Gregori said, pulling the camera off his shoulder.

Kyleigh nodded and waited for both people to leave before she removed her top and pants and changed into the robe. A short time later, Jessica returned with a stack of dresses over her arms. Her smile was bright as she said, "Ready?"

Kyleigh took a deep breath. "Ready."

For the next hour, she tried on different dresses and then paraded in front of her friends and the production team. Meg had returned from the bathroom, looking like her normal, boisterous self as she gave her unfiltered opinion like she always did. Julie was a little more tactful. Shawnee was a downright tyrant.

"No, absolutely not," she said as she touched the light material of the latest dress Kyleigh had on.

"What's wrong with it?" Kyleigh asked, trying not to get impatient. She was starting to get hungry, and she just wanted to get back to her store and finish her work.

"If you like it, get it," the director said, sensing Kyleigh's rising impatience. "But with this material under the camera lights, you'll look naked."

Kyleigh threw her hands in the air. "Fine. Jessica, what's next?"

The shop owner tried not to look nervous as she took her back to the dressing area again.

"Don't worry," she said, patting Kyleigh on the arm, "we'll find you something. In fact, I have a dress that just came in that might be the right fit."

She left only to return a few moments later. A small gasp escaped Kyleigh as she stared at the gown. It wasn't her normal style of dress. The gown had one thick strap made of silk flowers that went over her right shoulder. Delicate beads covered the sloping neckline. The bodice was tight along her breasts. Four rows of the same beading circled her torso. The rest of gown flowed to the ground in soft waves. As soon as it was on her, she never wanted to take it off. She felt like a Greek goddess.

"What do you think?" Jessica asked.

"I think if Shawnee objects to this one, I'll get married in sweats," Kyleigh murmured, turning left to right to see the dress from different angles.

"She'll approve of that one," Gregori assured her.

Taking a deep breath, Kyleigh said, "Well…let's go get everyone's stamp of approval."

As soon as she stepped on the pedestal in the main show room, a small gasp went through her audience.

"That's the one," Julie said.

"You look beautiful," Meg agreed, getting emotional.

Shawnee walked over to her, a look of satisfaction on her face. "Yes, this will do nicely."

As Jessica started pinning the dress in the places that needed altering, Shawnee's phone vibrated. The director rolled her eyes at whatever she read in the text she'd received, but she nodded to Gregori.

"Let's take a lunch break," she said. "I want to get some shots around town anyway."

"Sound good to me," Gregori said. He gave Kyleigh a thumbs-up before they left.

After Kyleigh changed back into her normal clothes, Jessica whisked away the dress so she could start working on it. Kyleigh didn't bother to ask what the price was. The show was going to cover it anyway.

As she returned to the main room where her friends were waiting, she noticed they both looked slightly ill as they sat in the shop's yellow-and-white-striped chairs.

"What? Did the dress look awful?" she asked nervously.

"No! Of course not. You looked gorgeous in it," Julie said. She rubbed her swollen stomach. "The baby's kicking more than usual. As much as I want to meet my little bean, I'm hoping they can hold off until after your wedding. I don't want to miss it."

Kyleigh snorted. "Even if you do miss it, it's just for the show. You can watch it on TV in a few months."

Meg and Julie exchanged glances.

"You're sure that you want to go through with this?" Meg asked.

Kyleigh tried to keep her features neutral. Julie and Meg had asked her the same question multiple times since they learned she was the chosen bride.

"Yes, I'm sure. This will be good for my store, not to mention it's only for ninety days. And the whole thing is making Holly so happy. With all the issues she's been having at school lately, I'm fine with doing this for her. It's not permanent."

"Okay, if this is absolutely what you want to do," Meg replied. She stood up and instantly started swaying. She grabbed onto the chair.

"Do you need to go to the doctor?" Kyleigh asked as she watched the color leach from her friend's face.

"I already have an appointment, but honestly, there's

nothing they can do for me. Not for the next six months or so."

Julie and Kyleigh stared at her with open mouths.

"Are you saying what I think you're saying?" Julie asked.

Meg beamed. "I'm pregnant."

Kyleigh ran to her friend and gave her a hug, "Congratulations. You and Tyler will be the best parents ever."

"Thanks," she said before turning to Julie, who hauled herself out of her chair as best as she could.

"Pregnant," Julie murmured before hugging her best friend. "And you said the baby is due in six months? So you're three months along."

"Yes," Meg replied. "I'm sorry I didn't tell you sooner, but I only recently found out myself. You know my anxiety sometimes messes with my body, and it can screw up my period. And I've been so busy at work lately that I hadn't really thought about my monthly nemesis. When I started throwing up the other morning, though, Tyler insisted I do a pregnancy test. It came back positive. I still have to see a doctor and get it confirmed officially, but given when I had a period last, I'm guessing I'm about eleven weeks."

Julie's eyes started to water. "Our kids are going to grow up the bestest friends ever."

Meg laughed. "They absolutely will. Can you imagine the amount of trouble they'll get into?"

"Please don't plan on corrupting my baby before they're even here," Julie joked.

"Pfft," Meg responded. "If anyone is the corrupting influence of our relationship, it's totally you."

They started heading out the door with Kyleigh, when she'd realized she'd forgotten her watch.

"Go on without me," she said. "I'll catch up with you later."

They nodded and left. Kyleigh hurried back to the changing room and grabbed her watch where she'd left it on the pink scalloped chair she'd used earlier.

"Oh, Kyleigh!" Jessica hurried over to her. "I'm glad I caught you. I had a couple of questions for you regarding the undergarments you're planning to wear with the dress. I do have some options I can show you if you don't know…"

By the time they were through, Meg and Julie were long gone. Kyleigh walked out of the building, lost in thought over the lacy bra and panties set she'd just picked out. There was no way she was going to sleep with her husband on her wedding night, so it seemed like a waste of money to purchase the sexy combo she'd just ordered.

She was so busy debating if she should walk back in and cancel the order that she almost missed the very pointed sound of someone clearing their throat. Kyleigh almost stumbled to a stop when she noticed Paul leaning against a fancy, red Aston Martin.

"W-what are you doing here?" she asked, silently cursing herself for sounding so breathless.

"I'm the show's host. It's bad luck to see the bride in her wedding dress before the big day. So I've been waiting out here for you."

Kyleigh met his eyes defiantly. "Isn't that only for the groom?"

"Sure," Paul said with a shrug.

"Shawnee said they picked out my future husband already," she said, hoping to see some kind of reaction from him. His face remained frustratingly impassive. "Anyone I know?"

"Probably," he said, giving her another one-word answer.

Kyleigh crossed her arms over her chest. "Probably?

That's all you're going to say? Not 'don't do it'? Not 'you're going to destroy the sanctity of my show'?"

Paul's full lips quirked upward, slow and sexy. Kyleigh tried to ignore how the sight made her heart speed up.

"I'll see you at the wedding, Kyleigh."

"Wait!" she called out. When he looked over his shoulder at her, she said, "Why did you come here? What did you want to see me about?"

He lifted a shoulder. "Maybe I just wanted to see you."

With that, he strolled around the Aston Martin and hopped in behind the wheel. The car soon roared to life, and Paul pulled into the street.

Kyleigh could do nothing but stare after him, watching the taillights until they disappeared from view.

Chapter Seven

Kyleigh was fairly positive she was going to throw up as Heather did her hair while Gregori filmed their every move. The wedding dress—which looked so beautiful two weeks before—hung like a noose from the rack they'd placed next to her. Gusts of wind hit the tent the bridal party was in, each blast making the vinyl material snap. Every time it did, Kyleigh's nerves frayed a little more.

She could hear wedding attendees arriving, laughter filling the beach where the ceremony was to take place. Back when she'd been an innocent idiot, she dreamed of marrying Paul on that beach. She half wondered if he picked out this spot himself as some form of punishment to her for insisting on doing the show. But then she had to remember that he was one of the most famous faces in the world these days. She very much doubted he remembered the significance of the beach and what it meant to her.

For what felt like the millionth time, she thought about telling them she wanted to back out. That this was all one huge misunderstanding. But even as she thought it, her eyes drifted to her daughter.

Holly stood in front of the long mirror stationed on one side of the tent, twirling her pink dress from side to side on the large blue outdoor rug. The bullying at school hadn't improved, but Holly had been holding her head up a little higher lately. Especially after Shawnee showed up at their house the other night with a bridesmaid dress that had Holly shrieking with giddy excitement.

At that moment, Shawnee entered the tent and looked around. She gave Holly an approving nod when she noticed her. "I knew that dress would be just perfect for you."

"I love it!" Holly replied gleefully. The A-line dress had a small scoop to the neckline that was perfectly suitable for a thirteen-year-old. The dress hugged the waist and the long skirt flowed to the ground, similar to how Kyleigh's own dress did. Heather had pinned half of Holly's hair back with baby's breath while leaving the rest to fall around her shoulders. She was adorable.

Kyleigh's heart melted at her daughter's animated expression, dulling the nerves roiling in her stomach.

"And how is our bride feeling?" Shawnee asked, running a critical eye over her. "You look pale. Heather, can you fix this?"

Heather gave her wife an exasperated look. "Unless you want her looking like a clown, then no. I've already put more than enough makeup on her face."

"Hmm," Shawnee murmured. She sat down in the chair opposite Kyleigh. "So this is when we do the pre-wedding interview."

Kyleigh nodded, rubbing her sweaty hands against the silk robe she wore.

Shawnee waited for Gregori and some of the other crew members to get into position before smiling brightly into the camera. "I'm currently with our bride, Kyleigh. Kyleigh, how are—"

"Wait." Kyleigh looked from Gregori to Shawnee. "Doesn't Paul usually do these interviews?"

She'd been binge-watching *First Comes Marriage* over the past few days to see what she should expect. She hadn't realized just how involved Paul was, acting as a mediator between the couples and meeting with them several times a week, even before the marriage. But she hadn't seen him since that day outside of Bridal Barn.

Shawnee cleared her throat. "He's with the groom's party right now."

"Oh…" Kyleigh didn't even know why she asked. She didn't need to see Paul at that moment. Even if a tiny part of her wanted him to burst into the tent and tell her to run. Now that she was faced with the realization that this was actually happening, maybe she wouldn't object so loudly if he did try to intervene.

"Let me ask you," Shawnee said, switching into professional mode once more. "How are you feeling on your big day?"

Kyleigh ignored Gregori who took a step closer to her, his camera locked on her face. "I'm, um, I'm nervous. I hope I'm not about to make a huge mistake."

"You're not," Holly said, coming to stand by her mom. She put an encouraging hand on Kyleigh's shoulder.

"And Holly," Shawnee said. "What are your thoughts on this whole thing?"

"I think it's great. And whoever my mom marries better be good to her or else." Holly glared at the camera. Kyleigh wrapped her arm around her shoulder and gave her a side hug.

"I think we're ready for you to get into your gown," Heather said.

Kyleigh swallowed before getting up on shaking legs.

"Any guesses on your future husband?" Shawnee asked

as Heather and Kyleigh went behind a privacy screen so she could step into her dress.

Kyleigh winced as she thought back to the eligible men who were her age and lived in the area. She was thankful that the camera crew was giving her space to get dressed so they couldn't film her reaction.

She still tried to sound hopeful as she said, "Considering how small Holiday Bay is, it has to be someone I know, right? Unless you shipped him in from another town."

"He very well might be," Shawnee replied, her voice light, not confirming or denying whether Kyleigh knew the man or not.

Heather finished zipping her into her dress before giving her a nod. With a steading breath, Kyleigh stepped around the screen.

A collective hush went through the small group gathered.

"Mom, you look beautiful," Holly said, awestruck, just as Julie and Meg entered the tent.

"We came to wish you good luck," Meg said, in a bright yellow dress that made her shine. Her pregnancy wasn't showing much yet, but she'd been battling morning sickness for the last couple of weeks.

"Hey," Kyleigh said, walking over to Meg and giving her a hug. "How are you feeling, Mama?"

"Like I want to throw up, but I gave the baby a stern talking-to this morning and told them to behave or else."

Kyleigh laughed before hugging Julie, who looked stunning in a lilac-colored dress. "And how are you?" Her eyes ran over her friend, her eyebrows going up as she saw how much bigger her friend's belly had gotten since the last time she saw her.

"I'm ready to get this show on the road." Julie laughed, giving her stomach a gentle pat. "My belly looks like that button on a cooked turkey that tells you when it's done. I feel ready to pop."

"Well, you look beautiful," Kyleigh assured her, though she couldn't help but wonder if Julie would make it through the wedding before going into labor.

"I could say the same about you," Julie said. "You look amazing. Your groom isn't going to know what hit him."

"Oh, I haven't…" Kyleigh said, waving at the mirror behind her.

"You haven't looked at yourself yet?" Meg asked, shaking her head in disbelief. "You look absolutely incredible. See for yourself."

Kyleigh turned and smiled at her beaming daughter who was next to the mirror. Closing her eyes briefly, Kyleigh made herself look at her reflection.

She stared at the woman in front of her, not registering at first that it was her. Heather had pinned her hair into a romantic updo embellished with the same rhinestones that matched her dress. Her makeup was soft and natural, done in a way Kyleigh could never replicate, no matter how many tutorials she watched on YouTube.

A commotion outside of the tent caused everyone to turn their attention in that direction. Kyleigh's heart thumped hard. For a half a second, she thought that maybe Paul was coming to stop her after all. It was a shock when a tall, older man with graying blond hair came through the tent flaps.

Kyleigh's jaw to dropped. He was last person she expected to see. "Dad. Wh… What are you doing here?"

Brock Sinclair glared at the cameras before turning to his daughter. "What the hell are you thinking? You're not seriously going through with this?"

Kyleigh instantly bristled. She and her father had always had a bit of a rocky relationship. Her dad ran his home like he ran his police station, with stifling rules and regulations. He tried to control so much of Kyleigh's life when she was younger that it had been a relief when he finally retired and moved to Florida with her mother.

Her mother came into the tent, petite in size compared to her husband. She wore a peach dress that was perfect for a mother of the bride. Her grayish-blond hair was cut chin length and styled to perfection.

"Sweetheart," her mom admonished, "why didn't you tell us you were getting married?"

"It's…" Kyleigh looked at the cameras. "It's complicated. How did you even find out about this?"

Brock glared again at the camera crew. "The way anyone finds out that their daughter is marrying a complete stranger. The show invited us."

Shawnee looked between father and daughter before hesitantly admitting, "Paul told me to invite him."

Kyleigh whipped around to the director. *"What?"*

Shawnee's face reddened. "Excuse me. I have to go maim my TV host." She stormed out of the tent.

Julie nudged Meg in the arm. "We should get to our seats. If you'll excuse us." She gave Kyleigh a sympathetic smile before exiting.

Meg looked tempted to stay, but she soon followed her best friend, giving Kyleigh a bright smile before she left.

Brock pointed at Holly. "Holly, grab your mother's stuff, we're leaving."

"Um…" Gregori started to say, but Kyleigh walked over to her father with her eyes flashing.

"Dad, I appreciate your concern, I do, but I'm a grown woman."

"Then stop acting like a teenager with her head in the clouds."

"Ouch," Holly muttered.

Kyleigh stiffened. "If you're not here to walk me down the aisle, then you can leave."

Brock looked at his daughter in disbelief. He repeated, "You can't be serious."

Somewhere in the distance, the wedding march began to play.

Heather looked uneasily between them before saying, "That's our cue."

"Grandpa, come on," Holly pleaded. "Please."

His eyes softened briefly as he looked at his only grandchild. Holly always did have him wrapped around her little finger. He turned his attention back to Kyleigh. "You're making the biggest mistake of your life."

"Brock," her mother muttered, but that was all. No defense of her daughter. No reminding her husband that Kyleigh was a grown woman. Lucille Sinclair had never been one to say no to her husband.

"It's my choice to make that mistake." Kyleigh grabbed the two sets of flowers, handing the smaller one to Holly.

Kyleigh eyed the arrangement of white calla lilies and blue irises that made up her own bouquet. Her heart did a funny leap. Paul had given her similar flowers once. They'd been on discount, he'd admitted sheepishly at the time, but she hadn't cared. She'd kept them even after they died, placing the bouquet carefully in her keepsake box along with the origami animals Paul had given her. After they broke up, they ended up in the trash with the rest of the box.

Heather's phone beeped with an incoming text. She winced when she saw the message. "Shawnee said you missed your cue, and we're getting behind schedule."

"Always the romantic," Gregori said. He asked Kyleigh, "Are you ready to start the rest of your life?"

"For the next ninety days, anyway," she replied.

"That's the spirit," Gregori said before saying to Holly, "After you."

She nodded, her face more serious than Kyleigh had ever seen it. She took one step and then another, making sure her rhythm matched the wedding march.

Kyleigh watched her go, tenderness for her daughter reminding her again why she was doing this.

It's not real. It's only for ninety days. I can give ninety days of my life if it means Holly can stand a little taller. A little more confident.

"I'm going to get my seat," her mother announced. With no further word to her daughter, she followed Holly out of the tent.

Her father stared at Kyleigh in disbelief, before he slowly, reluctantly offered his arm to her.

When she looked at him warily, he said, "What would people say if I didn't walk you down the aisle?"

Even with the ruddy color to his cheeks displaying his discontent and their earlier argument, Kyleigh could read between her father's lines. Despite their differences in pretty much everything when it came to Kyleigh's life, she never doubted that her father cared for her. The problem was he didn't ever seem to understand when that care bordered on control.

She took his arm, and together they stepped out of the tent.

Kyleigh sucked in air as she took in the scene in front of her. She hadn't been able to see anything when she first arrived at the beach. The show's crew had put a blindfold on her when they led her into the tent earlier, so she wasn't able to get a preview of what her wedding would look like.

She took it all in now. The beach had been transformed

into the venue of her dreams. White chairs lined either side of the aisle she walked down. Stationed at the end of each row were arrangements of calla lilies and blue irises that matched her bouquet. Up ahead stood a pergola wrapped in more of the same flowers. Behind it was the bay, shimmering in the setting sun.

Though she was tempted to look at her groom, she kept her eyes focused on Holly as she headed down the aisle. She was the reason Kyleigh was doing this. To ensure the store succeeded so Holly would have a secure future. To uplift her daughter when she'd been feeling so low.

Her daughter, in that moment, didn't seem to have a care in the world, as she reached the front of the aisle and took her spot to the left of the altar.

In fact, Holly seemed to be on the verge of freaking out as she stared at the profile of Kyleigh's groom. Her eyes then shot to her mom, before going back to the groom, her mouth gaping like a fish.

Curiosity getting the better of her, Kyleigh finally shifted her gaze to her future husband. His back was to her, so she only saw his black hair, sprinkled with the tiniest bit of gray. She frowned. There…was something familiar about that head.

As she took in his body and the way he stood, a warning bell started to go off in her head.

Danger, danger, danger.

She glanced over at the best man, and her stomach dropped. There was no mistaking the familiar man staring back at her with a sheepish grin. Who could forget James? He was part of the biggest boy band in the world—Paul Rodriguez's band. Even after Holiday Boys broke up all those years ago, she would have recognized James. They'd hung out together numerous times before Holiday Boys signed with their manager and left town.

Which meant…

That familiar figure started to turn. Kyleigh's eyes immediately shifted down to the white runner she was stepping on, unwilling to acknowledge the truth that was in front of her.

Her father stiffened beside her as he took in her groom-to-be. Slowly, she made herself look and accept the reality her brain was already screaming at her.

The beautiful flowers she'd been holding dropped listlessly to the ground.

And then…all hell broke loose.

Chapter Eight

Paul stood at the altar, feeling remarkably calm. He always thought he'd be a jittery mess on his wedding day. No, that wasn't true. After he became famous, he never pictured getting married in the first place. Too many women interested in him with the wrong intentions. But he was about to marry Kyleigh. And for some reason, that made all the difference in the world.

They were going into this for all the right reasons. There would be no ridiculous notions of love and happy-ever-after… not this time around anyway. Kyleigh had told Shawnee when Paul wasn't around that the show would give her store some nice publicity. He wanted to save his career, not to mention get his production company off the ground. Who would want to entrust them with their dream projects if his own show fired him?

This was a safe decision for both of them. They knew each other, despite how long ago it was that they dated. This was a good decision, one they'd both benefit from. Feelings *would not* be involved.

"You doing okay?" James asked quietly from where he stood to Paul's right.

"Fine, couldn't be better," Paul replied with a flash of smile at the nearby camera. He glanced at his friend, who looked slightly peaked. His brow furrowed in concern. "*You* okay?"

"Yeah," James said, turning to face the aisle. "Just… memories, you know?"

Paul felt instantly guilty. James and his husband had finalized their divorce last year, but that didn't mean the wounds weren't fresh. Paul should have asked Tyler or Jake to step in, but with their wives being pregnant, they'd both been too preoccupied with getting nurseries done and attending ultrasounds.

He nudged James in the arm. "Thanks for doing this, man."

James gave him a half smile that didn't reach his eyes. "I owe you, you know, for ditching our show."

"You never owe me for anything," Paul replied. "We're brothers from another mother, you know that. Through thick and thin."

James's lips quirked upward, real warmth appearing on his face. "Yeah."

Paul turned so that he was facing forward again, his eyes not missing any details. The crew had outdone themselves, getting the beach ready and turning it into a dream wedding venue. Paul focused on that instead of the little voice in the back of his mind, reminding him that he had another brother he could have called instead of James.

His blood brother, Dominic.

But he'd distanced himself a long time ago from his family. No point in opening old wounds now.

The wedding march began to play, and a rush of satisfaction went through him. Whether it was real or not, he was about to make Kyleigh Sinclair his. Even if it was only for the next ninety days.

Out of the corner of his eye, he saw a small figure stand

to the left of the altar. He heard a small gasp and turned his head slightly.

Kyleigh's daughter stared at him in stunned disbelief, her mouth hanging open. He tried to hide his own surprise. In all his careful planning, he forgot one detail. He was about to become a stepfather. Lord help him.

Paul gave her a quick wink, and her eyes almost bugged out of her head. Inhaling deeply, he turned around to face his bride.

The air caught in his throat as he watched a goddess walk toward him. He took in every detail of her gorgeous face. Paul was never one for sentimentality, but she looked like an angel as she approached. She had her eyes focused on the white runner she walked on, not glancing up to see who she was about to marry.

Look at me, baby.

An odd sensation formed around his heart, a pounding that he did his best to ignore. He wanted to see Kyleigh's reaction when she realized it was him that she was about to marry. As if she heard his silent plea, her eyes slowly lifted.

Kyleigh froze when she saw him, a look of horror popping on her face. Her bouquet fell to the ground.

Whatever feeling that had been reacting in his heart region stopped and crumbled. Paul was half tempted to run a hand over his head to make sure his hair wasn't sticking up at weird angles. He got that they were long past being anything to each other, but did she have to look at him like she'd rather marry the devil?

He tried his best to ignore the cameras that were zooming on both of their faces. He silently thanked Heather for slapping a pound of makeup on his face so the camera lights wouldn't drain him. His cheeks heated with humiliation. Kyleigh looked like she was about to throw up. Or turn tail and run away. That'd be a first in their show's history. Fan-freaking-tastic.

"What the hell is this?" the man next to Kyleigh demanded, and a lick of heady loathing rushed through Paul.

He had known it was risky to invite Brock to his wedding. The man had done everything in his power to separate Paul from Kyleigh when they were younger. He had always thought Paul and his family were beneath his. The man practically had a conniption when he found out Paul had gotten his dirty hands all over his precious little girl.

It didn't seem to matter that Paul was wealthier than Brock Sinclair's entire family put together. The man still stared at Paul as though he were a bug that had crawled out from underneath a rock.

Old rebellion ignited in him as he stared at the man who'd been responsible for taking so much from him. "What does it look like?" Paul responded, his voice calm despite the emotions rampaging through him. "You're interrupting my wedding."

"You think I'm going to let you marry my daughter, you son of a—"

"Stop," Kyleigh said. She was sickeningly pale. If she hadn't been clutching her father's arm in that moment, she might have collapsed.

The crowd around them began murmuring. He could see Heather and Shawnee whispering to each other where they stood in the back of the audience. Gregori kept inching his way closer and closer to Paul's face. He was tempted to shove the camera away, but if he broke anything, the network would take it out of his salary, and it didn't matter that Paul was a multimillionaire. He was not one to throw money away.

Straightening his shoulders, he walked toward Kyleigh and her father.

"You take one step closer, and I'll punch your lights out," Brock threatened.

Suddenly, Paul was amused. The man might have once upon a time been sheriff around these parts, but Paul wasn't a kid he could threaten anymore. He knew without a doubt thanks to years of practicing self-defense and karate—a necessity in his line of work considering the amount of stalkers he'd dealt with—he could lay Brock Sinclair on his ass if he really wanted to. And God did he want to, but Kyleigh's wide, pleading eyes made him resist the urge.

"If you're going to continue to interrupt the wedding," Paul stated, his voice a mixture of boredom and dry humor, "you'll need to leave."

Brock's face turned a vicious red color. A vein throbbed deliciously on his forehead. He ignored Paul, turning to his daughter. "Kyleigh, we're leaving."

"About that," Paul said. He began to fiddle with his cuff links which cost more than the suit Brock currently wore. "Kyleigh, here, is under contract. Now, be a good man and wish us well."

Brock took a menacing step toward him, and Paul's fists curled.

Do it, you bastard. I dare you to do it. He could see Shawnee hurrying toward him, but his laser focus was on the former sheriff.

"But…" Kyleigh finally spoke, the words barely above a whisper. "Surely, you can't want to marry me."

"I fully intend to marry you," Paul replied, his voice softer. He wanted nothing more than to take Kyleigh away from the crowd—away from her poisonous father—and explain. Explain what? He wasn't sure. All he knew was that he was going to do everything in his power to make sure this wedding happened.

"We... We can't get married," Kyleigh said weakly.

"We can, and we will," Paul responded stubbornly. At his tone, a spark of life finally ignited in Kyleigh's eyes.

There's my girl.

"I'm not marrying you, Paul," she hissed, probably hoping the cameras wouldn't hear what they were saying, but Paul knew the microphones were picking up every word.

"You are marrying me," Paul said simply. "You see, if you don't, I'll sue you for breach of contract. I'll take everything, Kyleigh, including your store."

Kyleigh took a step back from him, staring at him as though he'd turned into a monster before her eyes. He felt like one, but there was no way that Kyleigh wasn't going to marry him.

"You—you can't do that!" she snapped. Shawnee finally reached their sides. Kyleigh turned to her, her voice pleading, "He can't take away my store, can he?"

Shawnee looked apologetic. "As part of making sure our investment in the show pays off, we have a clause in the contract that allows us to recoup any costs you might create if you cancel on us."

"But I didn't even sign the original agreement!" Kyleigh said, frustrated tears turning her eyes into the color of sea glass. "Holly did it. I didn't even know she entered me until I received your email."

Shawnee looked at Paul, and he knew she was about to give Kyleigh an out. Paul wasn't about to give in.

"Then I'll also sue you for fraud," he replied.

Kyleigh looked like she wanted to slap him. "What? How—"

He nodded at her. "We paid for that beautiful dress you're

wearing and spent weeks generously promoting your store. Now, you're telling us it was all a mistake. That sounds like fraud to me. Doesn't it to you, Shawnee?"

"Leave me out of this," she muttered before walking away.

"And let's not forget that after I asked you *not to do the show*, you signed the contract anyway. Not Holly. *You.* I think that gives me a pretty good case in court. So what do you say?" he asked, pretending it didn't bother him how much she looked like she wished he was dead. "Marry me or lose your store."

"Kyleigh…" Brock warned.

Kyleigh lifted her chin, hatred pouring out of her. "I guess we better get married then."

Chapter Nine

Kyleigh reached for a glass of sparkling wine. She wasn't much of a drinker. She never had been, but she almost wished she had something stronger to numb the pain and feeling of betrayal that was coursing through her.

The wedding guests had moved to Florentina's Italian Restaurant in the heart of Holiday Bay. The show had rented out the restaurant for the night. A makeshift dance floor had been set up in one corner of the room. A multitude of string lights filled the ceiling space, casting the room in a romantic light.

Romantic? Ha! Kyleigh was ready to commit murder.

She couldn't believe that Paul—the man who'd once owned every inch of her heart—had threatened her very livelihood. And now she was married to him!

The rest of the ceremony on the beach had passed by in a blur. When it came to the part where the officiant told Paul he could kiss his bride, Kyleigh had turned her head at the last second so that his warm lips brushed the corner of her mouth. She wasn't certain what she would have done if he had actually kissed her. Probably headbutted him.

The dinner they'd eaten afterward had been awkward and stilted. Paul tried to speak to her a couple of times, but she'd firmly ignored him, too furious to even acknowledge him. The only relief she'd had from the whole miserable situation was that her parents weren't there.

Her mother claimed to have a headache and insisted that her father bring her back to the hotel, giving Kyleigh a sympathetic smile as they went. Her dad had looked like he was one step from throttling Paul or finding a way to arrest him, despite being retired from the force. It had been a relief to see him go.

The show's viewers would devour the drama, the cameras capturing every moment. Not a single shred of privacy was left untouched. Even now, as she glowered angrily at the brown bamboo tile that made up the dance floor, she could sense Gregori hovering nearby, capturing her every emotion. Maybe she *should* ask the bartender for something stronger.

Meg walked over to where Kyleigh was sulking in the corner. "How you doing, lady?"

"Just thinking about the different ways I can make the next ninety days as miserable as possible for my new husband," Kyleigh replied before downing the wine, slamming the now empty glass back on the nearby table.

Meg snorted. "I get it. I don't know what I would have done if I were in your position. Probably the same thing."

"Tyler never would have blackmailed you into marriage," Kyleigh muttered.

Meg looked fondly across the room at her husband. Tyler was walking over to where Paul stood with his fellow Holiday Boys, James and Jake.

The show's other cameraman, Leroy, recorded whatever Paul was saying as he flashed another one of his famous Hollywood smiles at the camera. She knew they'd be headed over to her next to film her post-wedding interview, but Shawnee had given Kyleigh a moment to collect herself, the director giving her an apologetic look before walking away.

"Oh, I wouldn't put anything past Tyler. He can be *real* stubborn about getting his own way. So can I. It leads to a lot of enthusiastic, heated sex." Meg wiggled her eyebrows.

Despite her efforts to stay in a bad mood, Kyleigh laughed.

Julie came over to them, rubbing her belly. "Hi," she said.

Kyleigh frowned at her. Julie looked paler than normal. "Are you okay?"

"Yeah, the baby's just moving a lot."

The DJ began to play music. Kyleigh watched Holly go over to Jake's son, Dylan, and ask him something shyly. He shrugged his shoulders before getting out of his chair. They walked over to the dance floor, and Dylan began twirling her around, much to her delight.

"That's sweet of Dylan," Meg said as she watched them.

Kyleigh's eyes narrowed as she examined the lovestruck expression on her daughter's face. "I think my daughter might have a crush on your stepson."

Julie shook her head fondly as she looked over at Dylan. "She'll be disappointed then. He just started dating a girl from college."

"Plus, Holly's what, thirteen?" Meg added. "Too young for Dylan. But it's kind of him to dance with her anyway."

Julie shifted uncomfortably, then asked Kyleigh, "But seriously. How are you feeling about everything?"

Kyleigh rubbed her forehead. "Honestly, I want to go home, get out of this dress, change into my comfy pj's and go to sleep."

"Aren't you a little excited, though?" Meg asked, cocking

her blond head. "You're married now. To Paul Rodriguez. Your former flame."

Kyleigh clenched her mouth together so hard, her teeth ached. "Yeah, what's not to be excited about?" she forced out. "I'm now married to Holiday Boys's most notorious womanizer."

"I don't know," Julie said. "I don't think he's as bad as his reputation says he is. I've known Paul for a few years now. He's always been so focused on his job."

Kyleigh scoffed. "Didn't he just break up with Monica Valdez? Everyone thought they'd get married."

Not that she paid attention to celebrity gossip. She couldn't avoid the variety of magazines stashed at the checkout counters with Paul's face plastered all over them whenever she went grocery shopping. Kyleigh knew more about his life over the past two decades than she'd ever wanted to know. Before Monica Valdez, there'd been Selena the supermodel, Beth the Olympic figure skater and dozens more.

Meg snorted. "Monica wishes she could have gotten an engagement ring out of their relationship, even if they only dated for a short time. Tyler told me Paul was never serious about her."

That didn't make Kyleigh feel any better. It just proved her point that Paul could never get serious about any woman.

Kyleigh looked across the room and found Paul staring at her. She turned away. "Let's not forget he also blackmailed me and threatened my store."

"Yeah, that was dumb on his part," Meg said. "He must have really been desperate to marry you."

But why? That was what Kyleigh couldn't wrap her mind around. Why would Paul have gone to such lengths? It was so out of character from the man she knew. It just went to show how much fame had changed him.

Julie sucked in a gasp of air, causing Meg and Kyleigh to look at her in concern.

"You sure you're okay?" Meg asked her best friend, her worry evident in the way she watched Julie rub at her belly.

"Actually… I think my water just broke," Julie replied.

"Oh…" Kyleigh said, grabbing Julie's arm to help support her.

"Let me go get Jake," Meg said. She hurried over to Julie's husband and whispered in his ear. His eyes snapped to Julie, spotting her easily despite the crowd of people between them. He ran over to her.

"Love, are you okay?" Jake said, wrapping his arm around Julie's waist.

"I think we need to get to the hospital," Julie said, her breathing labored.

"What's going on?" Dylan asked, coming up to them with a disappointed Holly trailing after him.

"Julie's in labor," Jake replied. "We need to go. Dylan, go grab her purse."

Dylan nodded, leaving to do as his father instructed.

"I'm so sorry to do this on your wedding day," Julie said.

A humorless laugh escaped Kyleigh. "It's fine." It wasn't like the day wasn't already ruined. Her friend bringing her bundle of joy into the world would be the highlight of Kyleigh's day.

Jake helped Julie out the exit. Tyler maneuvered his way over to Kyleigh and Meg, holding Meg's purse. She turned to Kyleigh, worry on her face.

"It's okay." Kyleigh gave her an understanding smile. "Go with them. Keep me updated, will you?"

Meg kissed Kyleigh on the cheek. "I will. And for what it's worth, congratulations."

The couple followed their best friends out.

Kyleigh turned to her daughter. "How are you holding up?"

Holly shook her head and turned to watch the people dancing. "I can't believe you married Paul Rodriguez."

"Yeah, me either."

Holly looked over at the man himself. "People are going to flip out at school when they find out that Paul is my stepdad."

"Keep in mind it's supposed to be a secret," Kyleigh warned. She really didn't want this going around town any faster than it needed to.

"I know," Holly murmured. "It's still kind of cool."

"It's also very temporary. Don't forget that either." Once the ninety days were up, she'd sign on the dotted line to end this farce as soon as possible.

"Yeah, I know," Holly replied, her face losing some animation. "But he'll be nice to you, right, Mom?"

Kyleigh looked at her daughter, taking in her concern. "I... I don't see why not."

"I couldn't hear what he said to you at the wedding when you found out it was him, but you looked upset."

"Oh, that." Kyleigh tried to put on a bright face. "That was shock more than anything. Like you mentioned, I wasn't expecting to see Paul up there. It's not every day a woman marries a Holiday Boy."

Holly nodded slowly, though she didn't look like she quite believed her mom. "Can I go get some more wedding cake?"

"Sure, don't eat too much, though. I don't want you getting an upset stomach."

"Okay." Holly hurried to the dessert table, her eyes on the prize.

Left on her own, Kyleigh started toward the bar to get some more wine.

She ran into Jessica on her way. The Bridal Barn owner beamed at her. "Kyleigh, what a beautiful bride you make."

She hugged Kyleigh, who returned the gesture affectionately. "You pulled off a miracle. The dress fits perfectly, considering the time constraint you were working under."

"Think nothing of it," Jessica said. "I can't believe two women who've gone on to marry Holiday Boys have worn dresses bought from my boutique. Will wonders never cease?"

Kyleigh forced a smile. Now that she wasn't hiding in the corner, more people were coming up to her to offer their congratulations, though most of them she didn't know. The show wanted to keep their marriage from leaking for as long as possible, so they hired a bunch of extras, instead of people she might actually want at her wedding. The cameraman followed her around, making sure to capture everyone who came up to offer their congratulations. It was all so fake.

But there was one group of people she expected to see that were missing from the festivities. Paul's family. She'd have to ask him about it later. After she was done plotting his demise.

Just as she turned in search of the bar to get that drink, she saw the other camera crew heading her way for the interview she owed them.

Kyleigh let out a quiet sigh. This was going to be a long night.

Paul leaned against the bar, his brow furrowing as he watched Kyleigh, who looked miserable even from across the room. Gregori was asking her and her daughter questions. Holly animatedly answered while holding a plate of wedding cake. Kyleigh looked like her face was made from stone.

"Hey," Shawnee said as she came over to stand by his side. She turned to the bartender. "Can I get a whiskey neat?"

"Sure thing," the man said.

Paul lifted an eyebrow. "You don't normally drink on the job."

"I feel like the occasion calls for it." Shawnee took the glass from the bartender and began to sip at it as she copied Paul's stance and leaned against the bar. They stood in silence as the guests laughed and talked throughout the room. Thankfully, Kyleigh's parents had left. He already had a hard enough time getting two minutes alone with his wife. He didn't need her imbecile of a father running interference, too.

He became aware of Shawnee watching him as he stared at Kyleigh.

"What?" he said impatiently.

"You know you screwed up today, right?"

"I did what I had to do to make sure our entire season wasn't destroyed."

"Bull." Shawnee took another sip of her drink. "I couldn't get why you were so adamant about this whole wedding and being the groom, but I think I'm starting to now. You're in love with her, aren't you?"

Paul felt a throb in the back of his head. "Don't be ridiculous. We dated for a short time years ago. We don't even know each other anymore. Both of us have long since moved on."

"Sure, keep telling yourself that."

A muscle in Paul's jaw flinched. "This season is going to bring in record ratings. My production company will be set after this."

"Paul, you and I both know you have more than enough money to start your own production company without any further help. You've been way too obsessed with success since I've known you."

Paul didn't tend to go into detail about his childhood with anyone. Not his parents' deaths. Not his brother's incarceration. Not living off beans and rice during his teen years because it was all his aunt could afford. That part of his life was very firmly in his past, best to be forgotten. Repressing his childhood trauma was what got him through life with his sanity intact.

But he said something to Shawnee then. "Growing up, wondering how you were going to afford to eat the next day can drive a person to want to succeed."

"You know, Paul, I love you like the annoying little brother you are to me."

"We're the same age."

Shawnee ignored him as she reached over and squeezed his arm. "You can rest once in a while. Maybe experience something other than fame and fortune. Like healing the woman's heart you just broke today."

"I…" He didn't know what to say to that.

Shawnee rolled her eyes before waving to the DJ. The man nodded and "Feels Like a Woman" by Zucchero began to play.

Paul stiffened. "How did you know this was our song when we were younger?"

"I had a hunch," Shawnee said. "Whenever you're feeling introspective, you play it. Now, go dance with your wife."

Paul looked over at Kyleigh, who was absolutely stunning in her wedding dress despite the misery on her face. He didn't want her unhappy. He wanted to see her smile at him like she used to. Before life went to crap.

Taking a steading breath, Paul took a step that would lead him in the only direction he wanted to go. Toward his wife.

The DJ took that as his cue. "Ladies and gentleman, it's time for the bride and groom to have their first dance."

He saw Kyleigh go ramrod stiff as he approached. Once he stood in front of her, he didn't say anything to her, merely held out his hand. For half a second, he was afraid she'd slap it away in front of the guests and the cameras. She certainly looked like she wanted to. Instead, she flashed furious eyes at him, but she placed her palm in his.

Paul pulled them onto the dance floor. Something inside his chest—a tightness that had been there since Kyleigh's horrified reaction to marrying him—loosened as he placed his hands on her waist and drew her near. Not as close as he wanted. But if he tried to pull her against him like he was tempted to, she'd probably knee him in the balls.

Her body was so tense as they began to sway to the song, he wondered if her muscles ached.

"Relax," he whispered against her ear.

When her body tightened even more, he tried to reign in the sudden impatience that was wending its way through him. "Is this how our marriage is going to be?" Paul asked. "You giving me the silent treatment the entire time?"

"You can't be serious?" she snapped. "After the stunt you pulled?"

"I know you're upset—"

"Upset doesn't even begin to describe how I feel right now."

Gregori and Leroy positioned themselves on either side of the dance floor. Paul shot a smile at them before returning to the matter at hand.

"Look, this is only for three months, Ky. Three months, and then you'll never have to see me again." Though his insides protested at that idea.

"Why?" she muttered.

"What do you mean?" Paul asked. "It's part of the contract. I—"

"No, I mean, why did you force me to marry you? You threatened my store, you bastard."

A muscle in his face ticked. "I did what I had to do to save this season. You don't know what it means to me."

"Tell me," Kyleigh insisted. "Because right now, I can't even look at you."

Paul looked at the cameras again, before whispering in her ear, hoping they wouldn't hear any further.

"This season will give me enough clout at the network that they'll let me move forward with a couple of projects I proposed to them. And don't pretend you don't get something in return. Once the show airs, your store will be a top tourist destination. Trust me. Every store we've featured on the show gets a financial boost. I promise you. Ninety days, and then we can get divorced."

Kyleigh's eyes flew to his. "Divorce? You mean an annulment."

Heat licked at Paul's belly. "Who's to say we won't consummate the marriage? The show does pay for a honeymoon, you know."

Her gaze narrowed. "I'm not going on a honeymoon with you." But the flush on her cheeks revealed what she was thinking.

He leaned down so he was even closer to her. "But we

used to be so good together. I wonder if I can still make you scream when I touch your—"

"Stop it!" she snapped, her cheeks a fascinating red. "I'm a mother now."

"You're still the sexiest woman I've ever met." His breath brushed against the shell of her ear, and she shivered in his arms. He smirked before pulling away.

She stared daggers at him. "Three months, and we go our separate ways. That's the agreement, right?"

"Right, and in the meantime, you and I play nice for the cameras. We'll do everything that other couples on the show have to do. Live together. Go on dates. Deal?"

She slowly nodded. "Deal."

Her face changed then, a diabolical expression appearing that had Paul frowning with caution.

"What?"

"I'm assuming we'll need to stay in my apartment. Unless you have a house in town."

"Actually, the show rented a house for us."

"I'm not disrupting Holly's routine. It's either my place or we live in separate quarters."

"Fine, your place it is."

"It's pretty tiny," Kyleigh mentioned.

"Not a problem," Paul replied, his mind already drifting to living in a small space with Kyleigh, brushing up against each other at every other moment. He wondered if her bed was small, too. They'd have no other option but to lie close to each other all night.

"Great," Kyleigh replied, giving him a bright smile that put him on instant alert. "You're going to love the couch. It's secondhand, but somewhat comfy."

"The couch?"

"It's the couch, or you stay somewhere else. I have to think of my daughter, after all."

"Fine," Paul gritted.

The couch wasn't ideal, but it'd let him stay close.

How bad could it be?

Chapter Ten

Paul woke the next morning feeling like he was ninety instead of forty. Every muscle in his body ached from sleeping on Kyleigh's couch, which was easily twenty years old. There was little padding left in the cushions.

"Good morning, sunshine," Gregori said, his camera already zooming in on Paul's face.

"Piss off," Paul grumbled, rubbing a hand over the whiskers on his jaw.

"What? You didn't sleep well? Personally, I slept like a baby," Gregori replied. He was also staying at Kyleigh's apartment. He'd set up an air mattress not too far from where Paul was sleeping. Had Paul known Kyleigh's couch was so uncomfortable, he would have gotten one, too.

"You try sleeping on this torture device," Paul snapped. He stood up with a wince. Stretching, he heard something crack in his back, which offered a slight reprieve from the ache he felt.

"You might want to put on some clothes," Gregori said. "As much as the audience will enjoy you shirtless, you're living with a young girl now."

Paul frowned as he looked down at himself. Normally he slept naked, but given that he was pretty sure Kyleigh still wanted to maim him, he decided to be respectful and wear boxer shorts through the night. If he was honest with himself, he hadn't even factored in Holly. It was going to take some getting used to living with a kid.

Grumbling to himself, Paul opened his suitcase, which was on the glass table in front of the couch. He rummaged through it until he found some sweats and a T-shirt. After pulling them on, he ran a hand through his hair, knowing he was probably sporting some nice bedhead.

"I need coffee," he muttered.

He glanced around. Kyleigh hadn't been lying when he said the place was tiny. He hadn't had time to really take everything in the night before. By the time the reception wrapped up and they'd done their wedding day reactions for the show, it had been late. He and Gregori had gone back to the hotel and packed up what they needed before heading to Kyleigh's. Kyleigh had opened the door looking just as unhappy as she had earlier in the day.

She'd also looked gorgeous with her face scrubbed clean of makeup and her hair hanging loose around her shoulders. She already had her pajamas on by the time they got there. They weren't meant to be sexy, but Paul bit back a groan when he saw her anyway. Kyleigh had on a loose T-shirt that showed a glimpse of her shoulder and plaid boxers that looked so soft Paul resisted the urge to feel them with his fingers.

He was half convinced that, despite their earlier agreement, she wouldn't allow them into her apartment, so he took it as a win when she did. She pointed to the couch before telling them to be quiet so they didn't wake up Holly. She'd left without so much as a goodnight before going into her room with a firm click of the door behind her.

Now that he got a full view of the place, Paul smiled as he took in the clean brightness of the room. Everything was slightly dated, but very much Kyleigh. One corner of the room had an overstuffed green chair. Next to it was a woven jute basket filled to the brim with yarn. A metallic pink crochet hook poked out of one spool. Various pictures hung on the wall. Above the couch was a painting of a gigantic sunflower, the thick paint causing the petals to pop. On the table beside the couch was a picture of Kyleigh hugging a laughing Holly when she was a toddler.

Directly across from Paul was a small hallway. There were two doors on the left, which he knew were Kyleigh's and Holly's rooms. To the right was the bathroom.

With a yawn, he moved to his immediate right where the kitchen was. He stumbled to a stop when he saw Holly there, eating a bowl of cereal at the kitchen table while she played on her phone.

She glanced up at him and narrowed her eyes. "You snore," she said by way of greeting.

"Okay," Paul replied.

He never knew how to interact with kids, especially young girls, despite the fact that they used to literally throw themselves at him when Holiday Boys first burst on the scene.

He looked around the kitchen, taking in the soft yellow walls and faded brown cupboards. A spice rack was attached to the wall to his left. Magnets covered the fridge, though Kyleigh had made space for a whiteboard with a grocery list on it. A window in the center of the room cast everything in morning light. Everything looked so homey.

Even though the space was small, it was much nicer than the kitchen at his home in California. He'd paid a very expensive interior designer to decorate that house. Gray walls and stainless steel appliances made up his kitchen. It lacked the warm energy that this space had. Maybe when he got home, he'd look at getting it redecorated.

Paul spotted a red coffeepot on the counter. After filling it with water, he opened a cupboard door to his left, hoping to find some coffee.

"The coffee's in the cupboard below the pot," Holly said.

"Thanks," he muttered.

Once it was percolating, Paul turned to find Holly still staring at him. Feeling awkward but aware of Gregori, who'd followed him into the kitchen with his camera, Paul sat across from the girl and gave her his best professional smile.

She merely lifted an eyebrow at him in return.

Paul fought back a genuine smile. Holly looked so much like a younger version of Kyleigh, it was uncanny.

"So…" he said, trying to start conversation. "How old are you? Ten?"

She stiffened, immediately indignant. "I'm thirteen."

Oh hell. He thought she was a tween. He could handle a tween. Teenage girls were another level. While he loved the fans when he was a teenager himself, some of them could get intense fast. Over the years, he'd grown an instinct to avoid teen girls at all costs.

He cleared his throat. "It's, uh, nice to finally get a chance to talk. Since I'm your stepdad now."

He internally cringed. Holly scrunched her nose, staring at him like he was an idiot. Gregori snorted behind him, and he wanted nothing more than to throw his friend and his damn camera out the door.

Holly sat back in her chair and crossed her arms over her chest. Her eyes narrowed as she asked, "Why marry my mother? You've never participated in your own show before."

He didn't know what to say to that. He didn't want to say to her or the camera that he'd married Kyleigh to save his career. Thankfully, the coffee sounded like it had stopped brewing. Getting up from his chair, he went over to the cupboards and started opening them until he found the coffee mugs. He poured a cup and took a deep sip of it, the heat making him perk up a little.

He realized that Holly still stared at him, waiting for his answer.

"Would you believe I care for your mom?"

"No," Holly replied instantly.

Paul frowned at her. "Why not?"

"Because everyone knows you're a player."

Paul was instantly offended. He ignored Gregori, who burst out laughing. "Contrary to whatever internet trash you read, I'm not like that." *Not anymore, anyway.*

Holly blinked huge, distrusting eyes at him. "Didn't you just get dumped by Monica Valdez because she said you were unable to commit?"

"First off, I dumped *her*. And considering I just married your mom, I'd say Monica is full of sh…poop."

Holly put her elbows on the table, her gaze unwavering. "But why my mom?"

"I—"

Kyleigh thankfully interrupted her daughter's interrogation when she appeared in the kitchen wearing a pink terrycloth robe. She winced at the sunlight as though the bright morning was too much for her. Given the dark circles under her eyes, Paul assumed she'd slept as poorly as he had. She still looked adorable with her cheeks flushed from sleep and her hair mussed. He couldn't look away from her as she trudged her way toward the coffeepot. He grabbed a mug out of the cupboard and handed it to her.

"Thanks," she said, not meeting his eyes as she filled her cup.

"You still take it with creamer?" he asked, not waiting for her answer as he walked over to the stainless steel refrigerator. Opening the door, he found a bottle of caramel-flavored nondairy creamer. "You use nondairy now?" he asked as he handed her the bottle.

"Meg and Julie are both vegetarians who try to avoid dairy as much as possible," she said. "I started buying it for whenever they came over for coffee, and now I get it out of habit." She finished preparing her drink. "Speaking of, I should see if Julie had her baby yet."

Leaving her coffee on the counter, Kyleigh drew her phone out of her robe pocket and pulled up her contact list. Paul turned away to grab his mug for a refill only to meet Holly's eyes. He did his best to ignore that inquisitive stare.

"Hey, Meg," Kyleigh said after a moment, her phone pressed to her ear. "I wanted to check in and see how Julie's doing?"

Paul poured himself another cup and leaned against the counter, staring at Kyleigh's profile. He took in the softness of her skin, the fine lines around her eyes and mouth. As the sun streamed through the window, it highlighted the streaks in her hair. There were some gray strands threading through the thick blond. Even at forty, she still took his breath away.

His heart did a funny jolt, and he rubbed at his chest. The caffeine must be kicking in already.

"Will you keep me updated?" Kyleigh asked. "Okay, thanks. If you need me to bring anything to the hospital, let me know." After another pause, she said, "Sounds good. Take care."

After she disconnected the call, Paul asked, "How's Julie doing?"

"She's still in labor," Kyleigh replied with a wince. "I don't envy her for that. Maybe I can swing by the hospital later this evening and drop off some food for everyone. I also want to pick up something for the baby."

"I'll go with you," Paul offered as Kyleigh stepped closer to him to get her coffee mug.

She gave him a startled look. "You don't have to."

"I want to," he insisted. "They're my friends as well."

Kyleigh nodded once. "Okay."

"Besides," he said, a smirk appearing on his face, "we have a big date planned for today."

Kyleigh's eyes widened. "What?"

"Part of the show," he said, nodding at Gregori. "I've got ninety days to convince you to stay married to me. We're supposed to date during that period."

"But I thought…" Kyleigh looked from Paul to Gregori and then back to Paul. She didn't finish her sentence, though, and instead took a sip from her coffee.

He could only guess what she probably thought. He'd told her yesterday that it was a ninety-day marriage, and he meant it. That didn't mean he wasn't planning on giving his all for the show. Plus, he wanted to spend more time with Kyleigh and get caught up on what she'd been doing with her life since they parted.

Paul leaned closer to her, so close he could smell the sweet caramel scent of coffee on her lips.

She instantly stilled as her eyes lifted to his, a question there.

He didn't know why he'd gotten into her personal space, only that he couldn't step away now that he was there. He watched in fascination as the pulse in her neck visibly sped up the longer he lingered.

"Ugh," Holly muttered from across the room before she got up and left.

Paul didn't even notice. He was too busy staring into Kyleigh's sapphire eyes, unable to look away. Against his better judgment, he reached out and twirled a strand of her blond hair around his finger, feeling the silky texture of it, before he tucked it behind her ear. Her hair was just as soft as he remembered.

Kyleigh looked at him, as if unsure. "Why'd you do that?"

He lifted a shoulder. "Because I wanted to."

Somewhere in the background, Paul heard Gregori moving, getting a better shot of them. It was background noise that wouldn't distract him as he enjoyed the nearness of his wife.

His wife.

His mouth ticked upward. "Whether you like it or not, Mrs. Rodriguez, for the next ninety days, you're mine."

Chapter Eleven

Kyleigh sat beside Paul in his rented Aston Martin. Cameras had been set up on the dashboard and side doors to capture their faces from every angle, not missing a single moment of their conversation. Gregori, Shawnee and some of the other crew drove behind them in a white camera truck.

Kyleigh had her phone out so she could read the text Meg sent her. There were still no changes in Julie's labor. The doctor didn't expect her to deliver for hours. Putting her phone in her purse, Kyleigh glanced at one of the cameras before asking, "Do you ever get used to it?"

Paul looked over at her before his eyes returned to the road. "What?"

"The constant cameras?"

He shrugged before steering them down a road that Kyleigh knew led to the outskirts of town. "You get used to it after a while, though I've admittedly never been in this position before." He nodded toward the ring on his finger.

The sight of it looking so right on his hand made butterflies form in Kyleigh's stomach, which she quickly squashed. She understood why Paul had pushed for their marriage. She was adult enough to acknowledge that they'd both gain something out of the situation. And while logically she understood it, Kyleigh was still furious at Paul for blackmailing her into marriage. She had to remind herself she'd only be married for ninety days… Well, eighty-nine now.

"But yeah," he continued, "After a while you get used to it. Especially when you've been in the spotlight for as long as I have. That said, there are times where I enjoy my privacy. There've been moments when I've had fans swarm me, even when I was doing something as mundane as ordering coffee or buying deodorant. I love meeting people, especially those who approach me respectfully, but I've learned to appreciate having boundaries more."

As they continued down the road, it dawned on Kyleigh that this was the first moment she and Paul had had to themselves since reuniting. She tried to think of something else to say, but she didn't know how to talk to him anymore. At one time, they'd practically read each other's minds. She didn't know him now, not as the man he'd become anyway.

Kyleigh peeked at his profile as he drove the expensive car down the road with ease. She understood why Hollywood had come knocking on his door. He was so incredibly handsome and had continued to age to perfection. It was crazy to think that she was sitting beside Paul Rodriguez, Holiday Boy and reality star extraordinaire, and not Paulo Rodriguez, the guy she met at performing arts camp.

He turned his head and caught her looking at him.

She immediately shifted her eyes to the passing landscape in front of them.

"What?" he asked.

"Nothing," she murmured.

"Come on, tell me. You look like you have something on your mind."

She bit her lip. "Okay. I was just thinking how strange it is to sit beside *the* Paul Rodriguez, megastar."

His eyes softened as he looked at her. "I'm still me, Kyleigh."

She shook her head. "It's just…you've come so far since Clarington. You're this hugely famous guy, who was someone I used to know back in the day. And now I'm married to you. It's strange."

He frowned for a second before his face cleared. "Okay, I acknowledge that my job is a bit different than what you're used to. But focus on me, the person, and not that guy on TV. We can spend the next few months getting to know each other again."

"And then?" she murmured.

Paul's face tightened for a second before it smoothed away. "And then, maybe we can walk away from this experience as friends."

"Hmm." The word *friends* sat strangely with Kyleigh. Could she and Paul ever be friends? She became distracted as he turned down another road. "Where are we going?"

"A place Tyler recommended. Wine & Stuff."

Kyleigh's mouth turned down. She'd never heard anything good about the winery. She was surprised the establishment had stayed in business for as long as they had, given that their wine was supposedly awful. But thanks to the recent Holiday Boys revival, Holiday Bay had become a tourist destination, and thirsty tourists had given the owners enough money to stay afloat for the foreseeable future.

After pulling into the parking lot and putting the car in Park, Paul gave her a wicked smile. "Let's go celebrate our nuptials." Not giving her a chance to respond, he got out of the car.

Kyleigh slowly followed his lead as the camera crew pulled into the spot behind them.

Several tourists stood outside, taking selfies beside a gi-

gantic wooden pirate the size of the building. A word balloon attached to its mouth read *Ahoy, Matey*. The statue
held a large wine bottle, the words *Wine & Stuff* scrawled
across its wooden surface. The florescent orange paint on
the brick building glared brightly under the afternoon sun.

Paul gaped at a metal parrot beside the entrance. He muttered under his breath, "I'm going to kill Tyler."

"Well…" Shawnee said as she came up to them. "This
will certainly have, um, audiences talking."

Paul gave her a disbelieving expression before he touched
Kyleigh on the back to guide her toward the building. She
immediately tensed at his touch.

"Relax," Paul whispered to her profile, tickling her ear
with his breath. "It's for the cameras."

Right…the cameras.

As they walked toward the building, a girl in the tourist group noticed them and let out a shriek. Before Kyleigh
realized what was happening, a crowd surrounded them.
She stepped out of the way as a determined woman about
her age, wearing a vintage Holiday Boys shirt, pushed her
way between them. Paul gave Kyleigh a *this is what I was
talking about* expression before charming his fans with a
charismatic smile.

"Crazy, huh?" Shawnee said as she stepped into the
empty space beside Kyleigh.

They watched Paul pose for pictures with the group and
sign the woman's T-shirt.

Kyleigh stared at the group, understanding what Paul
meant about boundaries. She knew he wanted her to treat
him like a man and not the celebrity he'd become, but it
was hard to do when people were yelling his name for an
autograph. How different this date already was compared
to their former ones. Paul had never been able to afford to

take her to places on dates back then other than fast food restaurants. Their nondates were some of the best she'd ever been on. They'd usually end up by the bay, talking for hours on end.

Paul glanced around the crowd, looking for Kyleigh. As soon as he spotted her, he said to the crowd, "It was nice meeting all of you, but we have business here."

"What kind of business? Something for *First Comes Marriage*?" the woman in the vintage T-shirt asked.

"Stay tuned," he said with a bright smile. He walked over to Kyleigh, muttering, "Sorry about that. I promise that doesn't happen all the time."

"It's okay. It's a part of who you are now," she said as they entered the building. "I guess I'll have to get used to it. At least for the next ninety days."

When Paul didn't say anything, she turned to look at him in concern. He gave her a ghost of a smile. "Right. Ninety days."

Kyleigh turned to take in the part of the winery that was really a gift shop. There were kiosks set up in the showroom, containing glass shelves that held touristy items. Shot glasses and magnets read Holiday Bay, MI.

She let out a small snort when she spotted one kiosk filled with Holiday Boys gifts. She walked over to it so she could get a closer look.

"When did you come out with this?" she asked, brimming with laughter. She held up a doll that was a poor replica of a Ken doll. She guessed it was supposed to resemble Paul. His name was written on the box, but it looked like the features had sat in the sun too long. The doll looked sun-bleached and slightly melted.

Paul stared at it in disdain. "That's not something I ever authorized. It's probably a cheap knockoff."

Kyleigh put the doll back on the shelf and tried to straighten her face as the winery owner, Sarah, hurried up to them.

Sarah and her husband, Ted, were quintessential hipsters. Sarah had her long dark hair piled into a messy bun. She wore a navy blue maxi dress that fell to her ankles. On her wrist was a bracelet of tiny bells that rang out whenever she moved. She smiled brightly when she saw Kyleigh, Paul and the show's crew hovering in her lobby. "Hello, everyone! Kyleigh! Fancy seeing you in these parts."

"Hi, Sarah," Kyleigh said in greeting, turning toward Paul so she could introduce them. "Do you know Paul Rodriguez?"

"Not officially, but I obviously know who you are," Sarah said, offering her hand to shake.

Shawnee walked over to them. "Sarah, I'm Shawnee, we spoke on the phone earlier this week. I appreciate you emailing me the NDA. Obviously, we need to keep everything you see in here under wraps until it airs on the show."

"Of course," Sarah replied. "I'm so thrilled and honored that you wanted to film here." She waved them to the back of the store. "I have something special planned for you today. We came out with a new line of wines. I have the samples already set out."

Kyleigh tried to keep the cautious expression off her face. They followed Sarah to the back of the store where a long bar was stationed.

Sarah pulled out two trays and placed four wineglasses on each. Grabbing the corkscrew, she removed the cork with a loud pop. "This is our newly launched Pirate's Trove Pinot Blanc. I wouldn't be surprised if we win some international awards for this one." She pulled out three more samples, each with a more ridiculous name. Captain Ted's

Cabernet Sauvignon, M'Hardy Merlot and Sarah's Scally-wag Strawberry Wine.

"Sarah!" a man called out from the back of the building,

"Ted's setting up for our monthly senior disco bingo," Sarah explained. "Hopefully, Betty won't throw out her hip like she did last time." Concern momentarily flashed across her face before she brightened. "If you need any-thing, give me a shout."

"Thanks, Sarah," Kyleigh said.

"So…" Paul said, eyeing the wine after Sarah left. "What should we start with?"

"The Pirate's Trove Pinot?" Kyleigh suggested.

Paul nodded. He handed Kyleigh her glass before grab-bing his own. He lifted it. "A toast."

Kyleigh's eyebrows lifted. "Okay."

"To us."

She put her glass on the bar. "I'm not drinking to that."

"Why not?" Paul asked. He nodded toward the cameras as if to remind her that they were there. Like she could for-get. Gregori and his team might be great at keeping quiet, but it was hard not to notice the camera in her face.

Through clenched teeth, she said, "To us."

Paul's mouth lifted, clearly humored by her reaction. He clinked his glass against hers, and they each took a sip.

Kyleigh paused as the wine hit her taste buds. She'd never been a fan of dry wine, but this tasted like sand and wet leaves at the same time. All the moisture in her mouth instantly evaporated. She half wondered if it would ever return or if the Pirate's Trove had destroyed her taste buds forever.

Paul also paused as if he were trying to categorize the taste. His mouth smacked together several times before he carefully put the wine back on his tray. "Uh, that's... interesting."

"Yeah," Kyleigh replied, putting her own glass back on the bar.

"Captain Ted's Cabernet next?" Paul asked.

Kyleigh wanted to moan in protest, but she reached for the glass anyway. She glanced at Paul who stared at his glass with equal hesitation.

"I didn't think you drank," Kyleigh said before taking a swallow of the new wine. She instantly regretted it. It tasted like berries and pencil shavings—heavy on the pencil shavings.

"I do sometimes. But not often and only on special occasions," he replied. He took a small sip of the cabernet and quickly put his glass down, muttering, "Oh god."

The wine was making Kyleigh's head buzz. ABBA's "Dancing Queen" started blaring from the back. "Yeah, I remember," she said in response. She grabbed the M'Hardy Merlot and swallowed half of it in one gulp.

"What does that mean?" Paul asked. He only took a tiny taste and didn't hide the groan that escaped him this time. "Why does this taste like rotten plums covered in dark chocolate?"

"Probably because that's what it is," she said, finishing her drink anyway. As the merlot settled in her stomach, the acridness of the drink made her insides sour.

"What did you mean when you said, 'I remember'?" Paul didn't let her comment go.

Kyleigh went back to the Pirate's Trove and finished it off. It didn't taste nearly as bad as she thought. She smacked her lips together and reached for Sarah's Scallywag Strawberry Wine. She swirled it around in her glass before taking a sniff of it. It smelled like poison. She drank it down in one gulp.

"Kyleigh…" Paul said.

"I just remember how drunk you were at Jake and Julie's bachelorette party. I was surprised, given you told me you never allowed yourself to get drunk because of what happened with your paren—"

Paul placed the glass he'd just picked up firmly back down on the bar. "That's not something we're going to discuss." He glared at Shawnee. "That gets cut. Understand me?"

Shawnee looked like someone just interrupted her favorite tennis match. "But—"

"No. My family is off-limits."

"So I guess that means I can't ask about Dominic?" Kyleigh asked as she reached for the Captain's drink. She didn't know why this place had such a bad reputation. The more she drank, the more delicious each wine sample tasted.

Paul didn't follow suit. "That is also very much off-limits."

"Do you even see him anymore?" Kyleigh asked anyway, even though the voice in the back of her head was telling her to shut up. This was Paul's private business. But as the wine sizzled her brain, she didn't think about that. She only thought about how much Paul had changed since he left her and how much that *really* bothered her.

"Kyleigh," Paul warned. "I'm not talking about my brother."

"Whoa," Shawnee interrupted though Kyleigh didn't think she was supposed to. "You have a brother?"

Paul's eyes turned glacial. "This will *not* be on the show."

"I've known you for how many years now?" Shawnee said, miffed. "You never once mentioned a brother."

"For the last time, we're not talking about this," Paul snapped before turning back to Kyleigh. "And the reason I got so drunk at Jake's bachelor party was because I never in a million years expected to run into you on that damn yacht."

"Pffft," Kyleigh responded. She giggled as the noise made her lips buzz. She reached for the remainder of her M'Hardy Merlot. She drank it down like it was water. The room was becoming nice and fuzzy now. "Yeah, I'm sure it was such a hardship running into me again. Was it guilt for standing me up on prom night?"

"Dude, not cool," Gregori murmured from behind his camera.

"I had my reasons," Paul gritted.

"Yeah, you had to go join a boy band and sleep with half the world." The room was starting to spin. She looked at her wineglasses through blurring eyes. They were all empty. She glanced over at Paul's and saw he hadn't even touched his last wine. She reached for it, but he grabbed her hand, stopping her.

"You're done," he said firmly.

"You're no fun," she grumbled.

"Shawnee, can you drive us back to Kyleigh's?" Paul asked, getting up from his chair and moving over to Kyleigh. "I don't trust myself to drive right now."

Kyleigh couldn't tell in her present state if he was feeling any effect of the wine or if he was too mad to drive, given that she'd just aired his dirty laundry in front of the camera.

Paul wrapped an arm around her, but when she tried to shake him off, his grip tightened.

"Oh, are you leaving?" Sarah asked, hurrying back into the room. "I wanted to see if you needed—"

"Thank you, the wine was delicious," Paul said, clearly lying.

"It was superb," Kyleigh added, wavering on her feet.

"Let me get the bill taken care of really quick," Shawnee said. "I'll meet you out front."

"You didn't answer my question," Kyleigh said as they headed for the front of the building.

"What's that?" Paul said, his tone stiff.

"Why'd you stand me up on prom night?"

"That's a conversation we can have when your head is clearer," Paul replied as he guided her outside.

"My head is perfectly…" Kyleigh's voiced trailed off as bile rose in her throat. She turned just in time to throw up in a nearby garbage can. As the horrible wine she'd consumed came back for a return visit, she felt someone hold her hair and rub soothing circles on her back. She continued to heave into the garbage.

Finally, she stood up on shaky legs and turned to thank whoever was helping her. Her mouth snapped shut when she saw it was Paul.

"You feeling better?" he asked, his earlier tension erased by amusement.

"No," she replied, before swiftly turning around to be sick again.

Chapter Twelve

Kyleigh woke up feeling like death. Her throat was sore from vomiting throughout the night. She'd been so sick she overhead Paul and Gregori wonder if she'd truly been poisoned.

She stumbled her way into the kitchen only to find Paul and Holly already there. She paused when she saw them. Paul looked uncomfortable. Holly looked combative, her arms crossed over her chest and her glare fixed on Paul. Gregori stood nearby filming the two of them, a wide smirk on his face.

"What's going on?" Kyleigh asked as she entered the room. She took some aspirin out of the cupboard.

"Did Paul give you a roofie or something?" Holly asked, causing Paul to scoff.

"What?" Kyleigh asked, swinging around to look at her daughter. She knew the quick movement was a mistake the moment her stomach roiled with nausea.

Her daughter finally stopped giving Paul a death glare to look at Kyleigh in concern. "Why were you so sick last night?"

Kyleigh swallowed the pain reliever before grabbing her mug to pour some coffee. "He didn't do anything. I drank some wine that didn't agree with me at Wine & Stuff."

Holly's expression thawed slightly. "Oh. I overheard Ebony's mom say that place should be condemned because it makes everyone sick."

"I won't be going back there anytime soon, trust me," Kyleigh grumbled as she gingerly sat in the chair next to Paul. "And you need to apologize to Paul for accusing him of that."

"But—" Holly started to protest but quickly shut her mouth when her mom gave her the *look*. She slouched in her chair and muttered, "Sorry."

"Okay," Paul replied. He still looked slightly offended, but he was gracious enough to accept her apology.

Kyleigh could feel his eyes on her, but she didn't meet them. She had enough of a recollection of her behavior the day before to make her cringe. She'd spilled his personal business in front of the cameras, and who knew what the network would use?

Guilt was a terrible thing when you were fighting off a hangover.

"So what's on the agenda for today?" Kyleigh asked, swishing her coffee back and forth inside her mug.

She wanted nothing more than to go to her store and bury herself in work, but the show was still covering Wendy's pay, allowing her to work full-time instead of her normal part-time. With Wendy at the store, Kyleigh and Paul could go on their show-sponsored dates. Since it was technically their honeymoon, Kyleigh was expected to take some time away from the store to focus on her new marriage. Shawnee had brought up the subject of them traveling somewhere nice, but Kyleigh flat out refused. She had Holly to think about, and it wasn't like this was a real marriage anyway.

"I thought you might want to go to the hospital today," Paul replied.

"I feel fine," Kyleigh insisted.

"Not for you, to go see Julie and Jake."

Kyleigh's head popped up. "Julie had her baby? I didn't get any calls." She pulled her phone out of her robe to make sure.

Paul grinned. "Yep, around 4:00 a.m. I called Tyler earlier to see how everything was going, and he told me. Meg planned on giving you a call this morning, but I told her you were sleeping, and I'd pass on the message."

Kyleigh looked down at her robe. "I'm the worst friend. I should have been there." Instead, she'd been busy throwing up on camera while embarrassing Paul.

"Technically, you *are* on your honeymoon," Paul replied. When she stared daggers at him, he laughed. "Jake and Julie will understand."

"I should hurry," Kyleigh said, taking another swig of coffee.

"Can I go, too?" Holly asked.

Kyleigh noticed her daughter was already dressed. "Sure. I'll only be a few minutes."

She actually took twenty before she was able to sit in the car next to Paul with Holly shoved into the small back seat of the Aston Martin. They stopped by Franki's Pasties for a dozen pasties before heading to the hospital. It didn't take them too long before they arrived at the small building in Clarington.

Paul swore under his breath when he noticed the press and fans already stationed outside, probably in the hopes of seeing a Holiday Boy. The camera van following them didn't help.

"You two go in," Paul told them as he grabbed a pair of aviator glasses from the driver's side door. He pulled them on and, with a quick set of his shoulders, went out to face the crowd. He was instantly swarmed, giving his normal practiced smile as reporters shoved microphones in his face to get the scoop.

Kyleigh wrapped her arm around Holly and pulled her toward the entrance. Gregori followed discreetly behind them, while the remaining camera crew filmed Paul speaking to the crowd.

"Excuse me, ma'am," a security officer said as soon as they entered the air-conditioned lobby. He frowned when he saw Gregori and his camera. "We're limiting guests today for security reasons. Do you have family checked in here?"

"Oh." Kyleigh looked over at Holly, whose shoulders drooped. "No, we're visiting my friend, J—"

"It's okay, Bryan." Jake's son, Dylan, came up to them. Holly instantly brightened. "That's one of my stepmom's close friends and her kid."

"Kid?" Holly said, sounding insulted.

"Never can be too careful these days," Bryan replied to Dylan. But he stepped back to let Kyleigh, Holly and Gregori through.

"Thanks, Dylan," Kyleigh said to the young man. "How's Julie…and your dad?"

"Both are exhausted, but they'll be happy to see you," he replied. He eyed the bag of pasties Holly held. "Are those from Franki's?"

"Here." Holly practically shoved them at him.

Dylan didn't notice the passive aggression. "Thank you," he said, then asked Kyleigh, "Do you want me to show you where the room is?"

Kyleigh smiled gratefully. "I appreciate it, but I want to stop by the gift shop and pick up a little something for the baby first."

"Sure." Dylan angled his head behind him. "The family

is in room 243 when you're ready." He turned and headed back the way he came.

Kyleigh and Holly entered the gift shop, while Gregori went to use the bathroom. As Kyleigh looked around, she noticed Holly's earlier animation was gone.

"What's wrong?" she asked. "Aren't you excited to see the baby?"

"I guess," Holly mumbled.

"Hey." Kyleigh reached out and grabbed Holly's chin. "What's up?"

"Nothing," Holly replied, not meeting her mom's eyes. "It's just that… Dylan's so stupid. He thinks he's so cool because he's in college now. And that he can just call me 'kid' whenever he wants. I'm plenty mature."

Kyleigh bit her lip to keep from smiling. She had a feeling she knew what was going on. Dylan and Holly had hung around each other multiple times over the past couple of years as their parents had grown close. It'd been obvious that Holly had a crush on Dylan, to which he seemed thankfully oblivious.

"Well…" Kyleigh tried to navigate carefully. "He is quite a bit older than you—"

"Only five years," Holly grumbled.

"When you're both the age that you are," Kyleigh said, "that might as well be a hundred years, as far as Dylan's concerned. Age doesn't matter so much when you're in your late twenties, early thirties."

"Whatever." Holly stomped away to examine some Holiday Boys toys on a rack located at the other side of the shop.

Kyleigh picked out several balloons, going for grays and beiges since Paul neglected to ask if Julie had a boy or a girl. Holly spotted a beige elephant and begged her mom to buy it for the baby. After they made their purchases, they walked out of the gift shop, just as Paul and the rest of the camera crew entered the hallway where Gregori was already waiting.

"All set?" Paul asked, his eyes warm as he took in Kyleigh.

"Yep," she replied before leading the way to the room Julie and Jake were in.

Another security member stood outside the door. He glared at the cameras following them. "No cameras inside."

Paul turned to Gregori. "Why don't you guys go get some coffee and come back in an hour?"

"Shawnee will kill me if I don't get a shot of Jake Reynolds's baby," Gregori argued.

"And I'll kill you if you do," a deep voice said behind them.

Kyleigh glanced that way and saw Jake walking up to them with his cousin James. James waved sheepishly at her, reminding her that he was best man at her wedding. She gave him a short smile in response.

"No pictures of my baby," Jake said firmly, folding his muscled arms over his chest menacingly. Even with the deep lines of exhaustion and the trace of a forty-eight-hour beard on his face, Jake could still pull off looking intimidating remarkably well.

"Agreed," Paul said, turning to Gregori. "I'll explain it to Shawnee. I'll call her after she returns from that scouting mission with Heather."

Usually when Shawnee went on a scouting trip with her wife, it had nothing to do with the show and everything to do with some needed couple time. Kyleigh overheard the married pair talking enough about their plans recently to know that.

"You're the boss," Gregori said before nodding at his team. Putting their cameras by their sides, they left the area.

"Hey, man," Paul finally said, hugging Jake. "Congratulations."

"Congratulations," Kyleigh repeated as she also gave the proud father a hug. "So...what'd you have, a boy or girl?"

Jake laughed tiredly. "Go see for yourself."

As soon as they entered the room, Kyleigh had to blink against the bright wave of pink flowing through the room. Pink flowers, balloons and clothes filled every empty spot.

Tyler and Meg sat on the hospital room's love seat. Tyler had his arm around his wife's back. Dylan sat in an armchair next to Julie's bed, eating a pasty. Lying in the hospital bed was Julie, looking beautiful but exhausted, her gorgeous red hair fanned out against her pillows. Cuddled in her arms was her new baby daughter.

"Hey," Julie said. "Thanks for coming."

"I'm sorry we weren't here earlier." Kyleigh handed Holly the balloons. "We should have come yesterday."

"They wouldn't have let you in, even with Paul. Security has been going a little overboard," Julie said with a glower at her husband.

Jake held up his hands in defense, looking completely unapologetic. "I'm trying to keep my family safe."

Julie snorted before looking back at Kyleigh. "They almost kicked James out, and he's blood related."

"But I have a date with Bryan later this week," James stated smugly. "So it was worth it."

Paul patted him on the back. "Congrats, man. It's about time you got back in the saddle."

"Yeah," James said, but the lightness in his voice didn't match the emptiness in his eyes.

Kyleigh peered down at the tiny bundle in her friend's

arms, taking in the cutest baby she'd ever seen. Even though she wore a pink cap on her tiny head, it did little to hide the shock of red hair sticking out of it. Kyleigh squirted some hand sanitizer on her hands from the table next to the bed before reaching out to touch a hand to the soft curls peeking under the cap.

"She looks just like you," Kyleigh observed.

Julie giggled. "That's what Jake said, too."

"And I stand by that." Jake walked over to Julie's other side before leaning down to kiss his wife on the forehead. "She's as beautiful as her mama." He ran a tender finger down the baby's cheek.

Paul let out a snort. "Man, Jake's going to be the most overprotective father ever."

Jake opened his mouth to protest, but Julie said, "She already has him wrapped around her little finger. Him and her big brother." She smiled at her stepson.

Dylan nodded as he chewed his pasty, his face serious as he said, "I don't see a problem with that. Just because I said she wasn't allowed to date until she was forty."

Father and son fist-bumped.

Julie rolled her eyes before turning back to Kyleigh. "Do you want to hold her?"

"Yes, please."

Julie transferred her daughter into Kyleigh's eager arms. Kyleigh began to rock the baby, taking in the sweet perfection of her features. Holly moved so she could lean against her mom, looking at the baby's face in fascination.

"So…" Paul said, as he came to stand beside them. "Does she have a name?"

Jake lay down on the bed next to his wife, ignoring her huff as she moved over to make room for him. He yawned before burying his head into her shoulder.

Julie patted his cheek before letting out a yawn herself. She responded to Paul, "Jane Martha. After our mothers."

Kyleigh smiled empathetically at her friend. "Your mother would have loved that."

Julie's mom, Jane, had been a longtime customer of Kyleigh's store. It'd been heartbreaking to watch the once energetic woman wither away with Alzheimer's. Julie had taken care of her mom for years until the older woman passed away right before Julie found out she was pregnant. Julie had been devastated. Even now, Kyleigh could tell by the sadness in her eyes that Julie was still struggling with the loss.

"Jane Martha Reynolds," Kyleigh repeated, then whispered to the infant, "You're the luckiest girl in the world, you know that?" She glanced up at Jane's parents, laughing a little when she noticed they had both fallen asleep.

"Maybe we should leave," Tyler whispered, getting up and offering Meg his hand. "Give the family a little time together."

James straightened from where he'd been leaning against the wall. "Sounds good to me. Dylan, will you let your parents know I'll be back later this evening?" He walked over to his younger cousin and grabbed a few pasties out of the bag Dylan was hoarding. "And I'm taking some of these with me."

"I guess we should go, too," Kyleigh said, reluctant to let go of the precious baby in her arms. But she remembered how tired she'd been after labor and how much she appreciated having some alone time.

"I can take her," Dylan offered, getting up from his chair, eager to hold his baby sister. Holly stepped out of his way. She stuck her nose in the air before leaving the room without saying goodbye to him. He didn't even notice as he took Jane from Kyleigh, cuddling her close.

"Tell Julie I'll give her a call later," Kyleigh said.

"I will. Thanks for bringing Janie the elephant and balloons," Dylan replied, nodding toward where Holly had deposited them on a table.

"You're welcome," Kyleigh said.

Paul put his hand on her waist and guided her back into the hallway. He froze as a nurse approached the room.

The man stopped when he saw Paul as well.

"What are you doing here?" Paul snapped.

Kyleigh frowned as she looked between the two men before it dawned on her who the other man was. It'd been years since she'd last seen Dominic, Paul's brother. He was an older version of Paul, though he had deeper lines on his face, and most of his black hair had turned gray, whereas Paul had only a few strands jutting through his locks.

"I work here," Dom replied, pointing to the badge attached to his scrubs. "I'm surprised to see you here. I didn't think you lowered yourself to visiting Clarington these days. You certainly haven't bothered to stop by and see me or Aunt Esperanza in the past twenty-plus years, Paulo."

Paul gritted his teeth. "Prison isn't really my scene."

Dom stiffened at that. "That was a long time ago. I've grown up a lot since then. Have you?"

Paul didn't respond. He tightened his hold on Kyleigh's waist, pulling her over to where Holly, James, Tyler and Meg waited at the end of the hall. James was busy flirting with Bryan, the security guard. Tyler and Meg were in their own world, whispering sweet or sarcastic nothings to each other. Only Holly had observed the altercation, questions on her face that Kyleigh knew Paul wouldn't answer for anyone, let alone her daughter.

"So how's married life going so far?" Tyler asked once they were all together.

"She hasn't killed me yet," Paul replied with an attempt at humor.

"Though I think Paul tried to off me," Kyleigh returned. "He took me to Wine & Stuff yesterday."

Paul glared at Tyler. "Yeah, thanks for suggesting it."

"You didn't," Meg said, lightly elbowing her husband in the stomach. "He took me there once. I thought I was going to die."

"Note to self, never trust Tyler again," Paul muttered. He glanced back to where his brother had been. Dominic was gone, probably checking on one of his patients.

"Bryan is about to go on break," James said. "We're going to head to the hospital cafeteria for a quick bite." He held up the pasties he'd stolen from Dylan. "Anyone want to join us?"

"I think we're going to head home," Meg said with a yawn. "It's been a long thirty-six hours."

Kyleigh felt instant remorse. "I'm so sorry. I should have been here with you."

Meg leaned over to give her a hug. "There was literally nothing you could have done. Julie wasn't kidding when she said Jake had this place on lockdown. We spent most of our time sitting on uncomfortable chairs in the visitor lobby, keeping Dylan company."

"Mom, I'm hungry," Holly said.

"Sorry, sweets. I guess we should have gotten more pasties." Kyleigh turned to Paul. "You want to go get lunch?"

The darkness that had lingered on his face since running into his brother lightened. "Yeah, I'd like that." He held out his hand to her.

She looked at it briefly before placing her palm in his.

Her heart fluttered as his fingers tightened around hers. Out of the corner of her eye, she saw Gregori and his crew hurrying over to them.

Everything Paul did was for appearances. For the show. And Kyleigh better not forget that.

Chapter Thirteen

They pulled into Franki's with the camera crew parking in the spot next to them. Holly got out first and hurried into the building, followed by Kyleigh and Paul.

"Two stops in one day?" Franki said, standing a bit straighter when he saw the cameras coming into his pasty shop. No matter how conscious Kyleigh felt about their constant presence in her life, she had to admit they would do wonders for the town's economy once the show aired. She made a mental note to make sure they had more stops at her shop. It'd been one of her motivating reasons for being on the show in the first place, after all.

"We gave our previous order to some friends," Kyleigh explained.

"I'm always happy to have repeat customers," Franki replied. "What can I get you?"

After they placed their order, Kyleigh and Paul sat down at one of the shop's white tables. Holly went to use the bathroom.

Paul absently watched her go. "She seems like a good kid."

"Even though she accused you of drugging me?" Kyleigh said lightly, fiddling with a saltshaker on the table.

"She was just trying to protect her mother. I can respect

that. I mean, I understand the urge to want to protect you," Paul said. Kyleigh's eyes widened at that but before she could question him about what he meant, he asked, "Does she see her father much?"

Kyleigh frowned. "Not really. Dan lives in the Upper Peninsula with his wife. He used to make more of an effort. When Holly was little, he'd take her for the summers, but after he and Ginger had kids, he became too busy. I offered to take Holly to him, but there was always some reason why he couldn't do it."

"How'd Holly react?" Paul asked.

Kyleigh's eyebrows pulled together as she thought back to those early days after their divorce. The days when Holly would wait eagerly in her room, her suitcase packed, before wearily accepting that her father wasn't coming for her. Kyleigh and Dan got into more fights than she cared to remember about his general disregard for his oldest daughter's feelings.

After it happened again last summer, Kyleigh finally put her foot down and told him she'd take him to court to rescind his custodial rights if he didn't start giving Holly the love and respect she deserved. Soon after that conversation, he started making more of an effort. He took Holly for the last part of the summer the previous year, and he'd promised her he'd be part of her upcoming talent show that paired fathers and daughters in a competition with mothers and sons. Personally, Kyleigh thought the idea was stupid. What were kids supposed to do if they grew up in a single parent home? But she'd been overruled by the PTA.

"Holly loves her dad, but I know it bothers her more than she lets on when her father cancels on her," she finally said in response to Paul's question. Deciding she'd over-shared enough as Gregori's camera zoomed in on her face, she asked, "Hey, can we feature the store a little more? I thought I'd be working this whole time and…"

"Of course," Paul said. "Maybe I can help you out. I bet I can sell a ton of stuff."

"I don't doubt that," Kyleigh replied dryly. She'd probably have people lined out the door for a chance to have Paul wait on them. She knew the same thing had a tendency to happen whenever Jake showed up at Julie's shop across the street. "But maybe we could do something else. Kyleigh's Knits offers different classes throughout the week. We have an upcoming ceramics class, and there's also a scheduled paint and sip workshop."

"Paint and sip?" Paul asked, his forehead wrinkling.

"Basically, you sit around socializing, drinking wine, and everyone paints the same picture, but you have creative license to paint it in whatever style you want."

"Yeah, that sounds good. I'll make sure Shawnee adds it to the schedule."

"Thanks," she murmured. Silence descended between them. She looked around the shop, while Paul's eyes stayed on her. Scrambling for something else to say, Kyleigh finally blurted, "I didn't know Dom was a nurse."

Paul instantly stiffened, and Kyleigh regretted bringing him up.

A muscle pulsed in Paul's jaw before he said, "Neither did I."

She forgot the cameras watching them. Forgot that she was out in public with an incredibly famous person. Instead, she thought back to the Paul she knew from years ago, the handsome boy who was her first love. Although she had never felt as close to another man as she had to Paul in those days, he'd always concealed a part of himself from her. Mainly, his family life.

Paul rarely let her come to his house back then, preferring to meet in Holiday Bay. While her parents had been upper middle class, Paul had grown up in poverty, raised by his aunt. Her father had tried to forbid Kyleigh from seeing him again after he arrested Paul's brother, but Kyleigh hadn't listened. They'd kept their relationship hidden from everyone, secretly meeting up and avoiding places where her father or one of his deputies might find them.

Nothing in her memories explained Paul's reaction to seeing Dom again at the hospital. She remembered how much Paul used to adore his beloved older brother. They'd clearly had a rift at some point, given how they'd reacted to each other in the hospital. If it had happened back when they dated, Paul never mentioned it to her that she could recall.

Awkward silence fell again. Paul didn't say anything else on the subject of Dom, and Kyleigh decided not to push.

She looked up as Holly made her way back to the table, but her daughter stopped abruptly when a mother and daughter entered the shop.

Kyleigh recognized the mother as Kate Meeker, one of the most pretentious people Kyleigh ever had the misfortune of meeting. Her daughter, Jenna, had bullied Holly for years, to the point where Kyleigh had had to go to the school and complain. Nothing ever seemed to get resolved, thanks to Kate being a practiced liar, even worse than her daughter.

"What are you doing here?" Jenna asked Holly. Her tone was so full of disdain, Kyleigh wanted to go across the shop and shield her daughter from the little brat. She didn't have to.

Because Paul had taken in Kyleigh's reaction. He turned in his chair in time to hear Jenna talk down to Holly. Saw as his stepdaughter wrapped her arms protectively around herself. And he stood up.

Crossing his own arms over his chest, he said, "Is there a problem here?"

Kate, too busy on her phone to care about her daughter's rude tone, looked up from the device in her hand, ready to dismiss whoever was speaking. She noticed the camera crew standing off to the side first before her eyes landed on Paul.

The petite blonde's hand instantly went to her bob, patting the thin strands into place. "Paul Rodriguez?" she squeaked.

"Yeah?" he said, his tone so dismissive, Kyleigh had to bite back her smile.

"I… I'm a huge fan." Kate moved closer, practically fawning over Paul. Kyleigh tried not to bristle as the woman tilted her head flirtatiously.

Franki walked over to their table, carrying a tray with their food. Paul's face was impassive as he looked at Holly. He didn't acknowledge Kate at all. "You better come get your food, Holly, before it gets cold."

"You know Paul Rodriguez?" Jenna asked in disbelief.

Holly raised her chin. "He's with my mom." She turned back to their table without looking at Jenna or Kate.

Paul put his hand protectively on Holly's shoulder and guided her to the table. He continued to ignore the horrible mother and daughter as if they weren't even there.

"Well!" Kate sounded offended. She and her daughter marched over to the counter, the mother tapping her foot impatiently as she waited for Franki to finish delivering their food.

After Franki placed the pasties on their table, he said with a wink, "Anything else I can get you?"

"I think we're all set, Franki," Kyleigh replied. "Thank you."

Considering how hungry Holly claimed she was, she only nibbled on her food until Jenna and Kate left the restaurant.

"Is Jenna still bothering you?" Kyleigh asked quietly as she watched Holly take bigger bites now that the other girl was gone.

Holly merely shrugged.

"You want me to destroy them? I've got connections, I can make it happen." Paul's tone was light, making his statement seem like a joke, but there was a seriousness on his face that Kyleigh wasn't used to seeing.

"Yes," Holly replied, but she giggled as she said it.

"On it." Paul held his fork up to hers, and they clicked the plastic together in a silent deal.

Kyleigh shook her head as she watched the two.

They finished eating and made their way over to Kyleigh's store so she could check in with Wendy. She spent the next few hours getting lost in work. When she finally came out of her zone, the sun was beginning to set.

She found Paul and Holly in the craft room, building houses out of stained glass while Gregori filmed their interaction. Holly's looked carefully crafted. Paul's looked like the slightest wind would make the whole thing collapse, despite the copious amounts of solder holding it together.

He cut another bit of stained glass, swearing when it snapped in half. "What the hell am I doing wrong?"

"You're cutting too far on the glass," Holly said. "I told you this."

Kyleigh's heart warmed at the sight of them working together. She didn't think Paul even liked kids, but here he was spending the afternoon with her daughter. The earlier stress on Holly's face was completely erased.

Though she hated to interrupt them, Kyleigh said, "Sorry I took so long."

They both looked up from their projects. Kyleigh tried to ignore how Paul's intent stare created a thrilling buzz over her skin.

"It's okay," he replied, his voice deep. "Are you ready to leave?"

"Yeah," she said. "Unless you want to finish your projects."

"I already finished mine." Holly proudly held up her cute pink-and-purple glass house.

"Mine is trash," Paul muttered.

Kyleigh tried not to laugh at the lopsided pile of glass in his hands. "It's...cute."

"That's me, always doing cute stuff." He winked at her.

Holly snickered while Kyleigh glowered.

They put away the equipment they got out before the three of them and Gregori left the store and returned to Kyleigh's apartment.

Holly set the table as Kyleigh started pulling out ingredients to make dinner. She couldn't hold back her surprise when Paul entered the kitchen and walked over to the cutting board. He started to slice up the cucumber she got out for the salad.

"What?" he asked when he noticed her watching him.

"I didn't think you knew how to cook."

He scoffed at that. "Once upon a time, I had to cook for my whole family. Believe it or not, I do know my way around the kitchen."

Gregori coughed but remained silent.

"What?" Paul said defensively to the cameraman. "I can cook."

"Remember that time you tried to cook French toast for the crew when we went to Fiji and half of us ended up with food poisoning?"

"I told you a million times, that wasn't my fault. The eggs they gave me were bad."

"Sure, Paul," Gregori joked. "Keep telling yourself that."

After they finished eating and did the dishes, Holly went to her room to read. Kyleigh and Paul moved to sit on the couch. Gregori sat in the armchair next to it, continuing to film them.

"Do you ever get bored filming people's everyday interactions?" Kyleigh asked the cameraman.

He shrugged as he switched out the battery for his camera. He put the used one in its charger and plugged it into the wall socket behind him. "Depends on the couple," he answered. "Sometimes they're so busy worrying about me and making sure I get their best angles, it gets real boring. It's much better when I can capture something that's real."

"And are you capturing anything real in Holiday Bay?" she asked.

He snorted. "I feel like I should get an award for this season."

She opened her mouth to ask him what he meant when Paul asked, "You want to watch TV?"

She pulled her attention away from Gregori to look at Paul. "What?"

He picked up the remote from the table next to him and nodded at the television across the room. "You. Me. Watch TV," he replied. He didn't wait for her response as he turned the power on.

A familiar game show theme began to play, pulling her

attention to the screen. They settled back against the couch and watched the show. Paul started shouting out the answers, his knowledge of popular culture outstanding.

"I guess it's a part of the job," she said when he got another question correct.

"Hmm?" He'd slouched down on the couch, his feet on the coffee table. He rolled his head to look at her.

She nodded toward the TV. "Knowing about this stuff."

He half smiled at her. "I guess it is. Plus, you travel the world enough, you pick up a lot of information about the culture you're in, even if it's on a subconscious level."

Kyleigh kicked off her shoes and copied his pose, placing her stockinged feet next to his. She could feel the heat of his leg against hers, their feet almost touching on the table. They sat in silence for most of the show, other than one or the other randomly shouting answers.

"You're not so bad at this yourself," he said after she gave a correct answer.

She lifted a shoulder in response. When the show went to commercial break, she glanced over at Paul. She was startled to see how relaxed he looked. She hadn't seen him look like this since they were kids. The joy of merely being still seemed to be enough for him in that moment. It must've been a nice change for him, considering how chaotic his life seemed to be.

She lightly touched her foot against his. When he looked at her questioningly, Kyleigh said, "Thank you for what you did earlier. For Holly."

He pressed his foot against hers and didn't move it away. "What was that about anyway?"

She stared at where their socked toes touched, trying to ignore how her body tingled at the contact.

She frowned thoughtfully. "Holly gets bullied a lot at

school. I don't get why. She's a good kid, and I'm not just saying that because I'm biased. Her teachers all tell me the same thing, that's she's quiet but smart. She never gives them issues and seems to get along with everyone, but over the past few years, that girl Jenna and her friends have gone out of their way to make Holly's life a living hell. At first, it was name-calling, but during the past school year, there have been a couple of physical altercations. I've gone to the school about it, but Kate—Jenna's mom—is president of the PTA. She lies and covers for her daughter all the time, and because she has close connections to the school, they tend to side with her instead of Holly. It's been very frustrating."

Kyleigh ran a hand over her face, not trying to hide the worry on her face. "I get scared. Holly's personality has changed so much since the bullying started. She was always such a happy girl when she was younger. Now, she's moodier and becoming antisocial. I don't think it's just because she's a teenager with raging hormones. Whenever she comes home from school, she seems so defeated."

Kyleigh stopped talking, looking over at Gregori in concern. Her shoulders loosened when she saw that he was fiddling with the camera and not filming them. That was all she needed—to give Kate and Jenna a platform to play victim.

Gregori seemed to feel her eyes on him. He looked up. "We don't exploit children. We won't air what you just said."

"Thank you," she replied, then looked at Paul to see his reaction.

The relaxation was gone, replaced by a scowl. "I wasn't kidding earlier," he said. "I could ruin them if you want me to. I've got the money and connections."

Kyleigh laughed, brushing him off despite the earnest

expression she saw on his face. Something inside her softened. "I appreciate it, but I'll figure out something. Even if I have to homeschool Holly or transfer her to a school outside of Holiday Bay."

The game show came back on just as Paul's phone beeped beside him. He picked it up and read a text message. He sat up, putting his feet back on the floor.

It was strange how cold Kyleigh's foot felt without the presence of his. "Everything okay?" she asked.

"It's Zan," he said, mentioning his fellow Holiday Boy and best friend. "His wife's been fighting leukemia. He said they checked her into the hospital." He stood. "I'm going to give him a call really quick. I'll be right back."

"Sure," she said, watching as he went into the kitchen.

She turned back to the show, but without Paul's presence, the warmth in the atmosphere disappeared. When the game show ended, she didn't have a clue who won.

Chapter Fourteen

Paul stared at the contract in his hands. Once he signed the paperwork his lawyer sent over, it'd be official. Paul would own his own production company. It was everything he'd dreamed of. Everything he'd worked so hard to get.

"Why aren't you more excited?" Shawnee asked. She and the other cameraman, Leroy, were filming him at Kyleigh's apartment. Kyleigh was at the store with Gregori and the rest of the crew.

"Hmm?" Paul murmured, only half listening.

"I said why aren't you more excited? This is what you've talked about doing for years."

"I am excited," he replied, trying to muster up some enthusiasm. Going by the look Shawnee was giving him, he didn't think he succeeded.

Paul didn't very well want to admit what his problem was. *Kyleigh.*

She wasn't there to celebrate it with him. Over the past two weeks, he and Kyleigh had spent practically every minute together. They went for walks around town. They spent time in her store. They did everything that a normal married couple did.

Except at night.

Kyleigh went to her room, and Paul slept on the blow-up

mattress he'd bought after that first night on the couch. He'd been tempted more than once to tiptoe into his wife's room to sleep beside her, if only to escape Gregori's loud snoring. But he also knew that if Kyleigh ever let him slip into her bed again, there would be no way they'd just sleep. He wouldn't be able to keep his hands off her.

Everything had seemed so crystal clear when he first married her. He would secure his place on the show, not only solidifying his status as host for all future seasons, but he'd also achieve the contract he now held in his hands. It was why he'd married her in the first place. That and the joy of seeing the horror on Brock Sinclair's face when he realized that Paul was about to marry his daughter.

But as he stared blankly at the words of the contract, his only thought was of his wife. He wanted to see her, wanted to share his news and see the expression on her face that she used to give him all the time when they were younger.

It didn't happen often, but there were times recently where he thought she looked at him with borderline affection. Then again, maybe he imagined it, given how carefully she hid herself from him. He wondered what it would take to break open that barrier of emotion she kept between them so he could see everything going on inside her head. He wanted to know how long it would take before she gave him that look again. Like he meant something to her.

He'd dreamed of that look enough over the years. And damned if it wasn't addicting. He needed her to be proud of him. He wanted to see her face when he told her that he was not only going to be the show's host but also the executive producer.

But it wasn't just Kyleigh who was on his mind. He hadn't stopped worrying about Zan and Mary since he talked to his best friend two weeks ago. Mary wasn't doing well. Her white blood cell account was dangerously high, and the doctors had indicated that they were running out of options for her. Paul had offered to come out to Maine when he spoke with Zan again the other night, but Zan had insisted that he stay in Michigan. Both his parents and his in-laws were in town helping with the kids, he said, but he'd let Paul know if there was something he could do.

Paul ran a hand through his hair. It wasn't fair, dammit! Mary was such a beautiful person inside and out. She deserved to watch her kids grow up. Zan deserved to have her by his side so they could grow old together. Paul didn't know what his best friend would do without her.

And despite his best efforts, he also hadn't been able to stop thinking about his encounter with his brother. It had been two decades since he saw Dominic last, since he'd even spoken to him. The last time he'd seen his brother was when Brock Sinclair showed up at their house and placed Dom in handcuffs before hauling him away to jail. Seeing him at the hospital, looking so put together, made a horrible feeling appear in the pit of Paul's stomach. Something that felt an awful lot like guilt. Guilt for cutting his family out of his life so thoroughly.

He'd been grateful to his Aunt Esperanza for taking them in after the accident. She'd done the best she could with two grieving boys. Even though she had to work multiple jobs to support her new family, she never complained. It was Esperanza who first heard Paul sing. She'd encouraged him to attend the performing arts camp where he eventually met Kyleigh.

He owed so much to his aunt, and Paul had tried to pay her back, making sure she lacked for nothing after he made it big. She'd stubbornly refused all his gestures, telling him that the only thing she wanted was for him to mend his relationship with Dom. The more she pushed, the more he distanced himself, until their relationship was nothing more than a few awkward calls and emails throughout the year, mainly for birthdays and holidays.

Shawnee lightly kicked his leg, pulling him out of his morose thoughts. "Hey, you okay?"

"I—"

The door to the apartment burst open. Holly entered, her face streaked with tears as she slammed the door behind her. She didn't say a word to him. She didn't even acknowledge them as she ran into her room, banging that door shut as well.

Paul looked at Shawnee expectantly.

She raised an eyebrow back at him.

"I don't know what to do with that," Paul argued, waving his hand at Holly's closed bedroom door.

Her eyes narrowed. "And you think I do? Besides, she's *your* stepdaughter."

"Yeah, but…" But he knew Shawnee was right.

Sighing, Paul put his phone face down, along with the opened email regarding his contract, and tentatively approached Holly's room.

Leroy started to follow, but Shawnee said, "Don't you dare."

As Leroy sat back down, Paul raised his chin bravely and took the remaining steps to Holly's door. He didn't know the first thing about calming an upset teenage girl. But he also didn't like seeing Kyleigh's daughter so upset. Since that day she'd accused him of drugging her mom, the two had an unspoken truce—to stay out of each other's way. Between him dealing with the show and her being at school, they rarely saw each other. Whenever they did, they usually had Kyleigh and Gregori there as a buffer.

Taking a deep breath, Paul tentatively knocked on her door. "Holly, you okay?"

She sobbed in response.

Rubbing his forehead, he said, "Look, can I come in?"

Her response was muffled, so he took that as consent and carefully opened the door.

Holly lay on her bed, her face buried in her pillow. She was crying so much, her tiny frame shook with each ragged breath she inhaled.

Paul cautiously walked toward her. "You want to tell me what's up?"

She shook her head, burying her face farther into her pillow.

Paul took an indecisive step back, ready to leave, but told himself not to be a coward. He crossed his arms over his chest. "Come on, maybe I can help."

Holly sat up, her blotchy face making Paul angry. She looked so much like Kyleigh. And if a part of Kyleigh hurt, it was an attack on Paul.

He grabbed her desk chair and sat beside the bed. "Tell me what happened."

"H… He b…bailed on me. AGAIN!"

"What are you talking about? Who did?"

"D… Dad!"

Paul's forehead wrinkled. "Take a deep breath and tell me what you mean."

Holly rubbed at her red face with the back of her hand. Doing as he instructed, she breathed in shakily before stuttering, "T… There's a competition at school on Saturday. A father/daughter talent show."

Paul nodded, remembering Kyleigh mentioning it.

"Dad said he'd come down from the U.P., but he called

me today and said he can't make it because his son has ton-
sillitis, and his wife can't handle it alone."

Paul noticed she didn't say, her brother or stepmom. It
was *his* son. *His* wife.

"Do you want me to shame him on my social media? I've
got seventy-eight million followers on Instagram," Paul offered, only half joking.

A tiny smile popped on her face before it melted into
bitterness. Too bitter for a thirteen-year-old. She stared
blankly at her hands. "I don't know what I'm going to do
now. I bet Jenna and Emily will make fun of me even more
than they already do."

Paul's mouth tightened. He remembered that stuck-up
little brat and her mother from Franki's. He sat back in his
chair, trying not to show his anger, when an idea popped
in his head. "Well, what about me?"

Holly looked up at him, her eyebrows pulling together.
"What about you?"

Paul shrugged, then said dryly, "I don't mean to brag,
but I was once in the most popular boy band of all time.
Believe it or not, I can carry a tune."

Her mouth dropped. "You'd do that for me?"

"Sure. Tell me what you need me to do, and I'll—"

He didn't finish as she threw her arms around him.
"Thank you, Paul."

He swallowed over the sudden lump in his throat. "You're
welcome."

Kyleigh walked toward her apartment, bone weary. She'd
had a busy day at the store. Traffic had picked up, thanks
to rumors going around town that four of the Holiday Boys
had been spotted in Holiday Bay recently. Though from
what Paul told her the other day, James had left town to go

work on a renovation project in Detroit. After the Holiday Boys broke up, James turned his hobby of flipping dilapidated houses into a successful business. It wasn't so much about the money for him as it was saving historical homes that had long been neglected.

From what Meg and Julie had told her, James was even going to have a home improvement show created by Paul at one point, but something had happened during that time and James abruptly quit the show. Kyleigh had never pried, but she saw the gossip on magazine covers in the grocery store. Apparently, James's husband had an affair around that time, divorcing James shortly thereafter.

But it wasn't just people seeking Holiday Boys out that made her day so busy. It had finally gotten around town that cameras were filming Kyleigh and Paul all over the place. Kyleigh was honestly surprised it took the news this long to break. While she wasn't allowed to confirm or deny that she'd been picked as the next contestant for *First Comes Marriage*, that hadn't stopped townsfolk from trying to get information out of her. She'd had to start hiding her wedding ring to avoid questions.

The hardest part of her day though had been her weekly call from her mom. While they tried to speak with each other once a week, her father also typically joined those calls. However, her father hadn't said a word to her since her wedding day. Kyleigh hated that there was tension between them, but she also couldn't forget his audacity in treating her like a child instead of a grown woman right before the ceremony.

As she entered the apartment, she froze in the doorway and took in the scene in front of her. Shawnee and one of the cameramen sat on her couch with their backs to her.

Paul and Holly stood in front of them, facing away from everyone.

"Five, six, seven, eight," Paul counted. They both swung around to face their audience. Neither noticed Kyleigh.

"Baby, I want to call you..." Paul crooned, singing and dancing to some music playing from Shawnee's phone.

"Baby, I miss your voice..." Holly sang, her soft voice high, but complementing Paul's.

Kyleigh folded her arms over her chest as she listened to the familiar song. It was one of the Holiday Boys's hits, one of the few written by Paul, since Tyler and Jake were the better known songwriters in the group.

Kyleigh had resented the song when it first came out, but she hadn't been able to avoid it since it'd been all over the radio. Maybe it had been wishful thinking on her end, but when the song first dropped, she thought it had been about their relationship, referencing the nights they'd sneak out to be with each other. Then again, considering how quickly Paul left her with barely a goodbye, maybe it had been about one of the million other girls he'd met after her.

She watched as Paul grabbed Holly's hand and twirled her once before they jumped into matching dance steps. The steps were a little too quick for Holly, who tripped on her own feet and started to fall.

Kyleigh hurried forward to catch her before Holly could hit her head on the coffee table, but Paul grabbed her arm first, steadying her.

"You okay?" he asked, letting her go when she found her balance.

"Yeah," Holly replied. "Can you show me that step again? Oh hi, Mom!"

Paul's face snapped to hers, his eyes widening in surprise.

"Hi," Kyleigh said, before waving her hand between them. "What's going on here?"

"Dad bailed on the father/daughter talent show this weekend, so Paul said he'd step in. There's no way I can lose with a Holiday Boy singing with me. Jenna and Emily are going to crap themselves when they see us..."

Holly's voice was a buzz in Kyleigh's ears as she stared at her husband. Paul gave her a sheepish smile, grabbing at the back of his neck as if he were embarrassed.

A knock on her door distracted her.

"Food's here!" Holly shouted, running to the door.

"I hope it's okay," Paul said, walking over to Kyleigh. "I figured you wouldn't want to cook after a long day, so I ordered Florentina's."

"Hey, Holly," a woman said in the doorway. She held several large bags of food.

"Hi, Izzy," Holly replied, grabbing one of the bags from her. "Come on in."

Kyleigh recognized the short, full-figured woman who entered her living room. Isabella had worked at Florentina's ever since she was legally allowed, considering her parents owned the town's only fine dining restaurant. Izzy paused when she got farther in the room, her face startling when she saw Paul.

"Hi, Izzy," Kyleigh said to the younger woman. "Do you know Paul Rodriguez?"

"Of course, hello," she said.

"And this is Leroy and Shawnee, they're coworkers of Paul's."

The three exchanged hellos. Paul stared at Izzy for a second before snapping his fingers. "I remember you! You spilled Zan's food all over his lap at Jake and Julie's wedding."

Isabella's face turned beet red. "Great, I'm so glad that's how the Holiday Boys remember me," she grumbled, then followed Holly into the kitchen.

"Nice one," Shawnee muttered before walking into the kitchen as well.

Kyleigh gave Paul a glare.

He responded by lifting a shoulder. "What? It was funny as hell."

When Isabella came back out, Paul paid her, giving her a tip so generous, she blinked at it twice before excitedly wishing them all a good night.

Paul sauntered over and touched his shoulders against Kyleigh's. "I might be a jerk," he murmured so close to her ear, she could barely hold back the shiver that longed to race down her spine. "But I tip well."

Kyleigh cleared her throat, ignoring his deep chuckle as he watched her reaction. Ignoring him, she walked into the kitchen but stopped so abruptly that Paul ran into her. He placed a hand on her hip, the heat searing through her clothes. She took a step away, and his arm dropped to his side. Kyleigh looked at the table full of containers of pasta, breadsticks and a large salad.

"Are we feeding an army?" she asked.

"I figured I'd get food for Gregori, Leroy and Shawnee since they're here."

Shawnee was already helping Holly get the table set.

"Thanks, Paul," Leroy said from behind them.

Much to Kyleigh's mortification, she only then remembered Leroy's presence, and the fact that he'd probably filmed every little interaction they'd just exchanged.

"Speaking of Gregori," Paul said, unruffled as usual by the constant presence of cameras, "where is our lead cameraman?"

"He wanted to take some more shots of the store before coming here," Kyleigh explained just as Gregori walked into the apartment, his camera at his side.

As they ate their meal, Shawnee and Gregori entertained them with stories that had taken place behind the scenes over the years from *First Comes Marriage.* Kyleigh couldn't remember the last time she had a more enjoyable dinner, laughing so hard that tears formed in her eyes at some of things they told them. She felt Paul's gaze on her more than once as he added his own details here and there.

Once dinner was over, Shawnee and Leroy left. Holly excused herself to go work on her and Paul's routine some more. Gregori sat in the corner of the kitchen, filming them on occasion but more preoccupied with texting his wife about his day.

Paul washed dishes as Kyleigh dried them. As she placed a plate in the nearby open cupboard, she peeked at Paul out of the corner of her eye. Something inside her warmed as she took in the adorable concentration on his face as he scrubbed at a particularly stubborn marinara stain.

"You're probably not used to this, huh?" she said, taking the clean plate from his hand.

"Domestic bliss?" he said lightly, causing her cheeks to pink.

"Doing dishes," she replied, ignoring how Paul's arms kept brushing hers as they worked in the small space.

"Believe it or not," he answered, "I actually do my own dishes. Aside from a cleaning service that comes in once a week, I like to have my house to myself. The only difference is I take advantage of having a dishwasher."

"Hmm," she said.

"What do you think my life is like? Orgies and constant parties?"

Something soured in her stomach at the idea of Paul in either scenario. "No, of course not."

"I spend so much of my day being around people, always having to be *on*, so to speak, that I've grown to really love the quiet when I can get a chance to enjoy it."

"Hmm," she replied, drying a glass with extra vigor.

Paul sighed beside her. "Ky…despite what you may have heard about me, I'm not this big party guy living it up with a bunch of different women each week. Frankly, I don't have the time. I'm too busy with work."

Kyleigh nodded, wanting to change the subject. "So where is home these days?"

Paul stared at the side of her face for a moment, before allowing the topic to change. "I have a few places, to be honest. I have a penthouse in New York, a home in Carmel, a condo in Miami. But I think my favorite place is a small cabin I have up near the Porcupine Mountains."

Kyleigh couldn't stop her shocked reaction at that. "You have a place in the U.P.?"

Paul grinned at her. "Surprised?"

"Very. I thought you left Michigan and never looked back."

Paul turned so that his hip was leaning against the counter. "I never forgot my life in Michigan. Not once in all these years."

"Oh…" she said by way of response. The air turned thick with everything left unsaid between them.

They finished doing dishes in silence, though Paul hadn't moved away from her as they worked. He seemed to actually be standing closer to her, the heat of his body warming her side. He unplugged the drain when they were through and put the dishcloth over the faucet.

"Thanks," she said, putting the last dish away and closing the cupboard door.

He turned so that he was facing her again. Tilting his head, he said, "For what? Doing the dishes?"

She didn't look at him as she wiped an invisible crumb off the counter. "Well, for that and getting the food, but what I really meant was for helping Holly." She turned toward him then. "Like I told you the other day, Dan hasn't been a very present father for her. I try to be everything she needs, but sometimes she needs her dad. I really appreciate you stepping in for him after he failed her again."

He reached out and brushed away a tendril of hair that had escaped her low bun. Her skin tingled where he touched. "You're welcome."

Paul's eyes seemed to ignite as he stared at her, warming her senses. The air shifted again, heating. Kyleigh swayed on her feet subconsciously, moving toward him. She forgot Gregori sitting in the corner of the room, probably filming their every breath. She forgot about Holly in the other room.

Paul's gaze drifted from her eyes to her mouth, before slowly lifting again, his expression turning questioning.

She didn't have an answer for him. The only thing she knew was that the world around them ceased, her vision blurring until he was the only being to exist. Her hand started to lift—to do what, she didn't know. Perhaps clasp onto his shirt to feel if his heart was pounding as hard as hers was. To maybe wrap her fingers around his neck to pull his mouth to hers, to see if his lips felt as good as she remembered. The temptation she felt was undeniable, and given the way anticipation filled his face, she bet that he felt it, too.

"Paul, could you help me with this step when you're done with the dishes?" Holly called out from the other room.

Paul jerked away from Kyleigh, and the spell between them disappeared.

"Be right there," he said, his voice sounding heavy. He looked at Kyleigh again, but she had already turned away, trying to cool her senses. She heard him let out a deep exhale before he walked away.

Gregori coughed from the corner of the room. Kyleigh glanced at him, and the older man gave her a knowing look.

"What?" she asked, feeling defensive for no reason.

"I got some great footage just now. Want to see?"

"No!" she replied adamantly. She ignored his laughter as she quickly exited the kitchen.

Chapter Fifteen

Kyleigh looked around her shop, making sure she hadn't missed any details. Her store was hosting the paint and sip class for anyone in the community who was interested. Paul had already told her he'd attend, and when they mentioned it to Shawnee, she exuberantly agreed that it would be a great idea. She wanted to get more footage of them going out on dates to show their audience what a "cute couple" they were. Her words, not Kyleigh's.

Kyleigh was still trying to adjust to the idea of them *being* a couple. Not that they were a real one. They still had two months left of their marriage, and then she would probably never see Paul again.

The thought made her sad.

The icy anger she'd held on to for his callous way of dumping her on her prom night, not to mention his behavior on their wedding day, had begun to defrost. Especially after she saw him helping Holly with her talent show. The relief and joy on her daughter's face as she learned the steps Paul showed her was something that Kyleigh wouldn't forget for a long time.

"What do you think?" she asked Holly as her daughter helped her set up for the evening's activity.

"It looks good," Holly said with a thumbs-up.

Earlier in the day, Kyleigh and Wendy had set up folding tables around the store's craft room. Kyleigh had bought some throwaway tablecloths from the dollar store over in Clarington and had tossed them over the tables to protect the surfaces from any paint spills. She'd placed vases of bright purple lilacs around the room to give it some added warmth. Each seat at the table had a kit of supplies that attendees would need for the event: paint, paintbrushes, compostable cups filled with water, paper towels and a small canvas.

To one side of the room, Kyleigh had left a table bare for the light appetizers she'd ordered. Next to it was a smaller table that held a black plastic container filled with ice meant for the drinks that would soon be delivered.

The bell above the shop's door went off, announcing a new arrival. Isabella soon appeared, pulling a cart filled with the order Kyleigh had placed from Florentina's.

"Hey, Kyleigh. Holly," Isabella said. "Where should I put everything?"

"Hi, Izzy, right over there." Kyleigh pointed to the empty table. "Holly, can you help her?"

"Yep," her daughter replied, already reaching for one of the food containers inside the cart.

"I brought nonalcoholic wine in addition to the alcoholic one," Isabella said, pulling a green bottle of sparkling juice out of a beige tote. "You said Meg was coming, right? I know she can't drink right now."

"Yes, though I need to double-check my list. I know the show screened the people attending, since both Tyler and Paul are planning on being here."

"Sounds good," Isabella said and began to pull things out of another bag for the charcuterie board Kyleigh ordered.

Kyleigh walked to the front of the store where Wendy

was stationed for the night, along with a couple of beefy, no-nonsense guys the show had hired for extra security. Wendy was shamelessly flirting with the tall blond one, who didn't even crack a smile at her antics.

"Wendy, do you have the list of people who are attending tonight?" Kyleigh asked.

Wendy pulled her eyes away from the man with a weighty breath. She grabbed the tablet next to her and pulled up the list of guests. "Yep, here you go."

"Thanks," Kyleigh murmured as she started to review it.

The list had Meg and Tyler as well as Isabella. Jessica from Bridal Barn had signed up with her husband. Two of Kyleigh's best customers, Leona and Bernice, had put their names down to attend. They were two elderly best friends who usually partook in all the store's workshops because they said it kept them young. A mother and daughter pair that Kyleigh didn't know also signed up. She wondered briefly if they were from Holiday Bay, considering she knew almost everyone in town, and she didn't recognize the names. She knew Wendy would need them to sign NDAs so they didn't say anything about what was filmed that night. Everyone else on the list were frequent visitors of Kyleigh's shop and would have already signed the necessary paperwork.

That was until her eyes settled on the final name, erasing every other thought and concern in her head.

"Wendy, was this last name supposed to be on here?"

Wendy gave her a grimace. "Yeah, I didn't know how to say no to that one."

Before Kyleigh could say anything, Tyler and Meg walked in. Meg looked radiant as always, her cheeks flushed with the joy of her pregnancy.

"I'm not saying you shouldn't have parked close," she

told her husband, "I'm simply saying I think you're a little *too* close to the fire hydrant."

"There was plenty of space," Tyler said. "You're being paranoid."

Meg shrugged. "Fine, don't blame me if the car gets towed. But if I have to hire a lift—and you know the only taxi driver in Holiday Bay is Walter Peddler—you need to acknowledge that the man shouldn't have a license, and you're risking my life and your unborn child's."

Tyler snorted. "I'll keep that in mind."

"Hey." Kyleigh hurried over to them.

"Hi," Meg replied. "I was telling Tyler on the way here that I'm really excited for tonight, but you'll have to plan another one of these when I can actually drink. I—"

"Lucas signed up," Kyleigh interrupted.

Meg's mouth snapped shut.

Tyler went rigid before wrapping his arm protectively around his wife. "We can leave," he said quietly.

Meg looked at her husband, and her shoulders loosened. She gave Kyleigh a dim smile. "It's fine."

"I can tell him to go," Kyleigh insisted. "You two shouldn't have to leave."

"Seriously, Lucas and I are fine," Meg assured them. "Well, I wouldn't say fine, so much as cordial. Don't worry about me."

"Are you sure?" Kyleigh asked. She never knew what happened between Meg and her former fiancée. They'd dated each other for years, since they'd both been in high school. One minute they were engaged, and the next, Lucas broke things off. Meg had been devastated at the time— much to the delight of the town's gossip network, who'd relished the breakup.

Many people in town still referred to Lucas as the prince

of Holiday Bay, thanks to his father being mayor for decades. And Meg had become their princess by association. Townsfolk had taken way too much enjoyment in her downfall. Especially when Meg walked around like a zombie for months after, her mental health spiraling.

She was open with loved ones about the struggles she'd gone through back then. The trauma of the breakup had opened up a deep trove of insecurities, leading her to having severe anxiety attacks. Thankfully, she was able to get the professional help she needed.

She'd also reunited with Tyler around that time. The former childhood nemeses had fallen deeply in love, and Kyleigh knew that her friend was happier and more secure in her life now than she'd ever been with Lucas. She'd made great strides in her mental health. Kyleigh didn't want her to take a step back, especially with her pregnancy going so well.

"You two look like worried mother hens," Meg said with a laugh. She hugged Kyleigh before kissing Tyler on the cheek. "I love you both for your concern, but I'll be fine. Lucas and I are on better footing now than when we were engaged. It'll be okay."

Kyleigh nodded reluctantly, then pointed to the back of the room. "Isabella is getting the snacks and drinks set up, so help yourselves."

"Oh! You ordered Florentina's?" Meg asked, her face lighting up.

Kyleigh smirked. "Just a charcuterie board and drinks."

"Good enough," Meg replied, grabbing Tyler's hand. Patting her baby bump, she told her husband, "Lead me to the food."

Tyler's eyes crinkled as he told her, "Your wish is my command."

After they disappeared, Kyleigh turned in time to see Gregori and his crew enter the building.

"We miss anything?" he asked.

"You'll want to keep the camera on some guy named Lucas," the blond security guard said. "There might be some drama between him and his ex. If there are any issues, let me know."

"There won't be any issues," Kyleigh said, glaring at the guard for airing her friend's dirty laundry.

"He finally speaks, and that's what he says," Wendy muttered under her breath as she stared the man down.

"Thanks for the heads-up," Gregori said. Pointing to Leroy and some of the other crew, he started giving instructions for getting things set up in the craft room. As Gregori got her mic'd up, the mother and daughter pair arrived.

"Are we late?" the mom asked. She was very pretty, about Kyleigh's height, with thick black hair pulled into a high bun. The shop's lights showcased the streaks of gray in her hair and gentle crow's feet around her eyes. She had to be only a few years older than Kyleigh. The daughter was a younger version of her mom, her eyes wide as she looked around the shop.

"Welcome," Kyleigh greeted, smiling warmly at both. "We actually haven't started yet."

"Are you Gloria and Ana?" Wendy asked. When they both nodded, she handed them paperwork. "We're currently filming a TV show here for HNC Network. We'll need you to sign these NDAs."

As Gloria and Ana took care of their paperwork, Jessica and her husband, Bart, walked in, followed by Leona and Bernice. As all of them had signed NDAs previously, Kyleigh directed everyone to the back of the store.

Finally, Lucas Beaumont walked in. Lucas looked just

as handsome as she remembered from seeing him around town. Shortly after he ended his engagement, he'd moved south to Grand Rapids, leaving poor Meg to face the gossips alone.

Kyleigh crossed her arms over her chest. "Lucas Beaumont, I didn't think this was your kind of scene. Shouldn't you be out kissing someone's butt on your dad's behalf?"

Lucas ran a hand through his stylish blond hair. Kyleigh couldn't help but notice how tired he looked. "Look," he said. "I don't want any trouble here. I just moved back to town, and I was looking for something distracting to do."

"Meg and her husband are attending," Kyleigh informed him.

He blanched at that. "I can go."

"Lucas?" someone said behind her. Kyleigh looked over her shoulder to see Meg standing in the aisleway. "Hi."

"Hey, Meg, you look good. Pregnancy suits you." He side-eyed Kyleigh cautiously before he walked over to his ex. "I know it's been a minute since we talked, but… I wanted to say congratulations. On everything. You deserve it."

Meg's face was soft as she examined him, worry forming on her face. "You look like crap."

He laughed despite the misery on his face that Kyleigh couldn't help but notice. "I feel like it."

Despite having every reason to chew the man out, Meg hugged him. "You and I should get caught up soon. Yeah?"

He tilted his head as he looked down at the much shorter woman. "I'd like that."

"Great." She linked her arm in his. "I heard a rumor you moved back to town."

"Yeah, last weekend…" The two made their way to the back of the store.

"Well, that was anticlimactic," Gregori said with his camera on his shoulder.

Kyleigh shook her head as she watched the former couple disappear from view. She turned her attention back to the business at hand. Gloria and Ana finished signing their paperwork, so Kyleigh motioned them in the direction that Meg and Lucas had gone.

"Wendy," Kyleigh asked her employee. "Does Lucas need an NDA?"

"No, he took care of it earlier when he signed up for the class."

"Okay,"

The bell above the shop rang one more time, and Kyleigh turned to see Paul and Shawnee walk in. She tried to ignore how handsome he looked with his soft black hair looking slightly windblown. He wore a dark navy T-shirt that showed off his muscled arms and jeans that looked painted on.

"Sorry, I'm a little late," Paul said, smirking at whatever he saw on Kyleigh's face.

She smoothed out her features. "We haven't started yet."

"Everything ready to go?" Shawnee asked Gregori, who handed Paul a mic. With expert ease, he clipped it on his shirt, barely noticeable against the darkness of his tee.

"Everyone's here," Kyleigh informed them. Shawnee nodded and headed to the back of the room. Paul lingered until Kyleigh pointed with her head for him to follow his director. With his lips tweaking up, he strode toward the craft room.

Kyleigh watched him go, staring at the way the jeans molded to his backside.

Gregori coughed, and she jumped, her face going bright red. "What?" she asked, when she noticed a broad grin on his round face.

He pointed to the side of his mouth. "It looks like you've got a little drool there."

Giving him a rude gesture, which caused him to laugh, Kyleigh made her way to the back of the shop where everyone started taking seats.

She and Wendy had set the tables up so that people could face each other and chat if they wanted. Despite not being on the clock, Isabella made sure everyone had snacks and wine. Meg and Lucas sat at one table, chatting away. Tyler added some comments here and there, but he watched Lucas like a hawk, ready to rip him apart if he did one thing to upset his wife. He kept his arm around the back of Meg's chair, and she leaned against him as if soothed by his presence, even as she chatted with her ex as though he were a long-lost friend.

Kyleigh guessed that was what they were. She didn't know how she would have reacted if she found herself in the same situation. At least when Dan had walked out on her and Holly, he'd had the decency to stay in town for six months or so, not giving people anything to really talk about. Not until he met his now wife, but at that point, some other scandal had popped up, and people had thankfully forgotten all about them.

"So…" Lucas said to Tyler as he fiddled with one of the brushes in front of him. "How are the Holiday Boys these days? Zan? James?"

Tyler gave him a perplexed look. "They're fine. Zan is supposed to have a new book coming out next year."

Though Kyleigh knew from conversations with Paul that Zan's only focus at the moment was on his wife.

"And… James?" Lucas asked.

Tyler's frown deepened. "He's fine. He's in Detroit working on a new renovation project."

Lucas didn't ask any further questions, though his body seemed to lose whatever steam he had left.

Meg reached over and squeezed his arm before turning to Tyler to ask if he'd locked their front door before they left.

"Of course," he replied, kissing her temple. "Stop worrying. I've got you taken care of."

Kyleigh turned back to the group gathered. "Ladies and gentleman, now that we're all here, we can get started," she announced.

Gloria and Ana were at the food table getting some snacks. When Ana turned and saw Paul, she let out a little meep.

Her mom put her arm around her daughter. "Sorry, she's a big Holiday Boys fan."

"Nice to meet you," Paul said, flashing the girl a smile.

"She didn't meep at me," Tyler grumbled jokingly.

"You're not as awesome as I am," Paul replied, winking at his bandmate.

Tyler threw a paintbrush at him, which Paul caught with ease.

"If everyone would like to take a seat, we can get started," Kyleigh said, giving the men stern stares. They both straightened, their faces changing into pure innocence. Kyleigh rolled her eyes at them. Holly settled into the seat next to Paul with Isabella on her other side, and the two started chatting.

Kyleigh began the class by walking them through how a paint-and-sip worked, explaining that they could choose whatever colors they wanted, but they should follow the pattern she would paint on the canvas set up in front of the room.

The atmosphere was light as people snacked on crackers

and cheese, drank their wine, and painted. Kyleigh helped them along, walking around to give people pointers.

She'd always loved painting. It was a gift she'd discovered when she attended the performing arts camp as a teen. She'd even minored in it at college.

When Kyleigh arrived at Paul's picture, she had to stop to take it in. He was supposed to be copying the picture of the beach with a sunset she'd drawn. The sun looked like a deflating tennis ball.

She leaned down and touched his hand. "It works better if you use gentler strokes."

"Hmm, I don't remember you having issues with my strokes before," he murmured so quietly only she could hear.

Her face burned. She didn't know whether to smack him on the back of the head or sit in his lap. He let out a soft chuckle, easily reading her. She huffed and stepped away from him.

Thankfully, Ana distracted him. "Do you ever visit Clarington, Mr. Paul?"

"Ana," Gloria warned her daughter. "Leave him alone. He's not here to discuss his personal life."

Ana looked at her mom, confusion written on her face. "But he's from Clarington, right? They have that painting of him and Mr. Zan on the side of the school."

"There's a mural of Zan and me?" Paul asked, apparently hearing that news for the first time.

Gloria looked embarrassed. "The school's art program painted it. You're hometown heroes."

Paul did a great job hiding his surprise at the news as he said to Ana, "I don't get back to the area much these days, I'm afraid. I mostly live in California now."

"So why are you here?" she asked.

He nodded toward Gregori and Shawnee in one corner of the room, and Leroy in the other, both cameramen filming everyone's interactions. "We're filming a project here."

"For *First Comes Marriage*?" Ana asked.

"Ah, that's a secret," Paul told the girl. "I'm not allowed to say anything about what we're filming right now."

"But…" Ana started to say, but her mom stopped her again.

"Ana, that's enough. You agreed that if we came to Holiday Bay and you ran into any nice Holiday Boys, you'd leave them alone."

"I am," she insisted. "I'm not bothering *him*."

She pointed to Tyler, who was whispering something into Meg's ear. She laughed before reaching over to gently squeeze his knee. Lucas was now talking to Leona and Bernice, asking them how their retirements were going.

"Oh!" Ana said excitedly, drawing everyone's attention. She pointed to the thin gold band on Paul's hand. "Are you married, Mr. Paul?"

A hush went over the crowd. Leona and Bernice craned their necks so hard, Kyleigh worried they might have possibly dislocated something.

"Uh…" Paul responded before looking in her direction.

Kyleigh's eyebrow rose at him. He'd got them into this mess, she certainly wasn't going to help him out.

Reading her just as clearly as he normally did, he stood up from his chair and walked determinedly over to her. "Actually, Kyleigh and I are married," Paul announced, wrapping an arm around her shoulder.

Kyleigh gave their audience a weak smile.

"Kyleigh! Why didn't you say anything?" Bernice said.

"We would have knitted you his and hers sweaters if we'd known," Leona added.

"We're trying to keep this as quiet as possible," Paul replied, "at least until the show airs, we hope."

If it hadn't been for the NDAs, Kyleigh knew the news would be all over town by dawn. There was already enough speculation as it was.

"You should kiss for the cameras," Isabella teased.

"Yeah, kiss her, Paul," Tyler said gleefully.

Meg nudged him in the ribs.

"Kiss, kiss, kiss," Ana insisted.

Gloria put her hand over her own eyes, as if giving up on trying to get her daughter under control.

"Oh, you know—" Kyleigh started to say, but before she could finish, Paul grabbed her by the waist and bent her backward in a deep dip.

"Paul—" she hissed just as his lips touched hers.

The mere touch of flesh against flesh ignited a spark inside her. Their wedding day kiss had been nothing. His mouth had brushed the side of hers after she refused to give him access to her lips, her fury and betrayal too much for her to stand any more intimate contact that day.

Paul probably only meant for the kiss in the workshop to last a second, something to give a good show to their audience and those ever-watching cameras. But as she felt him to start to pull away, her mouth followed his of its own accord.

Paul froze for just a second before he deepened the kiss, his lips going firmer, more persistent against hers.

Kyleigh's ears rang as heat pooled between her thighs. Her hands, which had been grasping his muscled arms for balance, moved to his neck, wrapping around it in a hold that wouldn't be denied.

Paul straightened them from their dip so he could pull her against him more firmly, not releasing his mouth from hers.

Someone catcalled.

Neither one of them cared. Kyleigh's body burned with desire, unable to break the grip he had on her if she tried.

"Okay, gross. Get a room," Holly muttered, causing some of the adults in the room to laugh.

"They're honeymooners," Jessica said lightly.

Her voice reminded Kyleigh why Paul was in Michigan at the moment, and not living his best life in California. She pulled abruptly away, her chest heaving. Paul's own skin appeared flushed, his hair slightly mussed.

"Young love," Bernice murmured romantically.

Kyleigh licked her bottom lip, tasting Paul on her tongue. Paul's eyes followed the movement, his gaze laser focused on her.

Kyleigh forced herself to say, "Okay, okay. Let's get back to painting."

Paul reluctantly went back to his seat. As Kyleigh showed the class the next step for their project, she was careful to avoid looking at him for the next hour. When the class was blessedly over, people started to get up to leave.

"This was your best class yet," Bernice said, patting her arm.

"Bring your handsome husband to the next one, okay?" Leona added.

"I'll keep that in mind," Kyleigh replied dryly.

"Let's see the ring," Bernice said.

"Oh…" Kyleigh pulled it from her pocket and put it on. She could see Paul look at her, a frown marring his handsome face.

"I didn't want to get paint on it," she explained, and he looked away.

She started to clean up as the attendees made their way

to the front of the store. Paul, Shawnee and Holly started to help put things away.

Paul came over to where Kyleigh was gathering the used supplies. "You weren't wearing your ring." He sounded hurt.

She gathered several paintbrushes that would need to be cleaned before she left the store. "Like I said, I didn't want to get paint on it." She frowned. "And…it's just easier not to wear it at the store. There are too many busybodies in this town, and our marriage was supposed to be a secret."

Paul didn't say anything more on the subject, to her relief. He grabbed the painting he'd done. "What do you think? Should I pitch it or sell it on an online auction?" he asked, trying to lighten the mood.

He showed her the drawing, and she snorted despite herself. "It's, uh, something."

It looked like the sun's rays were trying to drown the sun in blue and orange waves of sludge.

"Shawnee, you should be feeling pretty happy," Gregori said from across the room as Paul threw away the picture. "We got some great footage."

"I am happy," the director said. In fact, she was practically beaming.

Wendy entered the craft room. "Don't worry about this. I have a cleanup crew coming in the morning. Everything will be back to normal before we open."

"Oh…" Kyleigh said.

Holly left the room, saying she'd be right back.

Kyleigh wanted to prolong going home. Paul was going to take her and Holly in his car while Gregori followed in one of the show's vans. She wasn't sure if she could have a normal conversation with him at this point, not after that kiss.

Kyleigh wanted to brush it aside. To pretend that it had

all been for the show. But it hadn't felt like it. For a second, Kyleigh hadn't been sure if Paul would let her go.

"Here's your coat, Mom," Holly said, walking back in the room. She handed her the jacket she'd stashed in the office earlier. "Can we go home now?"

Despite her reluctance, Kyleigh said, "Yes, baby, we can."

As she drew on her coat, Paul walked over and helped her slide it on the rest of the way. His fingers brushed the back of her neck, causing her already heightened senses to go haywire. As if that wasn't enough, he placed his hand on her lower back, guiding her out of the store.

The night was unseasonably cool as they walked outside, which she was grateful for. The air helped cool her down.

Before they could even make it a few steps, she heard the familiar voice of Ana say, "Look, Papa, there he is."

Paul tensed next to Kyleigh. "What are you doing here?" he snapped.

Kyleigh looked over to see Dom leaning against a blue Blazer. Ana held his hand, uncertainty on her sweet face as she looked between Dom and Paul.

"Kyleigh." Dom nodded, ignoring his brother. "It's good to see you again. Sorry, I didn't get to say it last time we saw each other at the hospital."

"Um, you…" Kyleigh looked from him to Paul, taken aback by the hint of fury she saw on her husband's face. "You, too, Dom."

"Daddy, you know Mr. Paul, don't you?" Ana asked.

Kyleigh was aware of Gregori and Leroy standing nearby, filming the entire conversation. Shawnee came out of the store with the two bodyguards, but she held up her hand, stopping them from approaching Dom.

"Daddy?" Paul repeated in a whisper, but his brother seemed to hear him anyway.

"Yes, daddy. To Ana, here. And Gloria and I have another one at home. A son." Dom motioned toward the woman sitting in the car, who waved cautiously at them, her own expression mirroring the concern Kyleigh felt.

"Are you stalking me?" Paul asked him.

Dom rolled his eyes. "Contrary to what your oversize ego thinks, the world doesn't actually revolve around you. I had no idea you'd be here. Ana has recently gotten into painting, so Gloria signed them up for the class tonight. She thought it'd be fun to have a little mother/daughter time, since she's been pulling long shifts at the hospital."

"Oh!" Kyleigh said, trying to defuse the atmosphere. "Is she a nurse, too?"

"Doctor," Dom said proudly.

Gloria rolled down the window. "Dominic, we should get going. We still need to pick up Bastián from Esperanza's."

"You named your son Bastián?" Paul choked.

Kyleigh's forehead wrinkled before it dawned on her why Paul was reacting to that name. It was their father's name.

"Yeah," Dom said, his face softening. He opened his mouth as if to say more, but he shook his head. Opening the door for Ana, who hopped in the car, he shut it quietly before turning back to his brother. "See you around, Paulo."

Paul didn't say anything after his brother drove away. A muscle pounded in his jaw as they made their way to Paul's rental car. He remained quiet during the drive back to the apartment. Kyleigh and Holly filled the silence by discussing Holly's upcoming talent show that weekend. It was a conversation that welcomed Paul to participate, but he remained quiet, with a face like granite.

Once they got home, Holly went to her room to practice her routine. Kyleigh went into her room to change into her comfy clothes, a T-shirt and yoga pants, before returning to the living room.

Paul wasn't there. Gregori sat in the armchair, changing out the battery on his camera. He nodded toward the kitchen.

Kyleigh warily walked in to find Paul sitting at the table, a small glass of bourbon in front of him. The sight of that alone was enough to concern Kyleigh, considering he didn't typically drink, least of all by himself.

"Hey," she said, sitting down next to him.

He didn't respond, his eyes fixated on the glass. She noticed that the alcohol inside was filled to the brim, the glass untouched.

"Are you okay?" she finally asked when the silence stretched on too long.

He flinched at the question before running a tired hand over his face. "Honestly? I'm not sure."

"You didn't know Dom was married and had a family."

"No," he whispered.

Kyleigh stared at him, waiting for him to elaborate. When he didn't, she asked, "Why? From what I remember, you two used to be super close. Is this because he went to prison?"

Paul's face grew tense. He finally lifted tormented eyes to hers. "Ky, I know you're trying to help, but I really don't want to talk about this."

She knew she should respect that, but she couldn't let it go. It was obviously hurting him. He needed to talk to someone about it. "I'm trying to understand. You loved your brother. I remember how much you looked up to him. He made a mistake, but that was years ago. He was barely out of his teens. Why are you so angry with—"

Paul shot to his feet so quickly his chair tipped over and fell to the ground with a startling clatter.

Kyleigh stopped talking as she took in the rage and pain on his face.

"Because he took *everything* from me," Paul rasped. Seeing her stunned reaction, some of the tension left him. "I'm sorry, Ky." He ran a weary hand over his face. "I… I need to step out for a minute." He bent down and corrected the chair. With a regretful look on his face, he left the room, pushing past Gregori, who hurried in with his camera.

The front door closed firmly a short time later.

"I heard a bang," Gregori said, eying Kyleigh carefully. "Everything okay?"

Kyleigh turned to look back at the table and the drink that spilled when Paul jumped to his feet. The contents pooled around the glass, the scent of bourbon infusing the air.

"Honestly?" she said. "I have no idea."

Chapter Sixteen

Holly paced nervously backstage. "Paul isn't coming."

Kyleigh tried to put on a positive face. "He said he'd be here."

The truth was, Kyleigh didn't know for sure where her temporary husband was. She hadn't seen him in two days. Not since she'd pressed him to speak about his brother.

"Hey, kid," Shawnee said, appearing beside them with Gregori at her side. "Are you nervous?"

Holly looked ready to cry.

Kyleigh could see two girls standing behind the curtains on the other side of the stage, pointing in Holly's direction and laughing. She recognized them as two of Holly's biggest bullies, Emily and Jenna. If Paul didn't show up, Kyleigh would personally maim him.

"He's not coming," Holly whispered again, her defeat making Kyleigh want to tear up.

"Who's not coming?" a deep voice said behind them.

Kyleigh whirled around to see Paul standing there, a guitar strapped to his chest. He wore a black button-down shirt opened at the neck and dark jeans. He looked so handsome, and Kyleigh's heart surged in relief at the sight of him.

"Sorry, I'm a bit late," Paul apologized to the group before looking at Holly. "You ready?"

Holly nodded, now glowing.

Kyleigh glanced over at Emily and Jenna and could see, even from a distance, the shocked expressions on their faces as they noticed who was now standing next to her daughter. Kyleigh wasn't one to be petty, but she did take a little enjoyment at seeing the girls so envious after making Holly's life a living hell the past few years. She only hoped they would leave her alone now that they saw she had connections to the Holiday Boys, instead of taking their jealousy out on her.

A teacher came up to them, a clipboard in her hand. "Holly, are you ready? Is your father here?"

The teacher looked around the group before she noticed Paul standing there. Her mouth gaped as she took in the famous singer.

"Mr. Rodriguez. We didn't know you were attending our little show. What an honor!"

"I'm actually singing with Holly here," Paul said, nodding at Holly.

"Oh…" The teacher shifted the clipboard, appearing uncomfortable. "You see, this is for fathers and daughters only."

"He *is* my father," Holly spoke up. "My stepdad."

Kyleigh's insides panged at that announcement. She immediately looked at Paul so she could observe his reaction at being called Holly's dad. There was affection in his eyes as he clasped Holly on the shoulder, his wedding band glinting in the dim light.

The relief Kyleigh felt at his reappearance dimmed slightly. She'd been so focused on Holly's happiness when this whole fiasco with the show began, that Kyleigh hadn't thought about the ramifications of how this would affect her daughter when the marriage ended. Realizing that a bond had formed between Paul and Holly made Kyleigh feel ill at ease. Holly would be crushed when another father figure walked out of her life.

The teacher's eyes flew to Paul's ring before shifting her gaze to Kyleigh's hand, noticing the large diamond and gold band. "I see. I mean, I didn't realize…" she said, clearly shocked. "Well, I guess that's all right then."

"Miranda," another teacher whispered, running over to them. "We need our next performer."

Miranda nodded at Holly and Paul. "You're on."

Paul lifted a fist to Holly, who laughed before fist-bumping him back. Taking a deep breath, she walked onstage to light applause. A gasp went through the auditorium as soon as Paul appeared. In less than a second, a wild cheer roared through the audience.

Kyleigh peeked at the crowd and saw a hundred cell phones whip out to record Paul and her daughter. Nerves danced over her, replacing her earlier concern. She really hoped the two crushed it, so Holly didn't get bullied on a national stage.

"They'll do great," Shawnee said. "Don't look so worried."

"This'll be all over social media," Kyleigh warned. "Aren't you concerned it'll spoil *First Comes Marriage*?"

Shawnee shrugged. "Just because people know you're married, doesn't mean they'll connect it with this season of the show. Even if they do, it'll create more buzz for the season. It was only a matter of time before the news leaked that Paul's the one who got married."

As Paul began to play the opening chords on his guitar, Kyleigh muttered, "I want to wrap Holly in a protective bubble so no one can ever hurt her again."

"Spoken like a true mama bear," Shawnee teased.

"I forgot to ask you," Kyleigh said, "how did you and Heather enjoy Mackinac Island?"

The couple had traveled to one of Michigan's biggest tourist destinations the day after the paint and sip class. They had returned just that morning.

"It was magical," Shawnee whispered back. "Though I think I gained ten pounds from eating so much fudge."

Kyleigh smiled but didn't have time to respond as Paul and Holly began to sing. They danced in harmony with each other, their voices matching perfectly. Kyleigh thought she'd burst with pride when the song finally ended, and the crowd jumped to their feet, giving them a standing ovation.

Paul waved his hand at Holly, indicating he wanted her to take the spotlight. She smiled awkwardly, taking a little bow.

A sweet feeling bloomed inside Kyleigh as she witnessed yet another kind gesture from Paul to her daughter. Despite her concerns, she was so grateful that Holly had him in that moment.

As soon as the two walked offstage, Kyleigh gave her daughter a kiss on the head. "I'm so proud of you!" she murmured against Holly's soft hair.

"Thank you." Holly gave her mom a tight hug. Then she stepped back, at the age where she wasn't one to show affection to anyone, least of all her mom. She turned to Paul and gave him a huge grin. "Thank you, Paul!"

"It was all you. You killed it!" Paul boasted.

That sweet feeling grew again, and Kyleigh realized what it was. Tenderness flooded her at their exchange.

As if Paul sensed her watching him, he looked at her, his face softening at whatever he saw on her features.

"Thank you," she whispered.

He nodded, his eyes not leaving hers.

"We should probably take our seats," Shawnee directed.

The group entered the auditorium from the back, so that Paul's presence wouldn't take away from the rest of the performers. It didn't matter since people knew he was there. Whispers flurried over the crowd when they saw the megastar in their midst.

Paul did his best to ignore it as the three of them, along with Gregori and Shawnee, joined Leroy and the rest of the crew, who'd stationed themselves in the room earlier so that they could film Holly and Paul's performance.

"Great job," Leroy told Holly.

"You did amazing!" Heather added from where she sat on the other side of Leroy.

Kyleigh felt herself get emotional as she took in the proud faces of the crew and their unwavering support of her daughter. They sat there for another half hour, Holly getting more anxious as she sat.

The last performer to go was Holly's nemesis, Jenna, who sang with her father playing the piano loudly behind her. Even his banging on the keys could do little to hide how off-key Jenna sang. After she was done, she looked around, clearly expecting to get the same reception that Holly had. When she only received a lukewarm response, she stomped off the stage.

"Now there's a kid whose parents always told her she was great when she's clearly not," Paul muttered.

"Be nice," Kyleigh said, lightly elbowing his arm.

Paul grabbed her hand and laced his fingers with hers. "Just being honest." He went back to watching the stage as if everything was normal.

Kyleigh stared at their interlaced hands, the gold band on his hand glinting under the lights. He continued to hold her hand as if it was a normal thing for them.

Jenna's mom, Kate, took the stage, looking annoyed even as she forced a smile on her face. As president of the PTA, she was in charge of announcing the winners.

"What an amazingly talented group we have today," she said with insincere enthusiasm. "I'm so pleased to announce our winners. In fifth place, we have…"

As the father and daughter pairings were read off, Kyleigh could see Holly becoming more and more worried. Her eyes lost their sparkle as another name was called that wasn't hers and Paul's.

"And in first place…" Kate read, her mouth turning pinched before she said with a fake smile, "Holly Turner and Paul Rodriguez."

Holly jumped up from her seat. She grabbed Paul's hand and practically dragged him onstage.

Not that the audience noticed. They were too busy talking about the fact that Paul was Holly's stepdad. Heads whipped in Kyleigh's direction, the loud whispering turning into a frenzy.

"Maybe we should get you out of here," Shawnee said from a few seats down.

"I can't leave," Kyleigh said, waving at a couple of people she knew. After they'd been so careful, this would be all over town in the matter of hours. "There's a school dance after the show. I volunteered to chaperone."

Shawnee nodded, then jumped out of her seat, pulling out her phone as she ran out of the room. Probably on her way to do damage control. There was no way this wasn't going to leak to the press. Kyleigh had seen how Julie and Meg had been hounded by the paparazzi when they'd gotten wind of her friends' marriages to Holiday Boys members. She had a feeling her life was about to change forever.

Gregori was a few seats down from her, talking to someone on his phone. He hung up and gave his camera to Leroy. Getting up, he sat back down in the chair beside her. "Shawnee told me to not leave your side until Paul gets back."

"I'll be fi—"

"Kyleigh, is it true?" Candace Kent, one of the town's biggest gossips asked.

Kyleigh's smile was brittle as she got to her feet. She wanted to escape down the aisle, but people were blocking it. Shawnee was right to ask Gregori to sit with her. She was slowly being swarmed.

Kyleigh raised her hand at Candace, giving a weak smile as she showed off her wedding ring.

"How did this happen?" Candace practically squealed. Others started to crowd around, making the air feel heavy in Kyleigh's lungs.

"Um, Paul and I…" Kyleigh didn't know what she could tell them. What was she supposed to say that wouldn't reveal that this was all part of a stupid TV show that her daughter entered her in without her knowledge? Though… the marriage didn't feel as fake now as it had the day she said her vows.

"What can I say, ladies?" Paul appeared in the space behind her chair. "Kyleigh and I dated in high school, and when we reunited recently, I realized I couldn't let her go a second time."

He sounded so sincere, Kyleigh almost believed him herself.

Candace placed her hand over her heart as though what Paul said was the most romantic thing she'd ever heard. Kyleigh had to admit, it kind of was.

"Now, if you'll excuse us, I need to speak with my wife for a second," Paul said, looking pointedly at the people who were blocking her escape. They scurried out of the way as Gregori and Kyleigh quickly exited the row along with the rest of the crew. Paul met them at the end of the aisle and grabbed her hand again. The fever pitch of whispering turned into an inferno of voices.

They left the auditorium and met Shawnee in the lobby, along with the rest of the camera crew and Holly, who held a small trophy in her hand.

"I'm so freaking proud of you," Kyleigh said, hugging her daughter again.

"Where to next?" Paul asked. "Should we go to Franki's? Or should we get really fancy and celebrate at Florentina's tonight?"

"Oh, I don't think I told you, there's a dance in the gymnasium." Kyleigh turned to face him. "I volunteered as chaperone."

Paul grinned at her, causing her stupid heart to speed up. The traitorous organ. "Then lead the way," he said.

Kyleigh stared at him with raised eyebrows. "You want to hang out at a junior high dance? After what just happened in the auditorium?"

Paul shrugged. "I go where my family goes."

And there went that stupid organ again.

As they entered the gym, passing through a large balloon archway, Kyleigh took in the room. The PTA had really outdone themselves. Balloons and crepe paper filled every corner. They'd hired the local DJ, Saul Fleeter, who referred to himself as the Saul Man. He played hits mainly from the '70s and '80s. While several parents had gathered on the floor to dance, the kids started to clump in groups, bored with the music selection.

"Mom, I see Tearia and Ebony," Holly said, noticing her friends. She handed her trophy over to Kyleigh before rushing over to the other side of the gym. She joined two girls who started talking excitedly to her, both of them looking at Paul and giggling.

"Teens," Paul muttered.

"Well, folks, this has been a treat, but we're going to head back to our hotel," Shawnee said. Heather stood next to her, yawning.

Paul took the trophy from Kyleigh and gave it to his director. "Can you put this in the camera truck on your way out? We'll pick it up on our way home."

"Sure," Shawnee replied. "Good night, everyone."

The rest of the crew also left, with the exception of Gregori.

"Kyleigh, dear," Kate said, coming up to them, her face bearing her normal pretentious expression. "What a surprise to hear that you and Paul are married. You didn't mention it the other day when we ran into each other at Franki's."

Before Kyleigh could respond, Paul said, "Why would she? She doesn't know you. Not well enough, anyway."

Kate looked like she'd just eaten a prune. "I… I was merely making polite conversation."

"Sure you were," Paul replied, already appearing bored with her.

Kate's eyes flashed angrily before she said stiffly, "I appreciate you volunteering to chaperone, Kyleigh. If you could monitor the bathrooms, that'd be great. Make sure the kids are behaving themselves and not sneaking anything into the stalls."

Paul looked like he was about to say something else snarky, but Kyleigh placed a hand on his arm.

"That's fine," she responded before turning to Paul. "Want to join me?"

He frowned one more time before placing his hand on Kyleigh's back. "Sounds like a plan."

It took them a good twenty minutes to get to their station due to people wanting to chat with them or to compliment Paul on his performance with Holly. But now that the initial shock of having a Holiday Boy among them had started to wear off, the crowd left them alone for the most part. It wasn't the town's first rodeo seeing one of the famous boy band members in their midst. People seemed more excited to discuss the particulars of their marriage, which neither of them were willing to do.

They finally left the gymnasium, Gregori following a discreet distance away. As they made their way to the bathrooms, Kyleigh asked, "What was that about?"

"What?" Paul asked innocently.

"You know what," Kyleigh said, giving him a fixed look.

They arrived at their destination and Paul leaned against one of the lockers. Kyleigh copied him, feeling the cool metal against her back. She turned her head so she could stare at his profile. She didn't say anything as she waited for him to respond.

He finally turned so that he could face her more directly. "Holly told me about the kids bullying her at school. She also said that one girl's mom did everything in her power to make sure her daughter wasn't punished. I can't stand bullies. Especially when they go after people I care about."

Kyleigh's heart throbbed. "You care about us? Holly, too?"

He regarded her like she'd just asked the dumbest question he'd ever heard. She bit back a smile at that look.

"Of course I care about both of you. What do you think today was even about?"

Kyleigh's throat suddenly thickened as she tried to push down the emotions pulsing inside her, looking for a way to escape and reveal everything she felt. In the distance, she heard a slow song begin to play.

She turned her body more fully toward Paul. "Will you dance with me?"

Paul looked in the direction of the gymnasium. Gregori stood down the hall, letting them have space while still filming them.

"Yeah," he responded. He walked into the middle of the hallway and held out his hand to her.

She moved and found herself wrapped in his arms, the warmth of him heating her through her clothes. She placed one hand on his shoulder, the other going against his heart, feeling the steady beat under her palm.

They swayed against each other for several beats before she said, "I'm sorry about the other day."

He searched her face, his eyes open and inviting. "You were just trying to help me. I get it."

"But I shouldn't have pushed you. You've told me more than once that your brother is off-limits. I should have respected your boundaries."

"I shouldn't have reacted the way I did and left."

They swayed for another minute. The song in the gym switched to a faster tune. They didn't notice as they continued to move to a rhythm of their own making.

"Where did you go?" she asked. "You haven't been home for a couple of days."

His face softened even more at her calling her apartment *home*. "I stayed with the crew at the hotel. We needed to go over logistics for the remainder of the show. They wanted us to go parasailing, but I told them I wasn't doing anything like that until summer. Plus, you don't like heights."

Kyleigh glanced at him in surprise. "You remember that?"

Paul's hands tightened on her waist. "I remember everything about you."

She wanted to ask, *Then why did you leave me?* But she didn't want to want to ruin the mood by bringing up the ugly past. That conversation could be saved for another day.

"Paul, I..." she started to say, but she became distracted as Paul's gaze focused on her mouth.

His eyes drifted up to hers, silently asking her a question. Maybe it was the feel of dancing in his arms or the exhilaration of realizing that he cared for not only her, but her daughter, that made her nod.

Paul's head bent down to hers. His mouth lightly brushed hers, the feel of those familiar, firm lips sending electricity over her skin. She could feel his heart speed up under her palm. When he went to pull away, she chased his mouth, opening her lips to allow him more access.

He breathed in sharply through his nose before dipping his tongue into her mouth, and she welcomed it, caressing it with her own. Paul pulled her fully against his body. Kyleigh's hand went to his hair, tugging it in a way she knew he liked. Paul groaned in response. He leaned down and picked her up as her legs circled him. She soon found herself against the lockers again, Paul's body surrounding her. She felt like she was on fire as Paul rubbed against her, his body hardening. Her body responded, desire liquefying between her thighs.

A loud cough down the hall was as effective as a bucket of ice water being poured over them. They broke apart, their chests heaving. Kyleigh's cheeks burned with mortification when she realized that Gregori was still there, his camera thankfully by his side. As her head cleared, she realized she could hear the voices of several teenage girls coming their way.

"Dammit," Paul said, hearing them at the same time. He glanced down at himself, and her eyes followed. She almost moaned at the sight of his very clear need for her. Giving her a panicked look, he turned and practically flew into the boys' bathroom.

A group of girls came around the corner right then. Kyleigh's hand quickly flew to her hair, trying to straighten it.

"Hi, Ms. Sinclair," one of them said when they noticed her. "They put you on bathroom duty, huh? Must be pretty boring."

"Yeah," she replied weakly, her legs practically trembling. "You could say that."

Chapter Seventeen

Paul paced around the apartment, waiting for Kyleigh to get home. It had been almost a week since that unforgettable moment in the hallway. When he'd left the bathroom after giving his body time to cool down, Gregori—the eternal cockblock—had been standing beside Kyleigh, talking to her about the talent show. He'd given Paul a knowing look, and Paul knew that there'd be zero chance of picking up with Kyleigh where they'd left off.

Since then, Kyleigh had conveniently developed amnesia, pretending that nothing had happened between them. Well, he wasn't about to let her off that easily. They had a date on Saturday, and he planned on using every bit of charm he had on her.

Paul needed her to remember how good they were together. Not just physically, but in every aspect of their relationship.

Because Paul sure as hell wasn't about to let her go. Not again. He had less than two months to win his wife over, to make her want to stay married to him.

From the first moment he saw Kyleigh all those years ago, he'd fallen in love with her. If he was truly honest with himself, he'd never stopped. She'd been the driving factor in everything he'd done in his life, in his determination to become rich and successful so that he'd finally be good enough for her. Even though she used to tell him that she only needed him.

He wanted to hear her say those words again. That he was enough, Paul Rodriguez. Not the famous guy he'd become, but the man he truly was. He wanted to hear his name on her lips as he brought her to an explosive climax. Most of all, he wanted to hear her say that she loved him.

"What's up with you today?" Shawnee asked, looking up from her tablet. She'd been reviewing several proposals for Paul's new production company. "You're distracted. Would this have anything to do with your wife?"

Paul scowled but continued pacing around the tiny kitchen.

"Gregori said you two got a little hot and heavy at the dance," Shawnee said, smirking at him.

"Gregori needs to stop being a damn gossip." Thankfully, the cameraman had the day off, and the rest of the crew was with Kyleigh. Otherwise the man might have words for Paul. He didn't want to deal with the drama today. He was saving all of his mental energy for Kyleigh.

"Is everything all set for the date tomorrow?" he asked.

"Yep, everything is organized to a T. Heather is even donating a delicious bottle of wine we discovered on Mackinac Island so you can woo your wife."

Paul went on defense. "Who says I'm trying to woo her?"

Shawnee had the audacity to roll her eyes at him. "Anyone with eyes can see that you're crazy about the woman. You've been acting like a loon ever since you saw her name listed as a contestant."

He was instantly offended. He had not been *that* obvious. "I don't know what you're talking about."

"Sure, buddy, keep telling yourself that."

He opened his mouth to argue some more, when the front door opened with a bang. Holly walked in, tears streaking her cheeks. Oh hell. What now?

Shawnee took one look at her and started packing her stuff up. The wimp.

"I should get going," she said, smirking at Paul when he glared at her.

Holly stood there, staring blankly at the floor. Shawnee finished gathering her things, telling Paul she'd email him a couple of pitches for shows later that day.

Paul crossed his arms as he looked at his stepdaughter. "What's wrong? Are those girls bothering you again?"

Holly sniffed loudly. "No. They tried, but some of the other kids told them to shove off. I have a lot more people talking to me now that they know you and Mom are married."

Paul examined her cautiously. "Are you okay with that?"

She shrugged. "Better than being treated like a freak, I guess."

"So what's wrong then?"

She sniffed again before finally saying, "I ran into Dylan Reynolds. He was with this stupid girl who was wearing a college sweatshirt from the same school he goes to. He introduced us and said she was his girlfriend."

Paul tried to think if Jake had mentioned his son dating anyone. They hadn't really talked much recently. Jake and Julie were busy with their new baby, and Paul had wanted to respect their space, but it wouldn't surprise him. Dylan was a miniature of his father.

Paul didn't know what to do about this situation. He *really* wished Kyleigh was home. Rubbing at his jaw, he sat down on the couch. Holly sagged into the armchair nearby.

"Dylan is eighteen," he finally said.

"I know," she mumbled into her chest.

"You're thirteen."

She shot him a sharp stare. "So?"

"So...he's too old for you."

"He's only five years older."

"Holly, I mean this with all sincerity. If Dylan ever made a move on you while you were underage, I'd crush his di— face."

"You don't understand," she argued. "I love him."

"And you're welcome to tell him that in ten years. But in the meantime, maybe concentrate on boys your own age."

Not that she'd be allowed to date any of them. Not if he had anything to say on it. No snot-nosed little jerk was dating his daughter—err—*step*daughter.

"Boys my age are too immature," she said stubbornly.

Paul wished again that Kyleigh was here to handle this. He had no idea how to talk a teenage girl down from an emotional ledge about boys.

He leaned back on the couch, resting his head against the back of it. "Listen, I know it'll hurt like crazy, but you'll need to let this go—let *him* go. Dylan is a man now, and you still have several years before you finish school. But I'll tell you what. If it's meant to be, who knows what the future will bring."

Holly was quiet for a minute before she said quietly, "Like you and Mom?"

Paul froze at that. He looked over at Holly and found her staring back at him intently. He swallowed hard before saying, "Yeah, like me and your mom."

She nodded. "I know you didn't meet Mom until you were in high school. Were you ever in love with anyone when you were my age?"

No. The only woman he'd ever loved was Kyleigh.

Holly tilted her head as she observed him. "Oh…" she finally said. "Have you never been in love?"

"I've been in love," he replied without hesitation. Kyleigh had been his whole world at one point—still was, if he was being truthful.

"What did you do?" Holly asked. When he gave her a questioning look, she said, "You told me I need to move on. How did you move on after you had your heart broken?"

Well… Paul had spent the first month after he left Kyleigh getting blissfully drunk, despite his aversion to alcohol and being underage. They'd just signed their contract for the Holiday Boys and the producers had put them in a beach house to record their first album.

Zan came home to find him passed out in the backyard with a pool of vomit next to him. His best friend had thrown a bucket of water over his head and told him to get his crap together. Paul had responded by punching Zan in the face. Thankfully, James, Tyler and Jake came home around that time and pulled them apart before Zan could retaliate.

In the state Paul had been in that night, Zan would have kicked his ass if he'd been in a less forgiving mood. Seeing the black eye on his face the next day had made Paul feel so sick with guilt that he hadn't gotten drunk again. Not until the night he ran into Kyleigh at Jake and Julie's pre-wedding party.

Instead, Paul had used sex instead of alcohol to escape his pain and yearning for Kyleigh. At the time, he'd been completely cut off from his former life. Too pissed off at Dom to speak to him, too upset with his Aunt Esperanza for continually bringing up his brother and too heartsick after being forced to break up with Kyleigh. Even if he had wanted to speak to her, which he'd attempted to do several months after they broke up, his calls never went through, and it finally dawned on him that she'd blocked him.

So he'd let out his pent-up frustration by sleeping with any woman who offered. He soon gained a reputation in the tabloids of being a player, a man who went through women like tissues. Even though he'd long outgrown his promiscuous ways, the reputation had stuck.

"Paul?" Holly asked, reminding them that she'd asked him a question.

Since he wasn't about to recommend any of his methods to his stepdaughter, he said, "I have just the idea for what will make you feel better."

Kyleigh walked toward her apartment, nervous butterflies fluttering in her stomach. She'd kept herself busy at the store until Wendy told her to go home. She figured by the time she returned to the apartment, Holly would also be there. It was shameful and awful to admit, but she'd been using Holly and Gregori as barriers since that heated exchange between her and Paul the previous Saturday.

Just thinking about the feel of him against her, his hips creating friction between her thighs, made her want to jump in Holiday Bay to cool off.

She'd been so focused on being a mother and business-woman over the years, she'd forgotten that she was also a woman who had needs. Needs that she'd neglected for longer than she'd like to remember. But Paul's heated kiss had awoken them from their sleepy slumber. He'd roused a hunger inside her that she had a feeling only he could fill. But while their fiery exchange had meant something to her, she had to remind herself that she was probably just another body to him.

"You okay, Kyleigh?" Gregori said next to her, making her aware that she was staring blankly at her apartment door.

She gave him a short smile. "Yeah, I'm good." Taking a deep breath, she opened the door.

A bloodcurdling scream greeted her. She rushed into the living room to find Paul and Holly sitting side by side on the couch, a large bowl of popcorn between them and a horror movie on the TV. On the coffee table in front of them was a half-empty pizza in a delivery box and bags upon bags of candy.

"What on earth?" Kyleigh said, drawing their attention.

"Hi, Mom," Holly said. Her eyes looked slightly puffy, raising Kyleigh's instant concern.

"What happened?" she asked.

"Holly and I have agreed that boys are stupid," Paul replied with a grin that had her pulse racing. "We're celebrating that fact by watching a *Saw* marathon."

Gregori snorted before heading into the kitchen.

"I have to pee," Holly announced, pausing the TV. "Don't start without me."

"Noted," Paul replied, his eyes not leaving Kyleigh.

After her daughter left, Kyleigh lifted an eyebrow at Paul. "Care to explain what this is about?"

"She ran into Dylan Reynolds and his girlfriend on the way home from school. She came home upset. Since I didn't think marathoning rom-coms was a great idea, we settled on horror movies."

"And that's a better alternative?"

"What healthier way to get her frustrations out over a guy than watching a man cut off his arm? In a fictionalized setting, of course."

She opened her mouth to argue with that logic, but she became aware of the teasing light in Paul's eyes, the way he hadn't stopped staring at her since she walked into the room. She licked her lips nervously, and he watched the movement, his eyes heating.

"Um, I should go and change," she said.

"You joining us afterward?" he asked. "If you're too scared, I'll be happy to hold your hand."

"Pfft. I won't get scared."

Paul's lips formed into a sensuous smile. The flirt! "The offer's still on the table."

But when Kyleigh returned to the room to the sounds of some woman screaming on the TV, she sat in the armchair closest to Holly.

She did her best to ignore Paul's seductive laugh as he noted her evasive maneuver.

Chapter Eighteen

Kyleigh stared at the beast in front of her. "Horseback riding. That's what we're doing today?"

Shawnee had explained to both of them that they needed a little more one-on-one time with each other for the show's sake, so she arranged for Kyleigh and Paul to go on a mystery date over in Clarington. Horseback riding at Kerrington Stables, a small farm with trails carved throughout a large span of deep pines.

"You okay?" Paul asked, a hand going to her chin so she had no choice but to look at him. The car ride over had been awkward enough. He'd started by being overly flirtatious, but her nerves had made her respond as though she were made of cardboard and had the personality to match. He finally toned it down, going from flirty to giving her concerned looks by the time they made it to the property.

"Yeah, I'm okay," she said. She jumped when a horse neighed from a distance. "I've never been on a horse before."

"I think you'll like it," he said. "Holiday Boys made a video once where we had to hop on horses to avoid a group of screaming fans."

"I remember," she said absently.

"Big fan of ours, huh?"

She glared at him. "Holiday Boys were pretty unavoidable back then."

She didn't tell him that she watched every video, listened to every song of theirs in hopes of picking up some secretly coded message from Paul that he missed her as much as she missed him. She never saw it. What she did remember was that in the video, some brunette with big boobs finally caught him, and they rode off on the horse together. Rumor had it that he and the model had a short-lived fling after they finished filming.

"Well, howdy." A guy came up to them. He wore tight jeans and a flannel shirt with the sleeves rolled up over his taut forearms. A large black cowboy hat covered his head, but Kyleigh could see hints of blond hair peeking out from it. He was a good-looking guy, even though he had to be at least fifteen years younger than her. His eyes filled with interest as he looked her over.

Paul tensed beside her.

"Welcome to Kerrington Farms. I'm Matt, and I'll be your guide today."

"Nice to meet you," Kyleigh replied.

"We don't need a guide," Paul said shortly.

"Sorry, partner. It's our farm's policy. We have a lot of marshes on the back trails that we want inexperienced riders to avoid. Your friend, Shawnee, explained that you'll have a camera crew following you in a golf cart. That noise alone could startle the horses. Have either of you been on a horse before?"

"He has." Kyleigh nodded at Paul. "I haven't."

"Well, let me show you what you need to do." Matt gestured for them to follow him.

As they walked over to a nearby barn, Kyleigh could see three horses already saddled. One was cream-colored, one was multicolored and the third one was a black beauty with a patch of white between its eyes.

Matt handed them both riding helmets that had cameras attached to them, so that they could film while riding.

"This is Buttercup," Matt said to Kyleigh, patting the cream-colored horse. "She's real gentle. Perfect for a first-time rider."

He advised Kyleigh on how to get on the horse, followed by instructions on how to sit properly.

Paul's lips turned into firm lines, his face growing strained as Matt placed his hands on Kyleigh's to show her the correct way to hold the reins.

After Paul hopped on the black horse, and Matt jumped on the multicolored one, they headed into the woods with the ranch hand leading the way.

"You know," Matt said to Paul over his shoulder, "you look awfully familiar."

"I get that a lot," Paul practically snapped.

Kyleigh glanced over at him, taking in his stiffness.

"I know!" Matt said, letting go of the reins with one hand to snap his fingers. "You're in that band my mom loves."

Kyleigh snickered while Paul glowered.

Matt continued on ahead. Kyleigh and Paul rode side by side behind him, listening to him prattle on, giving different facts about the farm. A tickle started to form in the back of Kyleigh's throat and she coughed a few times before looking over at Paul. He didn't seem to be paying any attention to their guide as he stared moodily in front of him.

"What's your problem?" Kyleigh asked quietly, fighting down the urge to cough again.

"Nothing," Paul said, not meeting her eyes.

She ran a finger under the strap of her helmet which was

causing her skin to itch. "Nothing? You're acting like your favorite dog died, but okay."

"I don't think Matt needs to be so touchy-feely with the customers."

Her eyes widened as she stared at him. "Are you...jealous?"

"I'm not jealous," Paul said, his tone waspish as he still refused to look at her.

Kyleigh scratched absently at her arm. "I'm old enough to be Matt's mother. Or if not his mother, at least his cool aunt. You have no reason to be jealous." She itched at her other arm. Her entire body felt scratchy to the point where she was getting really uncomfortable.

"For the last time," Paul said, finally looking at her, "I'm not..." His voice trailed off, a look of horror appearing on his face.

"Matt," he yelled out to the ranch hand, who was still talking, mostly to himself. "We have to go back."

Kyleigh rubbed at her neck. "Why?"

Matt turned his horse so that he could join them, "What's the problem, partner? I wanted to show you the...oh!" He also stared at Kyleigh like she'd grown an extra head.

"What?" she said before going into another coughing fit.

"Are you allergic to horses?" Paul asked.

"How would I—" *cough* "—know? I've never been around them."

It was the worry in his eyes that made her finally look down at herself. Hives covered both of her arms, her skin a pinkish red. She started coughing again.

"Gregori!" Paul yelled at the cameramen following them in the golf cart. "You and Leroy take the horses back." He jumped off the black horse. "We're taking the golf cart."

Kyleigh didn't even protest as Paul walked over to her and placed his hands on her hips, pulling her off the horse.

He wrapped his arm around her waist and dragged her to the golf cart.

"Hang on, baby," he said as she started coughing again.

He placed her in the seat of the cart before jumping behind the wheel. Whirling it in the direction of the barn, he slammed his foot on the pedal, muttering to himself about how slow the damn thing was.

Kyleigh couldn't stop coughing. Her chest started to ache. She gulped in some needed air, but it only made her cough worse.

As soon as they arrived in the parking lot, Paul leaped out of the seat and ran over to her. Picking her up bridal style, he hurried to their car and carefully placed her inside. He got behind the steering wheel and started the vehicle, then hit the gas.

"Where are we going?" she said weakly. Her chest was starting to hurt.

"The hospital," Paul replied. "Just keep holding on."

She was grateful that they were in Clarington already, so they only had a short drive before the small hospital appeared within view. He pulled into the emergency room driveway. A nurse and doctor hurried out, pushing a stretcher. Kyleigh squinted through eyes that felt swollen.

"Gloria?" she said, recognizing Dom's wife.

"Hey," Gloria replied before turning to Paul. "Your show called the hospital and said you were most likely headed this way. Can you tell me what happened?"

"We were horseback riding when she started coughing and itching. I think she might be having an allergic reaction."

Gloria nodded, then turned to the nurse. "Marge, put her in room one." She looked back at Paul. "Do you know if she's allergic to any medications?"

Paul started to shake his head. "I'm not—"

"No," Kyleigh rasped. She felt like she couldn't breathe.

Gloria said calmly, "We'll get you feeling better. We're going to put you on the heart monitor and check your oxygen levels, okay?" Looking over to the nurse, she ordered, "Let's get the EpiPen in, and make sure we have two good IV lines. I want to ensure that steroids, antihistamines and fluids are running. Keep checking her blood pressure every three minutes. Paul, you're going to have to let her go so we can help her."

It was only then that Kyleigh realized Paul was holding her hand, clutching it firmly in his. He reluctantly let her go. As they went through the hospital doors that separated the emergency area from the lobby, she kept her eyes focused on his worried face until the doors closed behind them, blocking her view.

It had been an hour. Sixty-two minutes, to be exact, since Paul had seen Kyleigh. He paced around the tiny lobby, thankful that Bryan, the security guard, was on duty and keeping people away from him. He didn't want to have to perform right then, to have to sign autographs or take selfies with fans.

Paul couldn't get Kyleigh out of his head. How she'd sounded like every breath hurt, every inhale accompanied by a faint whistle. Her lips had started to turn blue by the time they'd arrived at the emergency room, her skin looking like one big rash. But worst had been the worry in her eyes.

He'd never forgive himself if anything happened to her.

"Paul?" a male voice said.

Paul whipped around at hearing his name only to freeze when he saw his brother.

"¿Qué haces aquí, Hermanito?" Dom asked, approaching in dark blue scrubs.

A muscle flinched in Paul's jaw. "Did Gloria tell you I was here?"

Dom's face tightened at his tone. "I haven't seen Gloria since breakfast this morning. If there's something medical going on, she wouldn't be able to tell me anyway, due to patient privacy."

Paul's fists clenched and unclenched by his sides as he turned away from his brother to stare at the gray doors Kyleigh had gone through. If he didn't get some answers soon, he was going to rip the dammed things down.

"Is it Kyleigh?" Dom asked.

"Why would you think it was her?" Paul responded coldly.

Dom laughed without humor. "Because she's the only person on this earth who can make you look like you're losing your freaking mind."

Paul's eyes didn't leave those doors. "It's been over an hour. I don't know what's going on."

"I could get an update, if you want?" Dom offered.

Paul looked at his brother, his eyes narrowed. Dom looked sincere enough, but he'd trusted him before and look where that got them.

Dom obviously saw the rejection on Paul's face. Shaking his head, he moved to leave before he turned back around. "How long are you going to penalize me, huh? You pushed all the family you ever had away because of a stupid mistake I made when I was a friggin' teenager. Why do you keep punishing me for it?"

"¡Porque me abandonaste!" Paul yelled, slipping into Spanish without realizing it. He hadn't spoken it since he'd left home, his parents' native language another thing he'd buried deep inside him, so that the language couldn't trigger more memories of all that he'd lost.

When Dom stared at him in frustration, Paul repeated in English, "You left me. After *everything*. After losing Mom and Dad, you left, too. But unlike you, they didn't have a choice. A drunk driver took that choice away from them. You did have one. You broke into that store. You got caught by goddamn Sheriff Sinclair. And he—"

He stopped talking. He couldn't go on. He pressed his palms to his eyes, pushing against them as if that would help erase the horrible memories swirling around his head.

"What?" Dom encouraged, sorrow etched deep into the lines of his face. "What did he do?"

Paul pulled his hands away to look at his brother. Anger and despair made him admit, "He said if I didn't break up with Kyleigh, he'd make sure they threw the book at you. That you were just another example of why my lowlife ass wasn't good enough for his daughter. Because of you, I lost Kyleigh, too."

A vein popped on Dom's forehead as he took in his brother's accusation. "I've done a lot of stupid crap in my life. I fully admit that. But Sinclair was a racist snob. You never would have been good enough to him."

"Well, your stupid decisions certainly helped confirm that."

"All right," Dom replied, holding his hands up in defeat. "But you weren't the only one to lose something. When I broke into that store, I was so lost. I got in with the wrong crowd. I escaped my grief after the accident by doing things I won't repeat to you. But I learned my lesson the hard way. I had to see Aunt Esperanza's face look a little more devastated every time she came to see me in prison. I lost you. And that's something I'll never forgive myself for, Paulo."

Dom rubbed a hand over his face tiredly. "But I've been trying to make up for it ever since. I finished getting my diploma in prison. I got out early for good behavior. After what happened to Mom and Dad, I decided to go back to school and become a nurse so I could help accident victims. I met Gloria, I got married and started a family. I'm proud of the life I've built. I'd love for you to be a part of it. To meet your niece and nephew. But I won't beg you. You said you lost your family. But we're all right here, Paulo, imperfect as we may be. We haven't left you."

"Paul?" Gloria called out as she entered the lobby. She paused when she saw her husband.

"How's Kyleigh?" Paul asked, hurrying over to her.

"She's stabilized. We'll want to keep her for a few more hours, but she should be good to go home later today."

"Are you sure? I can arrange for a private room if you think she needs it."

Gloria gave him a reassuring smile. "Her oxygen levels are good, and the rash has dissipated. She'll probably want to go home and sleep. I'm going to put a recommendation in her discharge papers that she should make an appointment to see an allergist. They'll be able to narrow down if it was the horses or something else that triggered the reaction. I'm also going to suggest she keep an EpiPen on hand moving forward, given the severity of her reaction."

Paul nodded. "Can I see her?"

"Of course," Gloria replied.

Paul looked back toward his brother, but Dom was no longer there. Giving Gloria a strained smile, they headed toward the triage area. He half expected her to lecture him on his fraught relationship with his brother, but she didn't say anything about it. She reviewed aftercare recommendations with him instead.

The tension in Paul's shoulders didn't ease until he saw Kyleigh's weak smile, which was barely noticeable over the oxygen mask she wore.

He ran to the bed and grabbed her hand, taking an unsteady breath as he examined her features carefully. Kyleigh looked paler than normal, and dark circles stood out noticeably under her eyes, but the red rash and hives were gone. As she took in a heavy breath, he didn't hear the terrifying whistling noise that he'd heard before.

"Hey," he said.

She didn't respond as she laid her head tiredly against her pillow.

"I'll leave you two now," Gloria said. "If you need anything, hit the nurse's button." She lifted a remote attached to the bed.

"Thank you," Paul rasped.

Gloria started to leave but turned to face him. Paul braced himself, knowing she was going to mention Dom. "Come see Esperanza when you're ready," was all she said before she left them alone.

The muscles in Paul's neck began to ache, and he moved his head from side to side to loosen the strain. Grabbing the chair in the corner, he pulled it up to the bed and sat down. He took assurance in the steady sound of Kyleigh's heartbeat, the rhythm amplified by the beeping monitor next to her bed.

"So…" he finally said. When she rolled her head his way, he said, "Best date ever or what?"

She murmured something, but he couldn't understand. He asked, "What?"

"Memorable," she said softly.

Paul chuckled, despite the somber moment. "Yeah, I guess going into anaphylactic shock can really make an impression." He picked up her hand and kissed it. He didn't miss how the beeping on the monitor sped up. Deciding to be a gentleman, he didn't point it out. Instead, he said, "Next time, you pick the date."

She gave a tired laugh. "Deal."

Chapter Nineteen

Kyleigh felt mostly back to normal the next day. A little exhausted but overall good. As she walked into the kitchen that morning, she took note of Gregori, Holly and Paul.

Gregori and Shawnee had been in the waiting room after the hospital released Kyleigh and had followed them back to the apartment. Holly had run over to her mother as soon as she saw her and given her a hug. After assuring her daughter that she was fine, Kyleigh had gone into her bedroom to sleep off the events of the day. As she drifted off to sleep, she could hear Gregori and Shawnee lecturing Paul on how they'd missed out on some great footage of him caring for her at the hospital. She'd been too tired to listen to his reply.

"Hey, Mom," Holly greeted her now. Gregori immediately swung his camera around to start filming her. She met Paul's intense stare and gave him a small smile. It must have reassured him because he went back to scrolling on his phone.

"Morning, baby," she responded to Holly. "What are your plans for the day?"

"If it's all right, I'm going to meet up with Tearia and Ebony. We're working on a project for school."

"That's fine. Just be home for dinner." Kyleigh grabbed

a cup of coffee and sat down at the table between Paul and Gregori. As she sipped from the mug, she noticed Paul becoming increasingly disgruntled. She tapped her foot against his, and his attention shot to her.

"Everything okay?" she asked.

He shook his head before putting his phone face down on the table. "The media got a hold of Zan's wife being in the hospital. They've besieged the building. Freaking gutter rats, every single one of them." Gregori lifted an eyebrow, his camera still focused on Paul, who responded, "Yeah, go ahead and put that in the show."

Kyleigh reached over and squeezed Paul's hand. "I'm sorry. Is there anything I can do?"

He stared at where she touched him. He flipped his hand over so that they were touching palm to palm. "Let me make up for our date," he said. "If you're up to it, why don't we go out for lunch somewhere? Anyplace you want."

Kyleigh remembered how he'd looked when she was in that hospital bed. The same worry lined his face now at what was happening to his best friend. She wanted to erase that look from his features forever. "Do you want to go get something to eat at Florentina's?"

The tension on his features eased, his eyes warm as he nodded. "Yeah, I'd really like that."

It was a warm day, so Kyleigh put on her favorite sundress with a light sweater, a blue little number that she knew brought out the color in her eyes. Despite her reservations when she and Paul first got married, something had shifted between the two of them recently.

Yes, Gregori and his crew were tailing them as they entered the restaurant. Yes, she knew that the circumstances of how this marriage had started weren't great. But she'd been forgetting more and more lately that this was a reality show and not a real marriage. More important, she didn't want to remember.

She was aware of Paul looking at her as they walked toward the hostess stand. "What?" she asked, giving him a half smile.

"Nothing. You look really beautiful right now."

"Oh." A faint blush appeared on her cheeks. "Thank you."

He looked pretty gorgeous himself in a dark polo shirt, black suit jacket and matching black slacks.

"Well, hello, you two," Isabella said once they reached the hostess station. She eyed the crew following them. "Just the two of you?"

"Yes," Paul said with a glower. Considering this show was his baby, he looked back at the crew with annoyance. Gregori simply rolled his eyes in response.

As they headed to a table in the dining area, Isabella said, "I'm so sorry to hear about Zan's wife. I hope she bounces back soon."

"Thank you," Paul responded with forced politeness.

Kyleigh reached for his hand again like she'd done earlier, wanting to comfort him. From what Paul told her on the ride over, Mary had been moved to the ICU. Zan had texted him that morning that her blood pressure had become erratic, going high before crashing. The doctors were doing what they could to regulate it, but Mary hadn't opened her eyes since that morning. She knew Paul was terrified for his friend.

He laced their fingers together, giving her an appreciative smile as they walked to a table next to one of the restaurant's expansive windows. Outside, the sun shone brightly, offering them glimpses of the bay in the distance.

They sat down, and a waitress soon came over to take over their order.

After the woman left, Kyleigh asked, "Are you going to need to go to Maine soon to see Zan?"

Paul rubbed his forehead. "I want to, but Zan said the press is really bad at the moment, and he doesn't want to draw more attention to the hospital than what's already happening."

Kyleigh thought back to how rabid the press and fans had been when Julie had her baby and four of the Holiday Boys had shown up to see their newest family member. Zan's family certainly didn't need to deal with that right now. She'd never really thought about the price the Boys had paid in exchange for fame and glory.

After their food was delivered and they began to eat, Paul said, "You know, the show's final episode will be filmed in a few weeks."

She nodded. It was hard to believe that they'd been married for two months at this point. "Yeah, I know."

Paul looked at the table, lost in thought. "Have you..."

He didn't finish. She cocked her head. "Have I what?"

Paul took a deep breath. "Have you thought about what you want to do?"

"You mean, have I thought about how we're going to end the show?" She knew what he meant. In the final episode of the show, they had to state on camera if they were going to stay married or not.

He nodded. "Have you?"

The vegetable lasagna she'd been eating suddenly felt heavy in her stomach. "Have you?"

He cocked a smile at her that made her heartbeat speed up. "I asked you first."

Kyleigh frowned at the table. "I don't know," she finally whispered.

"Kyleigh—"

"You left me before. I sat around on prom night waiting for you to show up. And instead, you sent me some cryptic message saying you didn't want to date me anymore. Who's to say you won't do the same thing again?"

"I won't—"

She completely missed the fact that he was as good as admitting he wanted the marriage. "I struggled for years after you left—"

"Yet you got married to someone else."

She looked at him with hurt eyes. "I rushed into a relationship with Dan after I read one too many tabloids about all the women you were involved with. You moved on. I tried to do the same thing."

"I came back for you," Paul said, so quiet she wasn't sure if she'd heard him correctly.

Kyleigh blinked at him, trying to comprehend what he'd just admitted. "What did you say?"

"I left you on prom night after I stopped by your house earlier that day. You weren't home, but your dad was. I foolishly told him that I wanted to marry you. I had this notion that I'd ask for his blessing first—do everything all gentlemanly. He told me to get the hell off his property and that there was no way he'd let his daughter marry someone like me who could offer nothing but poverty. I swore right then that I'd make something of myself and come back for you. I left, and my world imploded. Dom went to prison, touring was exhausting and then the band broke up right when we were dominating the world. I took what money I'd earned and started buying the rights to songs. Once I reached multimillionaire status, I came back to Holiday

Bay, thinking there was no way your dad could object to me now. When I came back to town, I went straight to your parents' house. Your dad greeted me again and told me you'd gotten engaged. So I left, never planning on coming back this time. And I've tried every day since then to get you out of my head."

Kyleigh shook her head in disbelief. "Why didn't you tell me about this sooner? About my dad?"

She wished she could say she didn't believe Paul. But she'd always known her father hated him with a disdain that never made sense to her. He'd made it clear on more than one occasion, but she had no idea how far he'd stooped to destroy their relationship. No wonder he'd gone practically feral at their wedding. They hadn't talked since, despite her weekly calls to her mom.

Paul leaned across the table, his face earnest as he looked at her. "Would it have made a difference? If I had told you about your dad?"

"I…" She didn't know. All these years, she'd thought Paul had left her and never looked back. He'd certainly acted like it, and she brought it up now. "But you *did* forget me, Paul. Your fans called you a player for a reason. It's well-known that you used to hook up with someone at every tour stop."

Regret shadowed his face. "I wish I could go back in time and change my behavior, but I can't. I was a heart-broken teenage boy. After I left the night of your prom, I had all these notions in my head about winning you back, but I couldn't quite forget what your father told me. That no matter what, I'd never be good enough. So a part of me did try to forget you. Once we had some distance from one another, I tried to convince myself that we weren't meant to be, that you'd find someone better. Someone your family would approve of. So I slept my way through groupie after groupie to try to erase you from my mind. But it wasn't nearly as many as people made it out to be. And no matter what, I couldn't forget you." He stared toward the view of the bay before giving her a sad smile. "And then when I found out you were engaged, I realized it didn't matter how rich I'd made myself for you, I'd lost you anyway. At that point, the Holiday Boys were done, and I'd moved on to the entertainment industry, getting into reality TV shows. I made myself care about fame and success only. Women became an escape from the daily pressures of my life, but I couldn't form a serious relationship with anyone. I didn't want anyone else."

Kyleigh went still before she whispered, "What are you saying?"

"I—" Paul's phone began to buzz. He pulled it out of his pocket to look at the text he'd received. His face went white.

"What is it?" she asked.

He looked at her with so much pain in his eyes, it took her breath away.

"I have to go to Maine."

Chapter Twenty

Paul hated funerals. He'd despised them since he had to attend his parents', watching as cemetery workers lowered their cheap caskets into the ground. He'd walked away when the workers opened the back of a nearby truck to pour dirt in the holes, unable to watch the last evidence of his parents' lives be buried under a deep layer of earth.

He wanted to walk away now as the minister Mary's parents hired to conduct the funeral went on and on about life in the ever after. He stood behind the row of white chairs the cemetery set out for the family. He could see the back of Zan's head, lowered, not looking at the grave or anyone around him. On either side of him were his children, Xander and Alice. Little Alice was only eight years old—far too young for a little girl to grow up without her mom. She was sobbing into her dad's shoulder.

From what Paul could see of Zan's son, the ten-year-old was trying to be stoic, sitting so stiffly in the chair on his father's right that Paul wondered if he'd been frozen into place.

As the minister continued, Paul stared at the purple coffin Mary was in.

He wished he'd been able to say goodbye to her. Guilt ate away at him for it. He understood and respected Zan's need to not have more publicity on them during such a difficult time, but he'd known Mary for fifteen years. He should have made more of an effort to see her while she was still somewhat coherent.

The minister finally wrapped up, and Paul forced himself to watch the casket lower into the ground. He gritted his teeth as Zan got to his feet and walked over to a wreath that stood where Mary's headstone would eventually be placed. He pulled a deep red rose from it and pressed the petals to his lips before throwing it onto the casket six feet down.

His children followed, throwing flowers on their mom's grave.

Paul had to turn away at that point. He looked at his fellow Holiday Boys instead. Tyler had flown in for the day, but he was leaving shortly after the ceremony. With Meg getting further along in her pregnancy, he hadn't wanted to leave her for too long. Jake would also be returning to Michigan that night, unwilling to leave Julie and their baby for long, but Paul knew his friends had needed to come, to be there for Zan and the kids, even if only for a few hours.

James stood on his other side. They were staying at the same hotel. James was going to stay for at least the next week to help out. Paul planned on staying for as long as Zan needed him. Would that screw up the show and the filming schedule? Probably. But he didn't care. He'd known Zan since they were little, had been his best man at his wedding to Mary, was godfather to their daughter. He would be there until Zan got sick of him and told him to leave.

He hoped Kyleigh would understand, though he knew she would.

They were overdue for a conversation when he got back. He'd been on the verge of telling Kyleigh that he wanted their marriage to be real during their date. He'd almost told her that he loved her. That he'd never stopped.

But when Paul received Zan's text telling him Mary had passed away, he knew he had to put that conversation on hold until he was in a better frame of mind.

But they would need to talk soon.

Given how she'd asked him about his past, about all the women he'd been with, he doubted she would believe him right then if he *did* confess his feelings. He'd have to work on finding an approach that would help him get back into her heart until she loved him, too.

Because there was no way Paul was letting Kyleigh go again.

If this miserable day brought him any sense of understanding, it was the realization that life was too short to wait on circumstances to align. He needed his family. Kyleigh and Holly both. He wanted to be the dad Holly needed. He wanted to grow old with Kyleigh, to never leave her side again. He just needed to find a way to convince *her*.

"Are you going back to the hotel?" James asked after the funeral officially ended and people started making their way to their cars.

Paul shook his head. "I'm going to head over to Zan's house. I want to make sure he doesn't need anything."

"We'll follow you over," Jake said. Tyler stood beside him, his face grim.

Paul clapped James lightly on the arm and nodded. He started to turn in the direction of his rental car, when he saw a familiar blonde at the back of the lingering crowd. The sadness inside his heart lightened slightly as he realized Kyleigh was there.

He walked over to her. "How... What are you doing here?"

She gave him a sad smile. "Shawnee gave me the details of where the ceremony was taking place. I hope that's okay."

"Yeah, it's okay," Paul replied, wanting nothing more than to hold her, half afraid she'd slip away from him like Mary had from Zan.

She looked over his shoulder. "Poor Zan. And his sweet babies."

He sometimes forgot that she'd grown close to Zan in the year she and Paul dated, though she hadn't kept in touch with him after Paul broke up with her.

She glanced back his way. "I can't imagine what those kids are going through. Just thinking of Holly having to grow up without me makes me crazy."

He didn't resist then. He pulled her into a close hug, burying his face in her neck to breathe in her sweet rose scent. He'd go crazy at the idea of losing her, too.

She began to rub circles on his back, murmuring over and over, "You're okay. You're okay."

He hadn't realized that tears had started to escape his eyes, dampening her dress. Pulling away, he brushed at his cheeks. "I'm sorry," he muttered.

"You never have to say sorry for grieving."

Clearing his throat, he said, "Speaking of Holly, where is she?"

"Izzy offered to watch her. She's staying with her until I get back."

Paul grabbed her hand to keep her close, and they began walking to the rental car. "When do you plan on leaving?" he asked.

"Depends."

"On?" Paul nudged her gently.

"On when you're leaving."

He wanted to kiss her, to make sure she never left his side again. It wasn't the time or place.

"I might not be leaving for a while. I need to make sure Zan's going to be all right."

She slowly nodded. "Will Shawnee and the team be okay with that?"

Paul shrugged. "They'll have to be."

Sympathetic understanding appeared on Kyleigh's face. "Oh. Well…realistically, I can probably stay for a week, but I'll need to get back to Holly and the store after that."

He let go of her hand to wrap an arm around her waist. His mouth brushed her temple. "Thank you for coming."

Kyleigh was weary to the bone. It had been such a long day. She'd decided at the last minute to go to the funeral so she could be there for Paul and to offer her condolences to Zan. Shawnee had used her connections to get Kyleigh on the list of people allowed to attend, which was sadly needed, given that every Holiday Boy was expected to be there, along with many other famous people.

For the first time in weeks, Kyleigh didn't have a camera crew following her. Though she'd begun to look at Gregori as a long-lost uncle, it was nice not to have her every expression filmed. Especially when she felt so conflicted over her marriage to Paul.

They'd seemed to have some kind of breakthrough at Florentina's. Though her younger self still ached over how they parted, she understood Paul's point of view. And once she cooled down, she'd give her father a call and give him a stern lecture about interfering with her life.

Paul reminded her so much of the man she'd fallen in love with back then, but he'd become a better version of himself. Life may have bruised them both in the time they were separated, but in the past two months of marriage, they'd fit back together like two puzzle pieces reconnecting.

She was in love with him. She knew that with absolute certainty. And maybe over the next few weeks before the show officially ended, she could show him that a relationship between them was worth keeping. But to stay married... They hadn't exactly started with the healthiest basis for a lasting marriage, what with all the blackmail and TV cameras.

But could they overcome the odds, stay married and live happily ever after?

Kyleigh walked down the hall of Zan's house after freshening up in the bathroom. The house was a beautiful brick mansion that overlooked the Gulf of Maine. She could hear the Holiday Boys on the floor below, talking softly to Zan. Kyleigh was about to head to the staircase leading downstairs when she heard soft crying coming from one of the rooms.

She bit her lip, unsure what to do. She knew it had to be one of the kids. Most of the guests had already left. Mary's parents were staying in the guesthouse behind the house, and Zan's parents were staying in a hotel down the road. She didn't understand why, considering the house was big enough to host most of the people living in Holiday Bay comfortably, but she supposed it wasn't any of her business.

As she started to walk by the room where she could hear the crying, she knew she wouldn't be able to live with herself if she didn't try to help. Lifting her hand, she knocked quietly on the door.

She heard a muffled, "Come in."

Kyleigh entered a pink bedroom designed for a princess. Soft pink walls perfectly matched the deeper shade of pink carpet. There was an open door on one side of the room, revealing a bathroom with pink wall tiles. On the other side of the room was a long, built-in bookshelf filled with every children's book imaginable. Against the wall closest to the main entrance was an open wardrobe brimming with stuffed animals. In the middle of the room was a large kid's bed shaped to resemble Cinderella's carriage. And in the middle of it was Zan's daughter.

She had her dad's dark hair and eye shape, but she had cornflower-blue eyes and pronounced cheekbones like her mom. She was a beautiful girl, reminding Kyleigh that Mary had been a world-famous model before she married Zan and started a family.

"Who are you?" The little girl sniffled.

"I'm… I'm Kyleigh. I'm here with Paul."

Alice perked up a little at that. "You know Uncle Paul?"

"Yes." Kyleigh smiled gently at her. She looked down at her watch. "It's pretty late. Are you having trouble sleeping?"

The little girl's eyes started to well with tears again. "Mommy used to read to me every night."

Kyleigh's heart ached in her throat. "I'm so sorry you lost your mom."

Alice looked like she was ready to start sobbing again.

Kyleigh looked over at the bookshelf again. "Would you like me to read you a story?"

Alice pointed to a worn book next to her bedside table. "Mom was reading *Little Women* to me."

"I can read a little to you, if you think it'll help."

Alice let out another sniffle before nodding.

Kyleigh entered the room and grabbed the book off the table. She looked around for a chair to sit in.

Alice scooted over. "You can sit next to me."

Kyleigh nodded before sitting on the edge of the bed.

She opened to where the bookmark was. She really hoped it wasn't the scene where Beth died. As she began to read, Alice curled up next to her, occasionally wiping her cheeks.

Kyleigh was at least a half hour into reading when she became aware of a presence watching them. She looked up to see Paul leaning against the doorjamb, an unreadable expression on his face.

Alice, who'd been starting to drift off, jerked upright. "Uncle Paul!"

"Hey, bunny." He entered the room and went to the other side of Alice's bed, giving her a small kiss on the forehead.

"Bunny?" Kyleigh asked.

"Yeah, 'cause as soon as she learned how to walk, she started hopping all over the place like a bunny."

Alice's tiny hand shot out to grab Paul's. "Uncle Paul, my mom died."

"I know." His voice was hoarse, like something was pressing on his vocal cords.

"What are we going to do now?" Alice asked, sounding small.

He sat down on the bed. "You're going to keep on living. And even though you're super sad right now, someday you're going to find a way to smile again. I know your mom loved you to bits and pieces, and that's what she would want."

"I miss her so much," she whispered.

"I know you do, bunny."

Alice looked from him to Kyleigh. "I like Kyleigh."

Paul lifted his gaze to stare intently at her. "Yeah, I do, too."

"Could you read a little more, Kyleigh?" Alice asked.

"Absolutely," Kyleigh told her.

She continued to read for a little longer. Paul eventually

got up to return to the Holiday Boys. Kyleigh stayed with Alice until she eventually fell asleep. Kyleigh carefully got off the bed and placed the book back on the bedside table. She brushed a stray hair away from Alice's damp cheek, her heart aching all over again for the pain the little girl was going through.

She quietly left the room only to find a ten-year-old boy sitting on the floor in the hallway. Unlike his sister, Xander was his father's miniature. But instead of having the deep abiding grief that his sister and father had in their eyes, Xander's were full of rage.

"Hey," she offered.

"That was my mom's favorite book," he said in response. "You shouldn't have read it."

Kyleigh shut Alice's bedroom door behind her as softly as she could. "Your sister asked me to. She was upset, and I thought it'd help her."

Xander got to his feet. He didn't meet Kyleigh's eyes. He shook his head, muttering again, "You shouldn't have read my mom's book." He turned on his heel and went down two doors to his own room, closing the door with a firm click.

Kyleigh let out a sigh. Her motherly instinct screamed at her to help him. Xander was in so much pain. Kyleigh wished she could protect them from all of the heartbreak they were experiencing.

Instead of heading toward the boy's room, she turned the other way. She didn't think Xander would appreciate her trying to help, and she didn't know either child well enough to press. She didn't want to cross his boundaries, and if he wanted nothing to do with her, she would respect that. But she would remember to say something to Paul about him. Maybe he could find a way to help.

As she tiptoed downstairs, she realized it was much later

than she'd thought. As she peeked into the room the Holiday
Boys had been in earlier, she noticed that Jake and Tyler
weren't there. They must have already left. James was also
gone, though she knew he was staying at the house instead
of a hotel, after Zan insisted. She and Paul had also been
offered rooms. She half thought she'd share a room with
Paul, but earlier he'd shown her where she'd be sleeping
and explained that he'd be sleeping across the hall.

"What are you going to do now?" Paul asked Zan.

They were sitting on a long, overstuffed blue couch in
the family room. Like the rest of the house, the entire room
was designed more for comfort than style. Despite Zan and
Mary's wealth, they'd obviously wanted their children to
grow up in a home and not a museum. This room had a large
stone fireplace, with the family's portrait over it. Books
lined one wall, several of them novels that Zan wrote. On
the other side of the room was a table that had four chairs
around it. Next to the table was a shelf filled with different
board games. The entire room spoke of warmth and love.
It was heartbreaking.

Paul sat facing Zan, one of his legs pulled up on the
couch while the other leg rested on the floor. Zan sat on
the opposite end of the couch. His face was drawn, his
shoulders hunched as he clasped his hands in front of him,
his fingers twirling the wedding band on his finger back
and forth.

Zan let out a loud breath. "I'm not going to off myself,
if that's what you're wondering."

Paul hadn't said that, but Kyleigh wondered if he'd been
worried about it. It was no secret how much Zan and Mary
were completely and utterly in love with each other. She
wasn't surprised that Paul worried about his friend's state
of mind now.

"I promised Mary that I'd keep going for the kids' sake." Zan leaned back and rested his head on the back of the couch. "You know what she told me a couple of weeks ago? She told me to get remarried. How the hell am I supposed to look at another woman when I don't even feel like I can breathe right now?"

He laughed, but Kyleigh had never heard a sadder sound in her life. The laugh turned into a pained moan.

"What am I going to do without my Mary?" he whispered. He started to cry silently, the tears streaking down his face highlighted by the table lamp nearby.

Paul moved so that he could wrap his best friend firmly in his embrace. "You're going to get through this," he promised. "You're going to keep going, because those babies upstairs need you. They're a part of Mary. But they're also a part of you, and they love you. Don't forget that. You're still loved by so many people. Just remember that if you get overwhelmed, you call me or any of the guys. We'll be here in a heartbeat. It might not feel like it right now, but you're not alone."

Kyleigh turned away from the room and headed back upstairs. She turned right instead of left when she reached the second floor and headed to the guest room she'd been given. As soon as she got into her room, she pressed a hand to her heart.

She hadn't been wrong. Paul was still the sweet, caring, protective person she had fallen for so long ago. The man she married the day of her wedding was the entertainer, not the man he actually was.

And *that* man was worth staying married to.

Chapter Twenty-One

After Paul landed back in Michigan, he drove his rental toward Clarington instead of Holiday Bay. He hadn't made a conscious decision. He just found himself aimlessly driving that way, lost in thought after spending the past two and a half weeks with Zan. He couldn't leave his best friend, who'd spent those weeks either walking around like a zombie or getting completely drunk out of his mind.

Zan had the decency to wait until the kids had gone to bed before losing himself in a bottle. Paul could do nothing but sit helplessly by. The few times he'd tried to intervene, Zan had bit his head off and told him to go home. So he'd stayed close, making sure that his friend didn't choke on his own vomit.

It was during one of those episodes that Mary's mother walked in. She and Zan had clashed plenty over the years, and when she saw the state he was in, she said that perhaps they needed to discuss custody of the children. Zan sobered up pretty quick at that threat and told her that she'd take his kids from him over his dead body.

And then he kicked her out of his guesthouse.

The next day when Paul went down for breakfast, Zan was already there, looking alert for the first time since Mary died. He made sure the kids came down for breakfast and ate, which had been something else Paul hadn't been able to accomplish, not with Xander anyway. Alice had clung to him almost the entire time he was in Maine, crying hysterically whenever he mentioned going home.

Xander had barely left his room. Paul had talked to Zan later that night about enrolling the family in grief counseling. It's what his school counselor had him do after the death of his parents, but Zan only said he'd look into it.

Paul had wanted to stay longer, though a part of him longed to get back to his own family. He missed Kyleigh and Holly, although he made sure to call Kyleigh every night. Talking wasn't the same as what he really needed. He wanted to hold Kyleigh close, afraid that if he didn't, he'd lose her like Zan had Mary. But he didn't feel right about leaving his friend, so he ignored Shawnee's increasingly frantic texts asking him when he would be returning so they could wrap up the show.

And then that morning, Zan told him how much he loved and appreciated him, but he needed to get the kids used to their new normal—which was just the three of them. Paul respected the decision, so he booked a flight home leaving that very day.

Though he was eager to see Kyleigh again after not seeing her for a week and a half, he found himself driving on a road he hadn't been down in two decades, and he soon entered Clarington.

It was bigger than Holiday Bay—at least big enough to have the closest hospital in the area. Down the road from the hospital were several chain restaurants and small businesses. Paul drove past the old pawnshop, which was now some hair salon named Barb's Beauty Salon & Spa.

He pulled to a stop at the corner of Main and State Streets, waiting for the light to turn green. If he turned right, Paul would head into the affluent area of Clarington. The large two-story colonial that Zan had grown up in was a few blocks away.

His family had been shining beacons in their hometown. His father was a pharmacist at the hospital, his mother the high school's principal. Paul had spent more than one afternoon in her office, getting the scolding of a lifetime. Zan's brother was the pride of their family, the class president who went off to the University of Michigan to get his doctorate.

Paul smiled as he remembered the shock and horror on the faces of Zan's parents when their son told them he was joining a boy band instead of going off to college. It was the only time Paul could ever recall Zan's mother shouting, considering what she did for a living.

Instead of turning right to head toward Zan's past, Paul turned left. Past the high school, where he could see the mural of Paul and Zan on one of the building's walls. Past the church where they buried his parents after their fatal accident. As he drove toward the outskirts of town, the houses became smaller, more rundown. The paved gravel underneath the rental car's tires turned to dirt. His fingers tightened as he turned onto his old road.

Thick trees blocked the view of his home, but as he pulled into the driveway, he finally got a glimpse of the house he hadn't been back to in twenty years.

He slowly braked so he could take it all in. The house wasn't much. His father and mother never had a lot of money. They used to get into terrible fights all the time about it, but they at least ensured their sons had a roof over their heads. The one-story farmhouse with the wood siding had a long, wraparound porch. Paul used to spend hours on the porch swing, sitting beside his mother, listening to her hum different songs. After she died, he continued to sit on that swing, crying on his Aunt Esperanza's shoulder, missing his parents with more heartache than a fourteen-year-old should have to bear.

It made the situation with Zan's kids all the more unbearable, because he knew what it was like to lose a mom at a young age.

When he'd left Clarington, the house had badly needed new paint, the stairs leading up to the porch practically crumbling. The roof had also needed replacing and used to cause leaks in Paul's bedroom when he was a boy. After he'd hit it big, he'd wanted nothing more than to see the place razed to the ground, as if that would help erase the pain of losing his parents.

Esperanza always refused to move. He'd wanted to pay her back a million times over for looking out for him and Dominic when they were younger, but all she'd wanted was peace between the brothers.

Paul stared at the house, taking in the changes. At some point, the old wood siding had been replaced with a cheery white vinyl siding. The porch steps and roof had been replaced. Flowers hung above the wraparound railing. It finally looked like the home Esperanza always wanted to turn it into, instead of the memorial it had been when he'd lived there.

Paul finished driving up to the house and put the car in Park. Taking a deep breath, he got out of the car. He was about to climb the porch steps when the front door opened.

Dominic came out slowly, wearing a T-shirt and jogging pants. "Paulo," he said, his raised eyebrows the only indication that he was surprised to see his brother. "What are you doing here?"

A little blur shot out of the door behind Dom. She came

to an abrupt halt at the top of the stairs, so fast that Paul's hands shot out to grab her in case she fell down the steps.

Ana cocked her head. "Hi, Paul!"

Paul swallowed hard. "Hey, Ana."

She beamed at him, clearly delighted that he remembered her name.

Guilt bubbled in his stomach. Did she even know that he was her uncle? He should have been in his niece's life.

Another little figure stepped outside. He was older than Ana by a couple of years and had curly black hair and brown eyes like his father.

"Bastián," Dom said. "This is your Uncle Paul."

Ana's eyes went huge. She started hopping on one foot, then another. "You're my uncle?"

Paul tried to smile. It hurt like hell. "Yeah, I am."

"You're my favorite Holiday Boy," she told him. "That must be because you're my uncle. Can I call you Uncle Paul?"

Paul cleared his throat before answering, "Sure, I'd like that."

Bastián leaned against his dad protectively, more cautious of this stranger in their midst than his sister. Looking Paul over, he said, "You're in Holiday Boys?"

Paul nodded painfully. "Yeah, that's me."

"Your music sucks," he replied.

"Bas!" his father said sternly.

"What? It does," his nephew said without a hint of remorse.

"I like it," Ana argued.

"That's 'cause it was made for girls," Bastián argued.

"Kids," Dom said, "why don't you go play in the yard for a minute so Uncle Paul and I can get caught up?"

"Are you gonna stay for lunch?" Ana asked.

"Oh, I…" Paul looked at Dom. "I—"

"He's staying," Dom assured her.

Ana let out a whoop before she ran to the corner of the yard where a tree fort had been built. Bastián looked uncertainly between the two men before following his sister.

Dom folded his arms over his chest. "Sorry about Bastián. He's overheard Esperanza and I mention you a few times."

"I take it the conversations weren't pleasant?"

"Probably about as pleasant as her conversations with you have always gone," Dom said without a hint of apology. "Gloria's working a double shift at the hospital, so I'm making her favorite. Lasagna. You don't want to miss it."

Paul didn't say anything. He turned to watch his niece and nephew play in the tree fort. "Where's Aunt Esperanza?"

"She's here." When Paul looked back at his brother, Dom said, "Do you want to see her?"

Paul moved so that he was facing his brother again. "Can we talk first?"

Dom's face didn't hide his surprise this time. He took a few steps back and waved his hand at the swing. Paul went up the steps and walked over to it, enjoying the familiar creak as he sat down. Dom sat next to him. Neither of them spoke.

Finally, Paul said, "The house looks different than when I was here last."

Dom nodded. "After Gloria and I got married, we decided we wanted to settle somewhere close to Esperanza to help her out. We bought this place from her after her fall. She said she asked you if you were okay with me buying the property, and you didn't object."

Paul didn't remember that conversation. But if his aunt

had tried to speak to him about anything relating to Dominic, he usually tuned her out.

Paul frowned. "Wait. What fall? Is she okay?"

"Remember how crappy the steps on the porch used to be? They crumbled underneath her feet a few years ago. She hurt her back pretty badly."

Paul could only gape at his brother in horror. "She never said anything to me," he whispered.

"You know how she is," Dom chided gently. "She's even more stubborn than you. She's always been the caretaker of our family and has never been one to accept someone fussing over her. Getting her to accept care from Gloria and me was a feat in itself, even though we both work in the medical field. We originally moved in to help Esperanza out and eventually bought the house from her. She mentioned something about moving into a senior community, but we couldn't imagine she'd be happy there for long, so we built her a small house on the property. We have dinner together every night."

Paul nodded, but his eyes burned. He should have been here. Esperanza gave so much to him, and he'd pushed her away. Pushed them all away for some stupid, selfish sense of self-preservation.

"What's on your mind, Paulo? Why'd you come today?"

Paul scrubbed at his face before tiredly leaning back in the swing. "Zan's wife died."

"I heard that on the news. I was sorry to hear about it. Zan's always been a good guy."

"Kyleigh came to see me at the funeral. She stayed with us for a week, trying to get the kids to eat, reading to Alice every night. Zan's a mess."

"I can imagine," Dom said, then let out a sigh. "Actually, I can't. I can't picture my life without Gloria."

"His wife—Mary—she was my friend. And God, Zan loves...loved her so much." Paul folded his hands over his chest, gripping them together. "I watched as he and the kids put flowers on the grave, and I... Life is so brutally short. Too short to hang on to things that only hurt."

Paul dared to look at his brother then, sorrow and regret in his eyes. "I shouldn't have pushed you out of my life. I... I was angry. I was angry at Mom and Dad for the accident, even though it wasn't their fault. I was angry because you left next. I was pissed that Sheriff Sinclair used you to make me break up with Kyleigh, even though he used his authority and position to make that happen. I needed an outlet for my anger. You were it, and you didn't deserve to be. And I—I'm sorry, Dom. I'm just so damned sorry."

Dom wrapped an arm around him, squeezing him to his side. "It's okay."

"It's really not," Paul muttered, even as he hugged his brother back. "I don't understand how you can stand to be around me."

"I mean, I heard Monica Valdez wrote a tell-all book about you. If she comes into town, Gloria and Ana are huge fans of her show. Maybe you can help me score some points by introducing—"

Paul jabbed his brother in the side, and Dom laughed, letting his brother go.

"Well, as I live and breathe," a voice said from the side of the house.

Paul jerked his head in the direction of the sound and saw his aunt standing there, beaming at the two brothers. He jumped to his feet and leaped over the railing of the porch to get to his aunt faster.

Esperanza was in her early sixties, but the sacrifices she

made for her two nephews showed in the deep lines on her face, aging her by at least ten years.

Paul reached the petite woman and hugged her close. He thought of what Dom said. How Esperanza had been injured, and never told Paul. He could have lost her and not even known what happened.

"I'm sorry," he whispered against the graying bun of hair on top of her head.

She pulled back and clasped his cheek in her hand. Her eyes brimmed with love he didn't feel he deserved as she said, "Welcome home, boy."

Chapter Twenty-Two

Kyleigh paced inside the store's bathroom. It was the only place she could get a little privacy. She needed to make a phone call, and she didn't want them filming her. She chewed on her inner cheek until she finally heard her mom's cheery voice.

"Kyleigh, hello."

"Hi, Mom."

"How are you doing? Are you almost done with that show?"

A pang went off inside her at the reminder. "Yeah, we only have a couple more weeks to film."

"Thank goodness that whole mess is finally almost over with. Maybe once it's done and you're able to get rid of that boy, then you and Holly can come see us. There's a nice man that your dad met at the country club here. He's a doctor. His name is—"

"Mom," Kyleigh interrupted. "Can I speak to Dad?"

"Oh…"

"It's been over two months. He can't avoid me forever, especially if he wants to see his only granddaughter again."

Her mom made a *tsk*'ing noise. "He won't react well to blackmail, Kyleigh."

"Holly and I are a package deal. If he wants to see her,

he's going to have to deal with me eventually." Kyleigh was unapologetic in her stance.

Her mom was silent for a moment before she said, "Just a moment."

Kyleigh could hear quiet arguing in the background before her father's gruff voice said, "Kyleigh."

"Dad."

"What I can do for you?"

Kyleigh's lips went thin. "I want you to tell me something, and I want you to be completely truthful with me."

He was silent for a moment before he said shortly, "What is it?"

"Did you tell Paul to get out of my life on my prom night?"

"Yes, I did," he said without apology. "The fool came to the house and asked for your hand in marriage. You were barely eighteen, and he had zero to offer. So I told him to leave and never come back. And I'd do it again in a heartbeat if it meant protecting you. He's no good. He never has been."

Kyleigh stared at her pale reflection, her eyes burning with unshed tears. "You made me think he dumped me because he didn't care about me."

"And he didn't. It should be a sign to you that he put his brother before you."

Kyleigh gripped the phone hard. "What do you mean about his brother?"

Her father went silent again.

"Dad, what did you mean?" she demanded.

"I figured he told you all that nonsense. It's all water under the bridge now. He married you anyway."

"Dad, if you want to continue to have a relationship with me then I want you to tell me everything. Now!"

She could hear him let out a hard breath. "I simply pointed out to him that it was in his brother's best interests if he didn't antagonize me. And the best way to avoid that was to leave you the hell alone."

Kyleigh pressed a hand to her throat, putting pressure against it to stop herself from screaming. "You threatened his brother. That's why he left."

"I did what I had to," her father said, sounding just like he used to when she was little and he tried to control everything she did.

"And…" Kyleigh swallowed. "Did he come and see me after he made it big and you still turned him away?"

"You were engaged to a good man—"

"Dan was a terrible husband, and he's an even worse father. How could you do this to me? To Paul? You destroyed our happiness."

"Now you're sounding like a hysterical teenager again. Grow up."

Kyleigh bit back the retort that was brimming on her lips. "Tell Mom I'll call her later."

"I—"

Kyleigh didn't want to listen anymore. She disconnected the call and hit Ignore when the phone rang several seconds later. She looked into the mirror and barely recognized herself.

All these years, she'd been so angry with Paul. At the wedding, he'd been so gleeful toward her dad, and now she understood why. She remembered his reaction after seeing Dom in the hospital.

He took everything *from me.*

A tear fell down Kyleigh's cheek, and she brushed it away with a hand that shook. Her father had destroyed so many relationships that night. Paul had always been so insecure about his financial situation when they were younger, and her father preyed on that. He'd ruined her relationship with the only man she ever truly loved. He made Paul resent his own brother. She didn't know how she would ever forgive him.

More important, she didn't know how Paul would ever forgive her.

Kyleigh leaned her head tiredly against the back of her couch later that evening. Gregori sat in the chair in the corner of her living room, eyeing her with concern. He'd evidently noticed something was off about her when she came out of the store's bathroom earlier that day, but when he asked if she was okay, she simply said she wasn't feeling good. Given the length of time she'd spent in the bathroom, he had no reason to doubt her.

Gregori's camera was on the table next to him, recording her as he always did. She was getting so used to the camera, she forgot it was there anymore. Gregori looked invested in the game show they were watching. It was just the two of them. Holly had gone to a sleepover with her friends, and Paul wasn't back yet from Zan's.

She picked up her phone where it lay next to her on the couch and opened her messages. There were several from her dad and a couple from her mom. She scowled and deleted all of them. Kyleigh wasn't in the mood to speak with either of them at the moment. She'd call her mom back when she wasn't so pissed.

She hadn't heard from Paul since that morning. At the time, he hadn't mentioned when he planned on returning home. She knew he needed to be there for his best friend, but she really missed him.

Kyleigh had grown used to him in her life, of coming

home and seeing him in her kitchen or helping Holly with something. It was weird how much of a presence he'd created in her life now that he wasn't there.

"So, Kyleigh," Gregori said when his show went to a commercial break. "The final episode is in two weeks. Have you decided if you're going to say yes to staying married to Paul yet or not?"

Kyleigh pulled at the neckline of her T-shirt. It suddenly felt too hot in her apartment. "Oh, I…"

Gregori's face flashed with disappointment before it smoothed over. "You know, I've known Paul for a lot of years now. He's a good guy. He works hard. Maybe *too* hard. I never understood what drove him so much."

Kyleigh's heart panged. She may not have known when she married him, but thanks to that revealing conversation with her father, she knew now.

Gregori continued, "The man already has more money than he knows what to do with. He's learned the entertainment industry inside and out, bought the rights to songs, helped adapt and produce movies that were originally books. As long as I've known him, he's always been searching for the next thing. But to be honest, I don't know if many people understand or see that side of him. I know he comes across as this playboy who only wants to be in front of the camera, but I always thought that was a persona. It's not the guy I know."

Kyleigh tilted her head toward the cameraman. "Why do you think he does it? Why does he need any of this still?" She nodded toward the camera.

Gregori folded his hands together and rested his chin on his fingers. "I think he did it to occupy his time until he finally found what he was looking for."

"And what's that?" Kyleigh murmured.

Gregori gave her an exasperated face. "You know what."
"I—"

The door to the apartment opened, and Paul walked in.

Kyleigh jumped to her feet, exhilaration racing over her at the sight of him. "Hey," she said. "I didn't think you were coming home yet."

Paul gave her an exhausted smile, the crinkles around his eyes deep with fatigue. "Zan told me to go home."

Kyleigh cast him a concerned look. "Is he okay?"

Paul glanced over at Gregori, frowning when he saw that the man was recording their reunion. "He will be."

Kyleigh nodded. "Did you just get in?"

"No." Paul took a step forward, and Kyleigh moved so he could step farther into the apartment. "I went to Clarington first."

Kyleigh's jaw dropped open. "Wow, why?" As far as she knew, Paul had always avoided his hometown like the plague, even before he was famous.

Paul left the suitcase he'd brought in with him near the door and entered the living room, all but collapsing on the couch. "I went to see my family."

Kyleigh plopped down next to him, regarding him intently.

He noticed her stare and cocked a half smile at her. "Don't worry. Dom and I didn't try to kill each other or anything."

"That's good," she replied, unsure what to say. It was so unexpected that he'd gone, but she was glad for him. Especially after what she'd learned that day.

Paul frowned. "I've been running from my past for a long time now. If I pretended it didn't exist, it couldn't hurt me, right? That was my thought process anyway. Instead, I lost everyone I loved. I missed being there for my brother when he got married. I missed seeing my niece and nephew as babies. I've got a lot to atone for, but I'm trying."

"It wasn't your fault," she whispered.

Paul laughed cynically. "I can assure you it was."

"I spoke to my father today," she said. Paul stiffened next to her. "He told me what he did to you. How he used Dom against you."

A muscle throbbed on his jaw. "You believe me?"

"Yeah," she whispered.

He let out a relieved breath. "I'm glad."

"I'm so sorry, Paul. I—"

Paul pressed a finger to her lips. "You don't have anything to be sorry about. You did nothing wrong."

"I wish you would have told me."

He smiled at her sadly, his face full of regret. "It would have ruined your relationship with your parents."

"It wasn't the greatest to begin with," she muttered.

Paul looked off into space. "If there's one thing I learned with my recent reconnection with Dom, it's that life's too short to hold on to the past. Besides, your father wasn't exactly wrong."

"He was absolutely wrong," Kyleigh insisted.

But Paul shook his head. "I didn't have anything to offer you then. We would have ended up like my parents, fighting all the time over money."

Kyleigh wanted to deny it, but she had to acknowledge that neither of them had been ready for marriage at eighteen. Instead, she reached over and gently squeezed his hand. "I'm glad you were able to make peace with your brother."

The look he gave her, a mix of tenderness and something else, had her leaping off the couch. "Do you want me to make you some tea or anything? It might help you unwind after traveling all day."

He eyed her closely, but only said, "Tea would be great."

She nodded and made her way over to the kitchen, ignoring Gregori, who grumbled to Paul, "What the hell was that even about? What'd her father do?"

"Not now, Gregori," Paul muttered.

When she came back into the room a short time later with a steaming cup of chamomile tea in her hand, Paul was already sprawled on the couch, fast asleep. She could hear Gregori in the bathroom, going through his nightly routine to get ready for bed.

Kyleigh reached inside the basket underneath the side table and pulled out a blanket. She carefully placed it over Paul's sleeping form, adjusting it so it covered him.

Running her fingers gently through his hair, she turned off the TV and headed for her room, her mind beginning to replay everything she'd learned that day.

Chapter Twenty-Three

Kyleigh lay in her bed, staring at her bedside clock. It was just past one o'clock. She'd been trying to sleep for the past hour, but her mind wouldn't stop racing with everything. Her father's revelation. Paul's return. Most important, she thought about Gregori's question and if she would say yes to staying married to Paul. She knew the show ended with that one big question. Stay married or get an annulment?

It was like a broken record, playing over and over in her head.

Stay married. Get an annulment.

Stay married. Get an annulment.

When she couldn't take it anymore, she got out of bed and quietly opened the door to her bedroom. She went into the bathroom, washed her hands in the sink and stared at her reflection in the mirror. Her hair was sticking up at weird angles from tossing and turning so much. Her blue eyes appeared dim under the overhead light.

She needed to get some sleep. She was supposed to meet up with Meg and Julie in the morning. She didn't want to show up at her friend's house looking like *Night of the Living Dead*.

She stumbled back to her room and was about to hop

back in bed when she heard a soft knock on her door. Frowning, she walked back over to it and cracked it open.

Paul stood on the other side. His lips lifted into a slight smile. The sight of it made her heart speed up. He was so unfairly attractive, even when he wasn't trying. "Can't sleep?" he asked lowly.

"How did you know?"

"I could hear you tossing and turning."

She shrugged. "What about you? You must be exhausted."

"I was," Paul replied. He tapped his temple, frowning. "I've got too much on my mind. I thought we could both use a distraction."

Kyleigh crossed her arms, trying to ignore all the directions her mind was trying to take her. One of those directions featured her and Paul and the bed behind her. The tips of her breasts hardened, the taut points obvious through the thin material of her T-shirt.

She immediately dropped her arms, hoping he wouldn't notice, but of course he did. He always seemed to notice everything about her. He glanced down at her movement, his eyes freezing momentarily at her obvious desire. His face became absolutely fiendish for a brief second before it smoothed away.

"What were you thinking?" she asked him, trying to ignore the heated look he'd just given her.

If he said her bed, she would either slam the door in his face…or grab him by the shirt and pull him inside.

"You want to go for a walk?" he asked.

"Now?" she said, taken aback.

"Why not?" he responded. "Most of Holiday Bay will be asleep. We're pretty much guaranteed to have the town to ourselves. Just you and me. No cameras. No people following us around."

Oh. Kyleigh actually really liked the sound of that. She glanced down at her T-shirt and boxers. "I'll have to change into something else."

"I'll come back in a few minutes. You think we can sneak out your bedroom window? There's a fire escape there, right?"

"Or we could use the front door like normal people," she suggested dryly.

"I don't want to wake up Gregori," Paul said. "I want this to be just me and you."

A rush of jittery excitement coursed over her. "Give me five minutes," she said and silently shut the door.

She couldn't believe she was doing this. Kyleigh and Paul had succeeded in sneaking out of the apartment without their trusty guardian following behind them with his camera. They'd used the fire escape to reach the ground, tiptoeing as quietly as they could down the steps.

Once they were a few feet away from the building, Paul flashed her a grin of triumph, which made her laugh like a giddy schoolgirl. They'd made their way to the center of Holiday Bay. Kyleigh could see her store in the distance. They headed toward it but stopped in front of Julie's store across the street.

"You think that's one of Dylan's pieces?" Paul asked, nodding toward a mahogany fireplace mantel in the window. It had an intricate design burned into the wood and at the center was a Petoskey stone, Dylan's signature addition to all his work.

"It's beautiful enough to be his," Kyleigh said. "Once he's done with school, I have a feeling he's going to be very successful in starting his own shop. Julie told me he's hoping to buy one of the empty storefronts in town."

She looked at the empty store next to Julie's. It used to be an ice cream parlor that also sold small sandwiches and snacks. Kyleigh would walk across the street on her lunch break and buy something sweet whenever she needed a sugar fix. It had also been her first job as a teen, scooping icy sweets for the locals. After a big corporation tried to take over the town, multiple businesses closed, including the parlor. Despite the connection to the Holiday Boys, downtown had never quite recovered.

"Yeah, Jake mentioned Dylan wanting to open a store," Paul replied, also looking at the empty shop. "I can see it happening. He's got a lot of talent."

They turned away from the window and continued, guided by the warm streetlights lighting their path and the faint moonlight shining down on them from above.

"I forgot how peaceful Holiday Bay is this time of night," Paul murmured. "Remember that time I sneaked over to your house in the middle of the night and we walked around town like this?"

She did remember. It was a few weeks before her disastrous prom night. Paul hadn't been able to wait to share the news that some big-name manager was interested in representing him and his friends, promising to make them one of the biggest boy bands of all time. He'd rushed over to her house and thrown rocks at her window like a lead in a romance movie. She hadn't known then that after that night their lives would change forever. While she'd been picturing happy-ever-after, he'd already had one foot in the limo that took him away from her. Her father made sure of that.

"Yeah, I remember," she said, sad for the girl she'd once been, so eager and in love.

"What's that unhappy look for?" he asked, nudging her slightly with his arm.

She shrugged, not looking at him. "I was just thinking about how much our lives changed after that night. You headed out to become a Holiday Boy, and I..:" She couldn't finish, but she didn't need to.

Paul looked suddenly despondent. "I'm sorry for leaving you like I did. I never wanted to hurt you."

"I'm not angry at you," she told him. And she meant it. No, her anger was all for her father now.

"It wasn't all bad after I left, though, right?" Paul said carefully. "You went to college like you'd always dreamed, got married, bought your store, had Holly."

"No, it wasn't all bad. I mean, I never wanted to be a divorcée, but I wouldn't trade Holly for anything. Honestly, it was better that Dan got out of our lives. He was never there for either of us much anyway, even when I was married to him. But I have no regrets. And even though I'm furious at my dad for what he did to you, he and my mom did support me throughout my marriage and eventual divorce. They loaned me enough money to start my store. I paid it back as soon as I could, but thanks to their help, I was able to make a living for myself and Holly all these years."

She could see Paul's face tighten at the mention of her parents, her father.

"I don't expect you to ever forgive him for what he did to you," Kyleigh said. "It was unforgivable making you choose between me and your brother."

Paul reached out and grabbed her hand, clasping it in his. He gave her a gentle squeeze, and she felt it then. The forgiveness that settled between them. For him. For the whole sad situation. She wondered if he felt it, too.

He didn't let go of her hand as they headed toward the bay.

"Do you think our spot is still there?" Paul asked, a wicked grin popping on his face.

Kyleigh's stomach fluttered. Long ago, they'd found a spot that overlooked the bay, far up and away from the beach. They'd discovered the location one day when they went hiking for some alone time. Some place where her father's fellow cops couldn't trail them to harass Paul, which had happened more often than Kyleigh liked to remember.

"You know it's a well-known make-out spot for teenagers now."

"We claimed it first," Paul said, holding her hand tighter.

"Doubtful," she replied, even as a wick of desire lit inside her. The small cliff had been their place to get away. They spent hours on that cliff, making love until one of them had to rush home.

"You want to see if we can find it?" he asked.

She raised an eyebrow at him. "You want to go hiking in the woods at night?"

Paul smirked. "You're so cute when you look at me like I'm crazy."

Kyleigh was thankful for the night's shadows as her face heated.

Paul put his free hand over his heart. "I promise I'll protect you from any owls or potential coyotes that might attack us."

"My hero," she said dryly before nodding at the Holiday Bay forest in front of them. "Let's do it."

Paul lifted her hand and kissed the back of it. She still felt the imprint of his lips on her skin after he pulled out his phone with his free hand. Activating the light, he led her into the woods.

"So what's going on with Holiday Boys?" she asked as they went down a path covered in leaves. The Boys had reunited a few years back and performed for the first time in decades at the fairground to raise money to save the local businesses. They'd gone on a small reunion tour shortly after that.

"I know there's talk of us going on tour again soon—worldwide, this time—but with Julie having her baby, and Meg pregnant, I don't think either Jake or Tyler want to be on the road anytime soon. Jake missed too much of Dylan's childhood due to being on tour. He told us he didn't want to make the same mistake with Jane. So maybe everyone will be ready in a couple years. I guess that'll also depend on where Zan's at mentally by then. I'm sure he wouldn't want to take the kids on the road or leave them with nannies. I don't know…we'll probably have to postpone for the foreseeable future."

She tried to see his expression in the light of the phone. "Are you sad about that?"

"Not really," he said, his teeth flashing at her. "When I was younger, I used to love traveling."

"I'm sure you enjoyed all those groupies." Kyleigh said it as lightly as she could, but she couldn't quite hide her bitterness at how successful he'd been at replacing her after they broke up. She'd forgiven him for leaving her like he had. There was still a part of her that was jealous of all those women who'd entered his life after her.

Paul had become an expert at reading her. He paused his steps, forcing her to stop, too, since he hadn't let go of her hand. "Ma'am, might I remind you that I'm a married man? That means something to me, even if we started under the guise of a reality TV show. For as long as you and I are together, I'll never cheat on you."

She stared at the seriousness on his face and nodded, her shoulders relaxing.

"Gregori said that after Holiday Boys broke up," she

said as they continued walking, "you started buying songs and screenplays."

Paul snorted. "Gregori is such a gossip. But yeah, that's about right. I'd always loved the entertainment world so I learned everything I could from the ground up. I was given the gig of hosting *First Comes Marriage*, and in between seasons, I continued to work behind the scenes on different projects in the industry. The show opened a lot of doors for me. It gave me extra money to buy the rights to songs. Every time you hear certain ones in commercials or on the radio, I get a percentage. I guess that's why I'm so protective of *First Comes Marriage* now. Without the show, I don't know if I'd have been able to achieve everything I wanted."

She stared at his profile, in awe of the man he'd become. They made their way deeper into the woods. Kyleigh knew they were getting closer to the cliff's edge from the increasingly loud sound of the waves crashing against the shoreline. They finally reached the overlook.

Paul took off the hoodie he wore and spread it on the ground. They lay side by side with their heads on the soft material. Kyleigh could feel the heat of him along the entire length of her body. It was as if he needed to be in contact with her, their feet, legs and hips touching. They stared up at the night sky, the stars shining brightly above.

"Look," Paul said, pointing upward. "A shooting star." He turned his head, and his breath whispered against her skin. "Make a wish."

She watched the star streak across the darkness and briefly closed her eyes. *Please let him fall in love with me, too.*

She'd known from the moment she watched him comfort his mourning friend that she was in love with him. Perhaps she'd never stopped. She'd certainly known when she met him all those years ago that he'd captured her, body and soul. Even decades later, she'd never quite been able to let him go.

"Do you know what that star reminds me of?" Paul asked. "Do you remember that play we were in at the performing arts camp?"

"Was that the play you wrote?" she said. "The one about the kid who had the power of the stars in his hands?"

"Yeah," he said.

"Didn't you put flashlights inside your gloves to get the effect of starlight? And then the one glove kept shorting out during the actual performance."

Paul chuckled. "I wanted to look so cool in front of you. Instead I looked like a flashing disco ball."

Kyleigh giggled. "That's right. I forgot you also had a sparkly shirt on."

Paul popped up on an elbow. "I was supposed to look like a constellation, thank you very much."

"You looked like a dork," she said with a grin.

He stared at her, and the mirth on his face disappeared. The atmosphere shifted between them, becoming charged.

Paul lifted his hand and brushed it down her cheek. "I meant what I said, you know."

She clasped his wrist, holding his palm against her cheek. "About what?"

"I'd never cheat on you," he whispered, looking more serious than she'd ever seen him. "In all the years apart, I never forgot you. No matter who I was with. It was just sex. It was always different with you."

"How so?" she said, her voice shaky.

Paul leaned down until he was a hair's breadth away from her mouth. "With you, it wasn't sex. With you, it was love. No one could ever come close to what you and I had. After I found out you were married, I tried to replace you. But it was like an itch under my skin that I couldn't scratch. It used to drive me nuts. Sometimes, I'd wake up in the middle of the night needing you so much that I ached."

"Paul..." she said, her voice hoarse.

He closed the distance between them and kissed her, tentatively at first, and then harder when she didn't resist, his tongue dipping inside her mouth to dance with hers.

Sparks flew over Kyleigh's skin as she wrapped a hand around the back of his head to hold him there, her fingers lacing through his thick hair. She tugged lightly on the curls, and he groaned. Paul shifted his body, settling between her legs. Their kissing became hotter, more urgent. Her legs wrapped around his waist, bringing him even closer to her and she could feel his hardness for her pushing against her core.

He pulled back, panting. His hands moved to the bottom of the sweater she wore. He looked hesitantly into her eyes. When she gave a nod of consent, Paul pulled it over her head. The night air did little to cool the inferno inside Kyleigh.

Paul stared down at the pebbled peaks of her nipples poking through the material of her bra. He leaned down and pressed his lips to her neck, kissing the sensitive skin there. She arched beneath him as hunger sparked over her skin. Paul made his way to her bra, pulling lightly on one of her nipples with his mouth, teasing it with those talented lips.

"Paul," she groaned as liquid want flooded between her thighs.

When he was done teasing her breasts, he moved even lower. He reached the top of her jeans and again waited for her consent.

She gave it by reaching for the button at her waist, undoing it as his eyes flared.

And then they lost the rest of the night as they rediscovered the meaning of making love.

Chapter Twenty-Four

Kyleigh chewed nervously on her inner cheek as Heather applied makeup to her face. It was crazy to think that she and Paul had been married for three months now. It was the big finale, the ending where they'd answer the question viewers cared about most. Would they each say yes or no to staying married to each other?

She and Paul hadn't had much time together after that incredible night when they'd pleasured each other in ways that still caused goose bumps on her skin whenever she thought of it. They'd snuck back into her apartment through her window. Paul had given her a lingering kiss that made her want to pull him onto her bed for another round, but he had to return to the living room before Gregori woke up.

As if sensing there had been a change between them, Gregori had tracked their every move for the next two weeks like a professional stalker. They could barely speak to each other without a camera being shoved in their faces.

She already knew what Paul was going to say when Shawnee asked him the question.

As they'd walked back to her apartment that night, he'd told her he wanted to stay married. He told her to think about it, but that now that they'd found their way back to each other, he didn't want to ever let her go again.

She savored the words and knew in her heart that she was planning on saying yes as well. She wanted to stay married to Paul. They'd already been apart for too long. She didn't want another day to go by without him in her life.

"You look nervous," Heather said as she started working on her hair.

"I am a little. A lot rides on how the show ends, doesn't it? I've seen other seasons. It's very dramatic."

"It is, but you'll do great."

Kyleigh glanced over at Leroy who was filming her today. "It'll at least be nice to have my life back. I'm looking forward to using the bathroom without the rest of the world knowing what I'm about to do."

Heather laughed as she completed the finishing touches with hair spray. "Well I, for one, have enjoyed watching the mighty Paul Rodriguez fall."

"What do you mean?" Kyleigh asked absently.

"Honey, I might be a lesbian, but even I can recognize a man head over heels in love." Kyleigh glowed at the words as Heather patted her shoulder. "Shawnee is one of Paul's closest friends. They've been friends since before I met and married her. I inherited Paul when I got Shawnee, but I'm proud to say he's a good friend of mine now, and I've never seen him like this before with a woman."

"Like how?" Kyleigh couldn't help but ask.

"Like the whole world rises and sets on you. The man is crazy about you."

"Heather, are you almost done?" Shawnee asked through the walkie that Heather had at her station.

Heather huffed. "She's always so impatient. Makeup is a work of art and shouldn't be rushed, even on subjects that are already perfect."

Kyleigh laughed before she glanced at her reflection.

Heather really was an artist when it came to makeup. Kyleigh never wore much. Heather simply added to her normal look, somehow magically emphasizing her high cheekbones and bright blue eyes.

"You're all set," Heather said after one more shot of hair spray.

Kyleigh nodded, murmuring her thanks. Leroy left to help Gregori get things set up where they'd be filming the final scene. They were at Kyleigh's store, since this was where they'd filmed their first scene. She remembered how Paul showed up that day, full of wrath, demanding that she drop out of the show. How things had changed in three months.

As Kyleigh walked to the front of the store, she paused to take stock of the place. She wasn't kidding when she said she couldn't wait for the cameras to be gone. While she was thankful that Wendy was able to step in and help during filming, Kyleigh would be glad when she had full control of her life once more.

She had almost reached the front of the store when she heard Paul and Shawnee's voices. A smile lit her face as she listened to the deep, warm timbre of Paul's voice. Until she realized what they were talking about.

"I'm telling you, the network is salivating over the footage I've sent them," Shawnee said. "You know, I didn't understand why you wanted to do the show in the first place, but it really was a genius move. The test audiences went absolutely wild when they realized it was you who was getting married. The network won't be so willing to fire you now. This season will guarantee your status on the show for years to come. Especially if Kyleigh says yes. If she agrees to stay married to you, the rest of the rights to this show are as good as yours."

"She'll say yes," Paul said, his voice rich with satisfaction. "Everything is going the way I planned."

Kyleigh paled. He'd told her on their wedding day that being on the show would help him push forward a couple of shows he'd want to produce, but she hadn't realized his job was on the line.

First Comes Marriage *opened a lot of doors for me... I guess that's why I'm so protective of the show now,* he'd told her that night on the cliff.

Bile rose in her throat. Had Paul only married her to save his status on the show? And what had Shawnee said? That once Kyleigh said yes, he'd be given the rights? Had this whole thing been a ruse? While she'd fallen deeply in love with him, had Paul only seen her as a means to an end?

Her brain scrambled over the past few months to see if she'd missed any clues that he wasn't being true. Her mind settled on her wedding day. She'd conveniently forgotten how he blackmailed her into marrying him, the blazing satisfaction on his face when her father had a conniption over their marriage.

So not only was she a means to an end, was revenge also behind Paul's motives?

She felt dirty. Used. She'd been about to sit down and tell the world that she'd fallen in love with her husband. That she wanted to keep the marriage. And the whole time he'd been using her for some ratings and a guaranteed win with the network.

She continued to the front of the store and sat down in the chair that Gregori nodded toward. Holly stood nearby, hopping from foot to foot in excitement. The expression on her daughter's face broke Kyleigh's heart. Holly loved Paul. She'd watched her daughter bond with the man, the father figure she'd always wanted.

"You okay, Kyleigh?" Gregori asked as he came over to light her with his meter. "You're looking a little ill. Do you want Heather to put some more makeup on?"

"I'm fine," she ground out, trying not to cry as Paul and Shawnee came into view. Her spine stiffened like steel when he gave her a loving smile.

Don't smile at me like that, you lying jerk!

Paul sat across from her. She could feel his eyes on her, but she didn't look at him. She kept her gaze on either her lap or at Shawnee, who'd begun speaking into the camera.

"I have the network on the phone," Heather said, behind Shawnee. She had told Kyleigh while she was getting ready that the heads had wanted to listen to their respective answers, probably to ensure they were all about to become even richer. Kyleigh's mouth lifted into a small sneer before she smoothed out her features.

"So," Shawnee said, her tone bubbly. "Paul. Have you come to a decision? Will you stay married to Kyleigh or go for the annulment?"

Paul gave that professional smile to the camera that Kyleigh had grown to hate. She thought it was because it didn't really show off the real him. It was fake, for an audience that adored Paul without knowing him. She'd foolishly cherished every smile he'd given her that she thought was real.

Paul looked at her with what looked to be sincerity in his eyes. "Kyleigh, I love you. I've been in love with you for two decades now. I never stopped loving you. I want to stay married to you. I want to help you raise Holly. I want the three of us to be a family. You're my whole world. You always have been."

Shawnee fanned herself as he spoke. "That's one of the sweetest things I've ever heard." She looked at Kyleigh next.

"And, Kyleigh, after hearing that speech, I can't imagine you're able to resist the man. But I'm required to ask anyway. What's your answer? Do you want to stay married or seek an annulment?"

"She'll say yes," Paul had assured Shawnee.

Kyleigh finally met his eyes. Concern flashed across his face as she raised her chin.

"No, I don't to stay married to Paul Rodriguez. I want an annulment."

Chapter Twenty-Five

Paul felt like he was going out of his mind. He hadn't seen or spoken to Kyleigh in over two months. After she'd told him that she wanted to get an annulment, she'd bolted for the door, grabbing Holly's hand and pulling her daughter with her.

Paul had wanted to run after her, but by the time he'd processed her rejection and jumped to his feet, Shawnee had been in front of him, handing him her phone with remorse on her face. He knew the procedure after a show wrapped. They had to tell the network if the marriage had worked or not. The executives were already promoting the show on heavy rotation, knowing they had a hit on their hands with Paul as the groom.

They'd threatened to fire him and ruin his career if he didn't fix it and make sure Kyleigh said yes to the marriage. One executive—a pompous guy named Marty—had even gone so far as to tell Paul that he was finished in the entertainment industry if he didn't change Kyleigh's mind.

Paul threw an expletive at him that would have made his Aunt Esperanza cross herself before disconnecting the call.

By the time he was able to escape to chase after his wife, he'd been too late. He'd arrived at her apartment only to find it empty. There'd been signs that she and Holly had been there. Clothes thrown all over the place, but they'd both disappeared.

Jake eventually took sympathy on him and texted that Kyleigh and Holly were staying with him and Julie. When he'd arrived at Jake's mansion, his friend met him at the door, crossing his arms over his chest, regret all over his face.

"I can't let you in," Jake had said.

"I need to talk to her," Paul insisted.

"I feel for you, man, I really do." Jake clapped him on the shoulder. "But Julie would send me to sofa purgatory if I let you in."

He'd shut the door in Paul's face before he could even respond.

Shawnee tracked him down after that and insisted he go back to California to meet with the network. Though he hadn't wanted to, she encouraged him to give Kyleigh some space while also trying to sort out the mess the show was in. The executives were furious that Kyleigh said no. Thanks to leaks from Holly's talent show, there was now a huge buzz for the season. Early viewers had worked themselves into a frenzy over Kyleigh and Paul's wedding episode. People were going rabid at the thought of Hollywood's biggest bachelor finally settling down. Audiences expected a happy ending, with many people across multiple social media platforms threatening to not watch the show anymore if the marriage didn't last.

Paul had wanted to tell Shawnee that he didn't give a crap about the show, but the crew depended on its success for their livelihoods. He'd worked with most of them for years now, had gone to several of their homes for the holidays. He couldn't let them down.

He spent the next month putting on a brave face and calming ruffled feathers at the network.

And then he formally resigned from the show.

He'd wanted *First Comes Marriage* to be a part of his new company. Had wanted it badly. He was grateful for the show and everything it had brought him.

But he didn't need it anymore.

He needed Kyleigh.

So he let it go. He spent the two months packing up his life in California while searching for property near Holiday Bay. It'd be nice to be close to Jake and Tyler again. Not to mention his brother and aunt. He wanted to be there for his niece and nephew and to get to know his sister-in-law. He wanted to continue to rebuild the bridges he'd burned down so many years ago between him and his brother.

Most of all, he wanted Kyleigh.

He bought a brick mansion that stood midway between Holiday Bay and Clarington. He could get to either location easily enough. And it was only a short drive to Kyleigh's store and Holly's school.

"You sure about this?" Shawnee said as he showed her around the house he bought. They finally stepped into a room that overlooked the bay that he thought Holly would like. Shawnee looked around the room in approval before turning her attention back to Paul. "You're really good with walking away from *First Comes Marriage*?"

Paul nodded. "It would take me out of Michigan too much, and I don't want to be away from Kyleigh."

Shawnee smiled. "You know, there was a reason why I picked her to be this season's contestant."

"I know," Paul muttered, trying to think of anything in the house that Kyleigh might object to. "You were right. She had that Midwest charm the show was looking for."

Shawnee walked over to him and patted him on the head. "Paul, you know I love you like the annoying little brother you are—"

"We're the same age," he grumbled.

"I chose her because of *you*," Shawnee said. "Because when I showed you that picture of her, you looked like you had your whole world ripped out from under your feet. It was the first time I think I've ever seen you get worked up over a woman in all the years I've known you. I knew Kyleigh was important to you, and I had a hunch you'd stop her from getting married to someone else. Now, I had no idea you'd actually go through with being a contestant. That was a lucky break—"

"Yeah, because it's going to give you record rating—"

Shawnee stepped up to him and whacked him on the back of the head.

Even though it was barely a tap, Paul rubbed the area anyway. "Ow."

"I don't give a flying fart about the ratings," Shawnee said, her eyes glistening with hurt. "If I gave a crap, I wouldn't have quit the show shortly after you did. I picked Kyleigh for *you*. So you'd get the chance to talk to the woman you were obviously in love with."

Paul stared in shock at his friend. "You quit the show?"

Shawnee sniffed. "I didn't like how the network treated you. Besides, I like the idea of being a part of a new production company from the ground up. If you'll hire me on as director, that is."

Paul frowned. "But… I plan on working out of Michigan. You'd have to move here. I can't picture Heather wanting to do that."

Shawnee snorted. "You do know Heather is from Wisconsin originally, right? She's been wanting to move closer to home for years now."

Paul was too choked up to say anything. He pulled Shawnee into a hug before releasing her.

"I'm sorry, I can't hire you on as director," Paul finally said.

"I—" Shawnee started to say, but Paul interrupted.

"I can't hire you on as director, because I want to hire you as co-producer."

Shawnee's mouth opened and closed several times before she said, "I can accept that."

They grinned at each other.

"You know," Shawnee said, walking over to the large window. "I couldn't help but notice there are a few empty businesses in Holiday Bay. We could probably buy one of the buildings and headquarter our company there. Maybe even set up a small studio."

Paul followed her and slung an arm around her. "Thanks, Shawnee. I couldn't have done this without you."

"Of course you couldn't. It's about time you recognized that you're hopeless without me."

Paul snickered. "Maybe we *are* related. Clearly, humility runs in the family."

"Obviously," Shawnee replied.

The relief he felt at not having to lose one of his closest friends when he officially moved was short-lived. He'd solved one problem.

Now, he just needed to find a way to get his family back.

Kyleigh felt bruised to her soul as she headed to Meg's house. She'd had a long day at the store, and more than anything she wanted to go back to her apartment and mope. She'd gotten really good at moping over the past few months.

After she'd told Paul that she didn't want to continue with the marriage, she'd spent the next week hiding out at Julie's house. Her friend hadn't said anything when she showed up with Holly, looking like someone had ripped her heart out of her body and stomped all over it.

She hid like a coward, hardly coming out of her room. Holly hadn't understood why she hadn't wanted to stay with Paul. She thought he was the best thing to ever happen to them, and Kyleigh didn't have it in her to explain that Paul hadn't really cared about them. He'd just wanted great ratings and a side dish of revenge.

Then about a week after their parting, Jake walked into the solarium she and Julie were in, wearing a sheepish expression on his face. He let her know that Paul had gone back to California. And another type of heartache began.

She'd fully expected to receive the annulment papers in her mailbox any day, doing her best to ignore the fact that they consummated their marriage while also trying to forget the searing pleasure she found in Paul's arms.

It had also been an adjustment not having Gregori and the rest of the crew following her around. She missed the older man's presence. He'd become important to her in the three months they'd been around each other. Sometimes she found herself watching his favorite game shows simply to block out all the noise in her head.

She pulled into Meg's driveway and took a deep breath before getting out of her car. The midcentury mansion was perfect for her eclectic friend, with its long slanting roof and large glass windows. She walked to the dark green double doors and raised her hand to knock just as it opened.

"Hey, Kyleigh," Tyler greeted her.

"Good timing," she said, trying to summon a smile. She

loved Meg and Julie dearly, but any time she saw a Holiday Boy, it was like a stab to her heart.

"I'm headed out to run some errands for Meg," Tyler explained. "Julie and Meg are in the family room."

"Thanks," she said as she entered the house.

Tyler shut the door behind him, and Kyleigh walked down the lemon-tiled floor, following the sound of her friends' voices. She found them occupying Meg's oversize, dark beige chaise longue. Meg sat with her feet up, rubbing her large belly. She was due the next week, and while Kyleigh knew her friend was nervous, she also remembered how uncomfortable she'd been toward the end of her own pregnancy and how she couldn't wait to get her body back to herself.

"Hey," Kyleigh said, going over to hug Meg before doing the same to Julie. She sat down across from them in a blue-and-yellow floral chair.

"Hi," Meg greeted. "Thanks for coming over."

"No Jane?" she asked Julie. Julie looked like her normal goddess self, even while wearing yoga pants, a T-shirt with a small stain on it and with her long red hair pulled up in a messy bun.

"No," Julie said. "Dylan volunteered to give me the morning off. He's watching his sister."

"He's a good kid," Kyleigh replied.

"Yes, he is. He's like his dad that way."

"So, Kyleigh," Meg said. "We wanted to talk to you."

Kyleigh looked from one friend to the other, not loving the determined expressions on their faces. "Why do I feel like I'm about to have an intervention?" she laughed forcefully.

Julie and Meg exchanged glances.

"We're worried about you," Julie said.

"I'm fine," Kyleigh said dismissively.

"You're not fine," Meg retorted. "You look like you haven't slept in months, and you've lost too much weight."

"I'm fine," Kyleigh repeated, more firmly this time.

"What happened between you and Paul?" Julie asked gently.

"Nothing happened." She didn't meet either of their eyes. "The show ended, and Paul went home."

"Jake said that Paul was a mess the last time he saw him," Julie said, her tone careful.

"I'm sure he was." Kyleigh didn't try to hide the anger she felt.

"See, that's what we're talking about right there," Meg said, rubbing her belly again. "The last time we talked to you about Paul, you seemed happy, like you wanted to stay married to him. And now you look like he ran you over with a truck."

Kyleigh jumped to her feet and walked over to the large window that gave a spectacular view of the bay through the thick woods.

"He didn't actually want the marriage," she admitted.

"What? I don't believe that," Meg replied.

"It's true." Kyleigh couldn't look at either of her friends. "I overheard him the day we filmed the last show. He didn't realize I was there. He only wanted to marry me to get high ratings for the show so they wouldn't fire him."

"I don't believe that," Meg repeated.

Kyleigh could see in the reflection of the glass that Julie and Meg were having a silent conversation between the two of them. She let out an exhausted sigh before she turned and sat back down in her chair with a tired plop.

"It's fine." She felt weary to her bones. "He made a bargain with me on our wedding day. If we stayed married, we'd each get something out of it. He'd get the network's attention so he could produce new shows, and I'd get free publicity for my shop. I just didn't realize that there was any fine print to the bargain."

She put on a brave smile before burying her face in her hands and letting out a sob.

Julie jumped up from the couch and came over to Kyleigh's chair, sitting on the arm of it. She wrapped her in a hug.

"I'm sorry, but that's crap," Meg said.

"Meg," Julie warned.

Kyleigh kept her face covered.

"I don't believe that's why he married you," Meg insisted. "I don't care what he said."

"What does it matter?" Kyleigh muttered, pulling her hands away from her face. "He went back to California, and he's probably already living it up with a new girlfriend or some model."

Meg's face took on that stubborn expression she was well known for in Holiday Bay. Usually when people saw that look, they ran in the opposite direction. "No, he wouldn't do that. He loves you."

"He doesn't." Kyleigh turned pleading eyes to Julie. She didn't want to talk about this anymore.

Julie pulled a damp strand of Kyleigh's blond hair from her face and tucked it behind her ear. "Being in love with a Holiday Boy has its challenges."

Kyleigh didn't meet her eyes. "Who says I love him?"

"Oh please," Meg muttered from across the room.

"If you want my two cents," Julie said, "I agree with Meg. Paul's in love with you. I've never seen him like this with anyone before."

"Well, he's given everyone enough examples over the years," Kyleigh muttered.

"Exactly," Julie said. "And the Paul I know would never *ever* get married unless he was deeply in love with a woman."

"He did it for his show," Kyleigh repeated.

"Paul's got more money than half of Hollywood," Julie said, her eyes lighting. "Trust me, no one can make Paul Rodriguez do anything he doesn't want to do. If it had been any other woman, he would have simply bought the rights to the show from the producers, despite whatever excuses he told you. He *wanted* to marry you."

Kyleigh sniffed but didn't say anything. She couldn't— *wouldn't*—believe her friends. She knew what she'd heard. Paul had told her himself how much the show meant to him. He would have done anything to keep it, including marrying her.

"Will you at least think about what we said?" Julie asked.

Kyleigh wiped at the tear streaks on her cheeks. "I'll think about it."

"Are we done with the intervention?" Meg asked.

"For now," Julie said lightly.

"Good." Meg let out a pained grunt. "Because I think I just went into labor."

Chapter Twenty-Six

Kyleigh cuddled Liam Hudson Evans in her arms, taking in the baby's perfect features. "Sorry, Meg," she told the proud momma. "It doesn't look like you contributed to this kid at all."

Meg laughed. "Yeah, he's definitely a carbon copy of his dad."

"He'll be a looker, for sure," Tyler boasted, earning a glare from his wife where he lay beside her on her hospital bed.

"Let's hope he doesn't inherit his father's ego," Meg grumbled.

"You like my ego," Tyler replied, kissing her on the cheek.

"You're such a sap," Meg told her husband, but it was hard to miss the love shining out of her eyes.

Kyleigh took that look as her cue to leave. Walking over to the bed, she placed the baby in his mom's waiting arms.

"I'll leave you three to have some family bonding time," she told her friends. She leaned down and hugged Meg as best she could. "Call me if you need anything, okay?"

"I will," Meg replied. "And you remember what we talked about before little man interrupted us."

Kyleigh gave a short nod but hurried out of the room

before her friend could mention Paul in front of Tyler. She kept her eyes on the floor so she didn't see the figure leaning against the wall opposite of where she stood. When the person moved, she finally looked up only to come to an abrupt halt.

Paul straightened before walking over to her.

Kyleigh lifted her head defensively. "What are you doing here?" she asked.

"I wanted to talk to you."

"And you thought this was the best place to do it?"

"If I asked you to meet me somewhere, would you have agreed?"

"No," she replied. Kyleigh turned to walk away from him, but Paul moved in her path.

"You and I are going to talk, Ky," he informed her, his face unrelenting.

"I have nothing to say to you," she said, moving around him. "Unless it's to talk about the annulment."

She only got a few feet before she heard Paul mutter, "Okay, we'll do this the hard way then."

Before she knew what was happening, she was in his arms being carried down the hallway bridal-style while patients and their family members gaped at them.

"Would you put me down?" she snapped, completely mortified. "You're making a spectacle of us."

Several people took out their phones and took pictures of them as they passed. Great, this would be trending within minutes.

"Like I said," Paul said in a rigid tone. "You and I are going to talk."

Kyleigh could see Gloria hurrying down the hall, looking at a chart. "Gloria, would you please call security? This man is holding me hostage."

Gloria looked up from her chart, eyeing her brother-in-law. "I better not get fired for this, Paulo."

"You won't," Paul assured her as he continued walking past the doctor.

Gloria sighed before pulling her phone out of her lab coat and pressing a button. "Go down the corridor and take a left."

"Roger that," Paul replied.

Kyleigh heard Gloria grumble something about idiot brothers as she headed to her next patient.

Paul followed Gloria's instructions and Kyleigh could see Dominic standing at the end of the hall, looking bored.

"Dom, help," Kyleigh said. "Call security. Your brother's kidnapping me."

Dom turned and waved his hospital badge over a panel next to a door. It let out a loud beep, and Dom pushed the door open.

"You've got ten minutes, little brother. Make them count."

Paul gave a short nod and went through the entryway. Dom shut the door behind them, and Paul put her back on her feet. She briefly registered through her haze of fury that they were in a supply closest, filled with toilet paper and cleaning supplies.

"You have some damn nerve," Kyleigh exploded.

Paul crossed his arms over his chest and leaned against the door, blocking her only way out.

"You didn't have to do this to discuss the annulment," she said when he didn't say anything. "You could have sent me the paperwork."

"You and I both know there isn't going to be an annulment," Paul finally spoke.

Kyleigh's cheeks flamed hotter than they already were. "Fine. A divorce, whatever."

"Not that, either, Ky."

Kyleigh's mouth opened. Closed. "We're not staying married."

Paul lifted an eyebrow. "We are, actually."

"We...we can't stay married."

"Why not?"

Kyleigh felt like she was going insane. "Because you don't want to be married to me. You only married me to get high ratings."

"That's not why I married you," Paul said.

"I overheard you, okay? I heard you and Shawnee on the day of the finale, discussing how happy the network was with the footage from our season. You only married me because you didn't want to get fired from the show, and you wanted the rights to it."

"Ah," Paul said, looking unbothered.

Kyleigh's temper was about to seriously blow a fuse. "Let me out of here."

"I quit the show."

She went still. "What?"

"I quit the show," Paul repeated. "I sold the rights I owned for *First Comes Marriage* back to the network. Then I sold my house in California and bought a place down the road from here."

"Wha... Why would you do that?" she asked, stunned.

"Because you're here."

"I don't understand," Kyleigh whispered.

"I married you because I saw your picture on the list of prospective contestants, and I couldn't bear the idea of you marrying anyone that wasn't me. I married you because I've been crazy, stupidly in love with you since I was seventeen years old." He stepped away from the door toward her. "I married you because you're my everything, Ky. Not the show. Not the ratings. I don't care about any of that. All I care about is you. You and Holly are my family."

He came to a stop right in front of her, cupping her cheek in his hand.

"I love you," he said. "I've always loved you. I'll always love you."

"Paul," she murmured right before his lips found hers. The kiss was gentle before it deepened into something that was pure need. He groaned in her arms when she traced his mouth with her tongue before nibbling gently on his bottom lip.

He pulled away, his chest heaving. "Say you'll stay married to me. I can give you the world now."

She closed her eyes as their foreheads touched. "All I ever needed was you."

He shuddered, and she looked at him questioningly.

"You don't know how long I've waited for you to say that," he told her before kissing her again. When they finally pulled back a few moments later, Paul wrapped his arms around her waist and started rocking them back and forth.

"So…" he said, his eyes shining with the love he had for her.

She teared up at the sight. She never thought she'd see him look at her like that again. "So?" she repeated, breathing him in.

"What do you say?" he asked, looking intently into her eyes. "Will you stay married to me?"

"Yes," she said.

"Even though we got married on a reality show?" he

asked as the tension left his face, replaced with pure happiness.

She grinned back at him. "Conventional is boring anyway."

He laughed before pulling her tighter into his arms. They both ignored Dom knocking on the door and telling them their time was up.

Neither of them cared. They might have found their way back to each other on a show built with the idea that first comes marriage, then comes love. But for Paul and Kyleigh, their love came first.

It always would.

* * * * *

Get up to 4 Free Books!

We'll send you 2 free books from each series you try PLUS a free Mystery Gift.

FREE
Value Over
$25

Both the **Harlequin® Special Edition** and **Harlequin® Heartwarming™** series feature compelling novels filled with stories of love and strength where the bonds of friendship, family and community unite.